Surry Hills, NSW 2010
t +61 2 9319-7199
f +61 2 9319-6866

NICHOLAS JOSE has published collections of essays and short stories, translations, and several acclaimed novels, including *Paper Nautilus* (1987), *The Rose Crossing* (1994), *The Custodians* (1997) and *The Red Thread* (2000). His most recent book is *Black Sheep: Journey to Borroloola* (2002). He has written widely on contemporary Asian and Australian culture and was president of Sydney PEN 2002–2005. He currently holds the Chair of Creative Writing at the University of Adelaide.

ORIGINAL FACE

NICHOLAS JOSE

# Original Face

GIRAMONDO

FIRST PUBLISHED 2005
FROM THE UNIVERSITY OF WESTERN SYDNEY
BY THE GIRAMONDO PUBLISHING COMPANY
PO BOX 752 ARTARMON NSW 1570 AUSTRALIA
WWW.GIRAMONDOPUBLISHING.COM

DESIGNED BY HARRY WILLIAMSON
TYPESET BY ANDREW DAVIES
IN 10/17 PT BASKERVILLE
PRINTED AND BOUND BY SOUTHWOOD PRESS
DISTRIBUTED IN AUSTRALIA BY TOWER BOOKS

NATIONAL LIBRARY OF AUSTRALIA
CATALOGUING-IN-PUBLICATION DATA:

JOSE, NICHOLAS, 1952– .
ORIGINAL FACE.

ISBN 1 920882 13 8.

I. TITLE.

A823.3

9 8 7 6 5 4 3 2

*The heart can push the sea and land*

# Chapter I

With a few incisions the skin of a human being may be removed in a single piece. So Daozi had heard. A surgeon could do it, a taxidermist, a butcher. He concentrated, using the technique he had learned in the cold storage rooms at the fish market, clenching his teeth as he directed his energy along his arm to the slim, sharp blade. His shadow got in the way in the half-light of the toilet block where he was working. There was blood everywhere, warm and sticky to the touch. The skinning took more cuts of the knife than he would have liked. The tattoo on the man's torso peeled off easily enough. The face was more difficult.

The night was silent but for occasional animal cries, and pitch-black beyond the circle of light cast over the picnic area by a solitary neon light. Daozi called out to the others, waiting in their cars in the darkness, when his job was done. Ah Mo sent the two Beijing brothers to help lift the thick plastic garbage bag that contained the body across to the concrete picnic table where he could see it in the light. The boss nodded with approval at the dragon tattoo, stretched across a piece of skin. Then he ordered the bag to be tightly tied and transferred to the boot of his car.

Daozi took off his clothes and placed them in another black plastic bag. He washed himself in the toilet block, shivering as he rinsed his hands in cold water from the tap. Blood sluiced away across the floor. He dumped his old clothes in the rusty iron bin outside, poured on some fuel and set the whole lot alight. While the fire warmed and dried him, he put on clean clothes.

Daozi: his name meant Knife. As a child he had beaten his own father with the blunt end of a knife to win approval from a ring of neighbours and guards. He had run in fear from his confused mother's arms only to be restrained by other un-relenting arms as his mother was taken away. That's what he remembered, in China, in the white light of trauma, so distant from this deep dark night of the Australian bush that could swallow any disturbance. He paced restlessly about the picnic area, in and out of shadow, rubbing his thin moustache. The first car drove away, leaving only Ah Mo, smoking under the light pole, and the woman, hiding her face behind her hair. Daozi caught her watching him from the car as he crossed the grass. For a moment he thought he would lose his balance, bound by passion that was also pain.

After silence had fallen on the moans of the dying man, the dead man's head had looked at Daozi. Tufts of hair stuck up from the scalp, eyes bulged from sockets, the mouth gaped open as if in a last unfinished act of communication. Daozi needed all his strength not to turn away, as if the effort of submission to this act of loyalty and rectification might yet knock him over. The faceless face was laughing at him. Everywhere, from dark cavities, in that circle of light.

The bridge flew out over the working harbour in a single span cradled by concrete towers and steel cables that tensed like black bamboo. It carried traffic east and west, high above silos and lumberyards and container terminals, in and out of the city centre. Lewis Lin, driving his taxi across, felt like he was flying on a thirty-second magic carpet ride into the blue. Not the old bridge, what the old-timers called the Coathanger – though that could take your breath away when you came from north to south into the view of water and crowded shoreline – no, this new bridge, a wonder of the world that Lewis had watched grow in his own time in the city, cantilevered out over the tidal water, the fish market, the warehouses and scrub-covered rock. On the day the two halves met in the middle to make a bridge he had joined the mob of well-wishers that crossed it on foot from one side to the other. From the crest he saw how the back half of the city worked, the new apartment blocks rising in Pyrmont where the old low workers' cottages had stepped down the hill, the scrap dredged from the harbour, rusting on barges, and the former bridge, still opening once a day for cargo ships to pass. And he followed the current with his eyes as it flowed out through the harbour to the sea.

Passengers joked that the new bridge should be called Madonna's Bra because of its uplift, two taut cones swelling from the seabed below. From a distance they could be a ghostly pair of circus tents pitched for a travelling show. Lewis knew that the bridge looked like all sorts of things. He had photographed it from every angle – its length, its inverted spearhead height, its vertiginous geometry. Below was history, he considered, what sailors and workers and traders had made in this place. Above was the sensation of flying into the future. And there in the middle, suspended, was the present, this fine summer Friday as he headed into the city at the beginning of his shift. As he came over the bridge he saw the city arrayed before him under a cloudless sky. It rippled like a curtain of glass and steel above the brick and earth and mirroring cobalt water. Lewis felt the exaltation of its insubstantiality as he swooped through Chinatown and entered the canyons around Central station. The traffic was thin.

There, as expected, he found a fare. A gentleman with a red face, a white beard and a sack on his back was stumbling out into the traffic to flag a taxi. He looked like Father Christmas.

'Pleasant Vale,' the old man said, squinting in the early morning sunshine when Lewis stopped to pick him up. He wasted no time before climbing into the front seat. 'Thank you, driver.'

Pleasant Vale! Lewis had to think about that one for a moment. Was it somewhere down the freeway in the direction of Canberra? There were passengers on Saturday nights who asked to be taken to places like that. When they were out in the middle of nowhere they jumped from the moving car without paying the fare and disappeared into the darkness.

'Pleasant Vale?' queried Lewis with a smile, as if he had not understood. 'Sorry?'

'Pleasant Vale, mate. Out Campbelltown way. I have to be at work before eight o'clock and I missed my train.'

The old man fumbled in the backpack for his wallet to let the wary driver see his money. Lewis swung out into the traffic.

'I manage the recycle centre,' the passenger explained. 'The garbage dump. The refuse depot. The tip! Whatever you want to call it. It's a rising tide. Rubbish. Trash. Waste. Never stops coming. You know what I'm saying?' He spoke with stagey elocution. 'It'll be waiting for me at eight on the knocker.'

The old man looked at the driver, assessing his background: glossy black ponytail tied in a red scarf, broad flat tea-coloured face, not more than thirty, dark glasses over the eyes. He reached for a packet of cigarettes and was preparing to light up when he noticed the No Smoking sticker on the dashboard. He sighed and put the packet away again. 'My daughter doesn't like me to smoke either. She's a dental hygienist. She lives round here in Surry Hills. She's got her own little terrace house thingy that she's renovating. I came in last night to give her a hand. Sanding the floorboards for her birthday. I must have dozed off to sleep on the sofa. She let me sleep through and I missed the bloody train.'

The passenger was talking and the driver only half-listening as he navigated towards the freeway. 'I picked you up outside Touch of Class,' Lewis observed, glancing at the man beside him with a wry smile. That was the heritage brothel on the corner of Riley and Foveaux. A tarted-up Victorian mansion with pink lacework and shrubbery as camouflage.

'As if!' the old man snorted. 'It's just a good place to get a cab.'

'Right,' said Lewis. 'Day or night. A lot of Asians go in there.'

The old man looked at the driver again. 'The girls, you mean. They're sex slaves, aren't they? You obviously know your way around, mate,' he said. 'Where you from?'

'China,' said Lewis curtly. 'Where you from?'

'Yugoslavia.'

'Yugoslavia? The former Yugoslavia,' said Lewis. 'You mean Serbia.'

Reg nodded. 'I've been here fifty years. It was Yugoslavia *then*. I'm a New Australian,' Reg laughed. 'How about you? Fresh off the boat? I'm Reg, by the way.' He looked at the driver's identification card on the visor. 'And you?'

'Lin. Lewis Lin.'

The exchange of names made them relax into silence. They stop-started along Parramatta Road, then through Ashfield on the old Hume Highway. Chinese signs, vertical and horizontal, crowded both sides of the road.

'Your zone,' noted Reg. 'You people don't mess around. All here to see what you can do out from under communism. I was the same once.'

Competing family restaurants, windows hung with glazed ducks, lined the strip where grocers or haberdashers or barbers had once been. 'Know what we call this?' asked Lewis. 'We say stir-fry the neighbourhood.'

'Stir bloody fry all right,' nodded the old man, settling back.

They drove out through changing stretches of suburbs until they reached the city's furthest fringes and the turn on to the freeway south. Lewis sat just above the speed limit of 110. When a sign came up for the Macarthur Park exit, the old man started to give directions. A few solitary eucalypts undulated upwards as reminders of the old pastoral scene that had made fortunes for the early pioneers. Now a technology park was growing up and government departments had moved in – overheated in summer, frostbitten in winter – to provide jobs for the sprawling population. The road from the freeway curved through grassy hills dotted with new homes on spacious lots: villas, chalets, haciendas. Services and sanitation heralded prosperity. That was the hope.

Residents put out their garbage in wheelie bins along the road – building waste, garden waste, anything they were getting rid of as they built their new lives. The bins were emptied twice a week by trucks that headed on down the road to the Pleasant Vale Recycling and Waste Depot. Tuesdays and Fridays. The dump manager had to be there to unlock the gates. Friday was the big day. Trucks arrived first thing, loaded up, hoping to get ahead of themselves for the weekend. If Reg was not there waiting for them, they would report him to the council and he would lose his job. He could not afford that.

'Go as fast as you like, mate,' he urged his driver. 'No speed cameras out here.'

Anyway, Reg Spivak liked his retirement job as dump manager. He believed in the work he did. He was committed to minimising the amount of garbage that ended up as landfill. And in between he had plenty of time to sit on a chair in the sun and read the books he salvaged.

7

'One day when all my garbage is drowned and smoothed over, my dump will be prime real estate.' Reg looked at Lewis out of the corner of his eye. 'Top Dollar Park. What do you reckon?'

The road narrowed through the last of the houses. There was a white line down the middle but barely room for two cars to pass before the bitumen dropped away to a crumbly shoulder. The cars coming against them were morning commuter traffic – cars ferrying kids to school, people straggling to work, trucks and delivery vans – and the dips and curves in the strip of road caused the vehicles to bunch up. There was no way to see what was up ahead. Lewis was trying to get in front when a black car appeared over the rise speeding straight towards him. The car had swung out to pass a gaggle of cars in its way, gambling on there being nothing in the oncoming lane.

'Jesus,' Reg yelped. 'I'm not in that much of a hurry.'

Then, as the line of cars accelerated down the hill, the black car could not get back in. Lewis swerved off the road into the dirt, trying to slow, and skidded as he bounced off the shoulder. He veered back just as the black car came whooshing past. They were a fraction from a pile-up. A head-on.

'Idiot,' said Lewis, his hands trembling as he rocked his car back on course. Burning rubber was in the air. The black car was racing into the distance.

'I got the rego number,' said Reg. 'Do you have a pen, mate?'

Lewis passed the pen from behind the sun visor and Reg scratched the number on a taxi company card. 'It's important

to remember things before you let them go,' he sighed philo-
sophically. 'Saints preserve us!'

'That was too close,' said Lewis, rolling his shoulders back to
steady himself.

'Maybe you should pull over for a minute,' Reg suggested.
'Did you get a look at the driver by any chance?'

'I didn't see a thing,' said Lewis. A BMW, 320 series. Black.
The car had flashed past him – two people in the front, maybe,
one in the back.

'Let's keep going then,' said Reg.

The road became a dirt track, passing ramshackle farms and
hillsides of brown-gold grass. The canopy of trees flashed tearings
of shadow and light as they approached the dump. No Through
Road: the old sign had bullet holes through all three Os. The
track ended in a set of padlocked wire gates and a fresher sign that
listed the charges for different kinds of dumping. The Pleasant
Vale Recycling and Waste Depot was supposed to turn a profit.

Reg got out of the car and opened the padlock on the gates
with a key from a bunch in his backpack. 'We made it,' he said
with more than usual feeling, ushering the taxi inside. The air
was thick with the whirr of cicadas celebrating his return.

'That's $76.40,' Lewis called out the window.

'What's the hurry, mate?' said Reg. 'You got time for a cuppa
before you head back, haven't you? Time to calm down for a
minute after our nasty shock.'

Lewis looked at his watch. The journey had taken an hour.
That meant another hour to get back. And it was hot. He wiped

the sweat on his face, feeling himself a stranger here. And wondered about the old man, vulnerable and exposed. But he said okay, appreciating Reg's offer. 'In all the time I've been driving it's never come that close before.'

'What hasn't?' asked Reg before he realised what Lewis meant. 'Oh that,' he said. 'The big one. Yeah, I'm glad my number didn't come up yet. Here, maybe you can use this.' He flicked Lewis the taxi card with the black Beamer's number on it and trotted across to the little cabin that was the manager's office. In a few minutes he re-emerged with two steaming mugs on a tray. Teabags floating in hot water. Milk. Sugar. Lewis had learned to drink tea with milk, the Australian way, but he drew the line at sugar. Reg took two spoonfuls. Then he presented Lewis with four twenty-dollar notes.

'I'll need a receipt,' said Reg. 'Don't worry about the change.'

Lewis rested his mug of tea on the roof of the car. He carefully wrote the date, the journey – City to Pleasant Vale – and the amount. Then he signed his name and gave Reg the card.

'Thanks, mate,' said Reg. 'You handled that pretty well.'

Lewis grinned. 'Chinese are bad drivers.'

'Not all of them,' chuckled Reg. 'That's obvious.'

'How will you get home when you finish work?' Lewis asked, looking round at the desolate rubbish dump and the bush. The place was way at the end of the road and he couldn't see another car.

'I'll be right,' said Reg. 'I can get a lift with one of the truckies. No worries.' The old man pricked up his ears. 'That'll be them now. Right on eight o'clock.'

The drowsy silence of the morning was broken by the sound of a truck rumbling down the road. Lewis put his half-drunk tea back on the tray while Reg went over to the gate. He was a stocky man with a barrel chest and the pigment in his pink face leached to grey in the dappled light. He waved the truck through as if he had been waiting there for it all night. The driver shouted a greeting, scarcely slowing as he rocked the huge machine through to the yard, lights flashing, signals sounding, pausing, crunching, reversing to the edge of the pit before letting the compressed garbage tumble out.

Lewis didn't want to stick around. He had made a good start on his quota for the day with the eighty bucks from Reg. The journey would not be over until he was back in town. He adjusted his sunglasses and headed back along the bush track, trees brushing by and the wind tugging at his ponytail through the open window. He reached the place on the road where the Beamer had nearly wiped them out. He saw the skid marks, snaking deep through the pink dirt by the side of the road, and the burnt scarring of his tyres in the bitumen. He breathed deeply, centring himself, properly acknowledging his scrape with bad fortune.

Reg liked to cast an eye over whatever was dropped into his pit. Anything useable, saleable or recyclable was supposed to be separated out. People were in such a hurry to rid themselves of things that they dumped it all in together without a thought for the future of the planet. What reached the dump was pretty far gone, admittedly, especially after being put through the compactor. Even the dump manager's expert eye was hard pressed to pick one thing from another in the mash of cans and plastic and ooze that tumbled out. It was quite by chance that the head had lodged in a pocket on top of the pile. It angled outward, and beckoned to Reg as he cast his gaze routinely back and forth over the garbage. The mass of blood and tufty hair with protruding eyeballs and a gaping hole of a mouth caught his attention in the moment before another load of extruded rubbish was dumped on top. A shiver went down his spine, telling him he had seen something even before he registered what it was.

'Wait a minute,' Reg shouted to Jimmy. 'Did you see something?' He ran over to the truck, waving at the driver to stop. 'There's something there,' he yelled.

The driver scowled. He could not hear through his earplugs.

'Just hold it for a moment,' Reg shouted. He fetched the long-handled spade and clambered up the stinking pile of rubbish to the place where he had seen the head. Delicately he shifted the waste to one side and there it was, black-red and sticky, with flies attaching themselves already. Reg closed his eyes and bit his jaw tight. He turned away, making an effort not to vomit at the mess of stained clothing, black plastic, foam pellets and scarcely recognisable flesh and bone.

Jimmy got down from his truck and peered over the edge of the platform. 'What is it?' he asked, walking forward. The back of the truck was still open above the pit, with bits dripping out.

'Body parts,' said Reg. 'A head.' He picked his way purpose-
fully across the mound of garbage and, ignoring Jimmy, went to
the office and called the police. Jimmy was bent double in the
yard, spewing his guts out.

'Not my day,' Reg said to himself after he hung up.

The sun was out in force in a bleached-blue sky by the time the
local police from Pleasant Vale arrived. They were the first on
the scene. Then Homicide from the city, dogs, Forensic, and the
specialists in really messy cases. Vehicle after vehicle trundled up
to the gates that were locked on police orders. People threatened
to dump their rubbish on the road if they weren't allowed in, but
Reg turned them away.

'Can't you see the yellow tape?' he shouted at them. 'It's a
crime scene.'

By mid-morning the team of investigators in overalls, boots,
masks and rubber gloves had a body in their bag, newly dead.
'Freshly skinned, with the head disarticulated,' one of the girls
cheerfully told Reg. They had bags of torn clothing that may
have belonged to the deceased and shreds of the black plastic
garbage bag in which the body had been dumped in a wheelie
bin somewhere down the road. They checked Jimmy's truck
for blood and other signs and interviewed the driver about his
collection route. They examined all the bins along the road and
the bins that had been taken back inside people's yards, trying
to match any traces to the matter found on or near the body.

By midday the television was there. When the investigators

left, Reg was ordered to keep the place closed until further notice. Only Detective Sergeant Rogers from Pleasant Vale police stayed behind to talk to him. He was a large, pneumatic young man with a milky, freckled complexion and ginger hair to match. Going by appearances, Reg judged him to be benign. He sat on the wonky chair in the manager's office and asked if Reg had noticed anything unusual that morning.

Reg decided to try the police officer's humour. 'Apart from a body, you mean?' he replied, earnestly tucking his chin under.

The detective laughed.

'No, nothing else,' said Reg drily.

When at last they had gone and he was left alone behind locked gates to guard the site, Reg fetched a large tub of plastic flowers from the shed where he kept the best of the things he salvaged. The flowers were creamy white, discoloured by the sun. He walked them across to the pit and flung them, rattling and scentless, at the mound where the deceased's head had been recovered. Reg inclined his own head solemnly under the baking sun, giving thought to the remains that were now on their way to their next chilly resting place. He was affronted by this intrusion of death into his world and, although he was a pagan, he found himself making the sign of the old Orthodox cross against his heart. A human life, passing so close, left its mark. Reg could feel the spirit hovering all about him, edged free from its mangled body. It spooked him.

# Chapter II

The day turned out pretty ordinary for Lewis after all. He took the taxi back to the depot at the end of the twelve-hour shift having made half as much again as the money he was contracted to pay the owner, Spiros. The depot was at the back of an auto shop off Canterbury Road. Spiros was waiting for him, complaining that the next bloke had let him down and there was no one to drive the night shift. Spiros couldn't stand to have a cab off the road. He was in debt to his father-in-law for the licences. He asked if Lewis could help him out.

Lewis shuffled on the spot. He was hungry. He was fatigued in a delayed reaction from the incident with the out-of-control Beamer that morning. But he needed to keep the owner of the cab on side and some extra fares would improve his average. He said he was prepared to work through to midnight on condition that he could take time off for a meal at home.

'Eat next door,' urged Spiros. 'My shout.'

There was a yeeros place next to the auto shop and a Maccas on the main road that Spiros favoured.

'I can't digest that stuff,' said Lewis. 'Sorry. There's food at home. Just give me one hour.' The food he ate on the road never satisfied him, not like the food his brother cooked.

'Fair enough,' said Spiros, patting Lewis on the back. 'I appreciate that. I owe you one, mate.'

Lewis lived with his brother Alan and Alan's wife Nancy and their two kids in a rented house in Concord. His widowed father had recently joined them from Beijing. The house had no frills but was big enough for all of them, a white-painted single-fronted brick box with lawn front and back that the landlord mowed, a concrete path that ran from the rusty front gate all the way round the house and straight down the back to the clothes line, a prodigious old lemon tree and a garden shed that Lewis had turned into a darkroom.

'Hi Pa,' Lewis called out in Mandarin when he walked in, adjusting his eyes to the gloom.

The old man barely understood a word of English but he liked watching television. He sat in the deep moss moquette-covered sofa in the living room most of the day, except when he shuffled out to the front porch to smoke. His daughter-in-law wouldn't let him smoke in the house because of the kids. 'Anyone with you?' the old man asked, rising to his feet. He was gaunt and shorter than he used to be, and his hair had receded far from his temples in a professorial manner. He lived in hope of Lewis bringing home a girlfriend – Chinese, Australian, didn't matter.

'Just me, Pa,' said Lewis. The old man responded with a smoker's cough.

'Five minutes,' called Alan from the kitchen where he had all the gas rings firing. The cooking smelled good. Alan's job as a house painter started early and finished early. Each day after work he would clean himself up and prepare the meal, letting the aroma of their food drive the toxic smell of stripper and paint from his hair and skin. Alan was Lewis's older brother and he was in charge of things. He was the good-looking one with a smooth relaxed smile that always came on his face when he cooked. Lewis put in money for the household, but Alan and Nancy kept the house going.

He could hear Nancy in the bathroom with Ming and Jack. The kids were splashing and giggling as she got them ready for bed. Lewis went out the back to check his prints, slamming the wire door behind him and striding down the path. When he was not driving the taxi or asleep, Lewis spent his time doing photography. Even while he drove, he was looking for subjects – an angle, a vista, a detail of the complex and ungainly city, a serene abstraction. Or he would dream up something to create with his camera, using his bedroom as a studio. He liked photographs that told a story in dark and light. The best ones were always accidents. They held meanings that could happen no other way.

He unlocked the shed and stepped into the darkness, fumbling for the switch to turn on the one bright bulb. He had enlarged a couple of prints – shots of Bondi Beach with unidentifiable figures standing by the shore – and studied them critically. He wanted the viewer to feel the vantage point of his invisibility. That was how he saw himself. But looking at the blown-up prints, he was dissatisfied with his work. He turned off the light, locked the shed and went back inside, where he poured himself a large glass of orange juice from the refrigerator and flopped down next to his father on the sofa. He needed to fill up on food and be on his way.

His father asked how the day had gone. The old man had a sunken, vacant quality, as if he were waiting to return from this foreign land that kept him apart from his dead wife. Lewis tried to cheer him up by telling him about the eighty dollar fare out to the garbage dump. That made his father guffaw. People spent their money in crazy ways in this country. As if there were no reason to save.

The television burbled on. The news. The same old stuff. Floods in India, bumper economy in China, and the President of the United States grinning from the side of his mouth in the White House garden. Politicians walking through revolving doors, journalists glowering to camera. Then came an item of breaking local news. An earnest young reporter in a badly knotted tie was standing against a locked wire gate out in the bush and frowning in the glare. Lewis raised an eyebrow. The place looked familiar. The camera jumped to a sign. *Pleasant Vale Recycling and Waste Depot*.

'Police are investigating the discovery of an unidentified body at a rubbish dump in south-western Sydney,' the journalist announced through unmoving lips. 'The body is said to have been badly mutilated. Police are regarding the death as suspicious and have appealed to the public for any information.'

A hotline number flashed across the screen. There was a shot of an old man with a white beard, figure bent, face averted from view, walking across the yard. The camera followed him, panning to a mound of garbage in a pit at the centre of the dump, before returning to the reporter's crinkled mouth and gleaming eyes for a solemn over and out.

'*Aiya!*' said Lewis, sitting sharply forward on the sofa as he recognised his fare, Reg Spivak. Was the old man *dead*? His passenger of that morning? His father had not understood the item and his brother had missed it as the wok sizzled and smoked. Lewis stood up, as if expecting a knock on the door any moment. In his shirt pocket was the taxi company card where Reg had written the registration number of the black BMW. He went straight to the darkroom in the garden shed and put the card between two layers of blackout plastic where no one would find it. Already, as he locked the shed behind him, he felt certain that the speeding car was implicated in the grisly news.

The food was on the table when Lewis came back in.

'Eat up,' Alan encouraged the family.

Lewis sat down and started eating straightaway. He could live on his brother's soy-fried chicken wings and peppery radish greens. Cooking was his brother's art, as photography was his. Alan had an eye, just like Lewis with his camera. And the dishes were not only colourful, they tasted good too.

'Eat up,' said Alan.

Nancy sat at the table, Ming and Jack perched on each knee. She made her fingers into worms that crawled up their arms. 'Stop it,' squealed Ming, the four-year-old girl, grabbing the chopsticks. She wanted to feed herself.

'Come on, Pa,' said Alan. 'Time to eat.'

'Hey, Pa,' said Lewis in Mandarin as the old man took his place at the head of the table, 'they had on the news that they found a dead body where I dropped off my long ride this morning. I wonder if it was already there when I arrived with my passenger. In all that garbage. Maybe I should go to the police.'

'Did you see something?' asked Nancy. 'It's nothing to do with you, is it?'

'What if they come looking for me? The police?' Lewis countered, not knowing if he was excited or anxious.

'You're teasing,' said Nancy. 'How would they find you?'

'They could trace the taxi if they wanted to,' said Lewis, chewing. He wondered again about Reg. The dump manager had been late for work. Was that suspicious? Lewis wondered if Reg might be involved. It was strange, after all, for someone to spend eighty dollars on a taxi ride from the inner city to a dump way out. Would Reg lead the police to him? Lewis knew he had signed the receipt that the old man asked for. That was information. Lewis had told Reg his name.

'Why would they be interested in you?' grinned Alan as he ladled out more rice.

'It's not your business,' said Nancy.

Lewis belched and stood up. 'I better get back to work.'

'You eat too fast,' Nancy sighed. 'We'll tell them you don't live here, if anyone calls.' She wished that Lewis would find a wife and move into his own house. Then his life would be more stable. He tired her with his coming and going at all hours. She worried that he would turn into one of those Chinese bachelor uncles who never leave the family home.

'Keep out of trouble,' his father added in the Chinese phrase that Lewis had heard all his life. Every day during the Cultural Revolution his parents said it, when he was a child in Beijing and every kid who stepped out the door might be stepping into calamity.

'I only saw it on television,' said Lewis dismissively. His paranoia made him feel stupid. There was no way they could trace him so fast. Or was it his wisdom, seeing round corners? He pulled his red bandana out of his pocket and tied it round his head as a disguise. He put on his dark glasses, even though it was evening. It was a weird look with his blue uniform. As he went out the door, he tried to imagine what he looked like. He was always doing that. He wondered if he was good-looking. Standards varied. He knew he wasn't tall enough for most Aussie girls. Sometimes passengers showed an interest in him. But he preferred not to be liked for his looks alone.

The silver taxi floated on the quiet street like a swan. Wide mown nature strips gave uniformity to the house fronts, to fences and hedges, walls and leafy screens, all in a line. At this

hour the residents were inside, engaged with meals and television, homework and the telephone. Maybe in a couple of houses
voices would be raised, but not always the same houses. If a
house was dark, it meant the people were having a night out.

Lewis answered a call from base to a nearby address and
picked up a young couple who had a babysitter to look after their
kids. They were heading out to a dinner party where they would
drink a lot of wine. He dropped them a couple of suburbs east
then headed into the city, crossing the Glebe Island Bridge in
flying mode for the second time that day.

It was quiet, especially for a Friday. Lewis felt entitled to
knock off early. But like every other taxi-driver in Sydney when
business slowed, he made his way to the airport where fares were
guaranteed as the last planes crowded in ahead of the eleven
o'clock curfew. Then he waited in the line of taxis, inching
forward, reading his book by the dim light in his car. It was a
book on photography. But he didn't agree with the author when
she said that photography could never tell the truth.

The airport was squeezed into a fringe of land between the
city and the sea, a convenient location except for the people
living under the flight paths who were being buried alive by
noise and pollution. Surely it made sense to relocate the airport
out where he had been that morning, Lewis thought, down the
freeway in the rolling hills beyond Macarthur Park where there
was nothing. But no politician would make the decision to move
the problem elsewhere so the existing structures became more
and more of a maze. More and more planes burning off their

fuel into blue waters and suburban yards. More and more people waiting in taxi queues, and the line of taxis waiting to pick up growing longer and longer.

Lewis, approaching the head of the line, watched as passengers pushed their laden trolleys in all directions, shoving and jostling. Seniors, disabled, babes in arms, those with tight connections, jet-lagged international visitors confused about the time: everyone had a reason to demand special treatment. Half the people were puffing away on cigarettes after their release from long hours in smoke-free airports and planes. They puffed fast, determined to smoke one or even two cigarettes before they got to the head of the queue. The taxi marshal, a big Pacific Islander in a yellow plastic jacket, was happy to ignore the chaos. No one could get his attention. But a blonde girl in big black leather boots caught his eye and he sent her to the head of the line with a cheeky wink. When she stepped off the kerb, however, and the next taxi happened to be a capacious wagon, a family of five voluble long-distance Europeans pushed forward from the back of the line and claimed it as theirs.

Gazumped! Welcome to Sydney, thought Lewis. He watched the girl give the family the finger as she turned swiftly to the car behind. The man whose turn it was stepped aside chivalrously, gesturing to the girl to go ahead. He even opened the door for her with a weary grin. Lewis was next. He honked lightly to catch the man's attention. He had bags hanging off each shoulder and looked round slowly. A boofy suit was crossing in front, jumping the queue as if he hadn't noticed that it was there. Lewis leaned over and opened the passenger door in the suit's path, then hopped out, chopping the air with his hand to make the suit jump out of the way. The man with the bags came forward. He had a matted mane of hair and a tawny beard to match and was still wearing his dark glasses in the middle of the night. Lewis had opened the boot and began to help him stow the aluminium equipment boxes on his trolley as well.

'What a zoo!' the man said as they drove away at last.

'It's Sydney,' said Lewis.

'Always good to be home,' the passenger laughed in response.

'Where to?' Lewis asked.

'Centennial Park.'

'Centennial Park,' Lewis repeated, his heart sinking. He had drawn the short straw after all – just about the shortest fare possible from the airport. That was the roll of the dice. But this passenger seemed to be a human being. Even though he was moving like a zombie, he was polite. He had his own rhythm and didn't need to push. Lewis was curious about him. Maybe if he could find out who he was that would compensate in part. He tooted a taxi in front that had stopped in the middle of the road for a pick-up. 'Which way do you want to go?' Lewis asked.

'Your call, mate. It's a short ride for you. Sorry about that.' Without much energy the passenger was making a gesture of being considerate. 'Been waiting long?'

'One hour,' Lewis grinned.

'Bugger that for a joke,' said the passenger, slumping sideways in the seat.

'Southern Cross Drive,' Lewis said, swinging the car away from the airport towards the city. 'Should be quicker at this time of night.'

'Sounds good.'

The man had the fetid sleepy smell that Lewis had learned to associate with long-distance flyers, especially big middle-aged men like this one who probably didn't fit the aircraft seat any better than they fit the car seat. Sometimes the smell was disguised by aftershave or toothpaste. The man yawned and said 'Excuse me', then scratched himself before patting his pockets automatically to check his things.

'Away long?' Lewis asked.

'Three weeks,' the man said, nodding as if to affirm the time.

'Working?' asked Lewis.

'Yup.'

'In the States?' Lewis pursued. It was a reasonable supposition, since most of the late night arrivals were off the big flights across the Pacific.

'Yup.' The man turned and smiled to show that his taciturnity was exhaustion not rudeness. 'I've come in from LAX,' he said, pushing his dark glasses up into his thick hair. His face was open and tanned but his eyes, slightly hooded, were sunk deep in a scribble of friendly lines.

'What were you doing there?' asked Lewis, smiling back expectantly.

'I'm in the movie business,' he said, stifling another yawn. 'I was shooting a movie.'

'That's interesting,' said Lewis.

'That's my equipment in back. I carry, my own stuff. It's insane. That's why I've got neck pain and never get any sleep during the flight.' He turned his neck from left to right until there was an audible click, then reinstated his dark glasses.

Lewis shrugged. He could only envy the man. Low dark vegetation flashed by as Southern Cross Drive curved north. In the distance was a vista of towers, illuminated against spuming cloud. Making movies had to be better than driving a taxi.

It proved to be a fast trip. Each traffic light turned green as they approached in a kind of synchronised dance. Lewis caught a glimpse of himself in the mirror. His black eyebrows bobbed. That's all he could see, a reflection of a part of his face that made him look like someone else. His passenger was staring blankly at the night. Lewis hoped he appreciated their luck with the traffic lights. Maybe he'd get a decent tip. He could not begin to imagine what the man was seeing.

'I never know why the directors are the famous names,' said Lewis, 'when it's the guy behind the camera who makes what you actually see in a movie.'

The man started, as if he had been falling asleep. He stared at Lewis defensively, as if a personal space had been broached. Then he relaxed into a grin as his thought processes came together. 'I could never figure that one out either. It's a bit of a war between the director and the cinematographer often enough. Too late for me to change sides now.'

'Huh,' said Lewis. The taxi had reached Centennial Park already, taking the road that bounded the dark grassy void, creeping over speed humps like a prowler. Lewis waited for his passenger to signal a particular house.

'That's it,' the man said, pointing to a wide two-storey sandstone house with a grand porch and an orange glow through the curtains of the front bay window. It looked like a security light to Lewis. No one was waiting at home for the returning hero.

'Fourteen dollars and five cents,' Lewis read off the meter. 'Fourteen bucks.'

The man pushed his dark glasses up onto his head and peered at the money he pulled from his pocket. He handed over a twenty-dollar note. 'Keep the change,' he said. 'Oh, and I need a receipt.'

Lewis wrote the receipt details on a taxi card, then he got out and helped unload the bags and equipment boxes, carrying them through the iron-spiked gate and up the stone steps.

'Careful, that's serious stuff,' said the man. 'Thanks, mate.'

'Your receipt,' said Lewis. 'The number's on it if you ever need another taxi.'

The front door had a solid brass knob in the shape of a pineapple and was surrounded with lead-lighting. The man was fiddling with his key. Then he stopped and turned to Lewis, picking up the deeper current of the conversation, now that the surface things had been handled. 'I guess you've got a point,' he said. 'The Director of Photography is the one that matters and nobody knows their name.'

'The DOP,' said Lewis, showing that he knew. Then he seized the moment to ask, 'What's your name? Maybe I do know it.'

'I'm just another dopey DOP,' laughed the passenger, as if it were a superficial matter after all. He turned to the door with his key and the taxi card wedged between his fingers.

'Maybe I've seen your movies,' Lewis insisted over his shoulder. 'What's your name?'

'I'm Bernie Mittel,' the man said. He was facing Lewis again.

But Lewis's expression was blank. 'Tell me one of your movies,' he said brightly, not skipping a beat. 'I really want to know.'

'Maybe you've heard of *Transformations of the Buffalo*,' the DOP said in the tone of worn, heavy irony that was his defence against disappointment. 'I shot that. Actually I won an Oscar for it.'

Lewis's face split into the cheesiest grin. 'Really? Wow!' He had heard of that one, even if he hadn't actually seen it. 'You're famous!'

'It's all relative,' said Bernie Mittel, feeling better for some recognition. He glanced at the card the taxi-driver had given him. 'Lewis Lin,' he read. 'Well, goodnight, Mr Lin.' He opened the door and put the first of his bags inside.

'Let me help,' said Lewis.

'I'm fine,' said the DOP. 'Thank you. Goodnight.'

# Chapter III

Bernie Mittel woke with an empty stomach, sprawled in a naked diagonal across the tangled sheets. He was tanned from head to toe except for his midriff and a pale stripe where the camera hung from his right shoulder. He had lugged it all over the shoot, bare-chested in the Arizona sun. No wonder his body ached. And now the phone was ringing.

He picked up because he thought it would be Jasmine. There was a message from her when he came in last night, the only voice message he had not deleted. But this time the voice was Josh Blane's, calling from Los Angeles where it must still be Friday.

'Hey, Josh,' said Bernie sleepily. He looked around to locate himself. The day in Centennial Park was heavy and settled. Through the shutters on to the balcony he could see the glossy foliage of the treetops across the road. Shit, he told himself, Sydney, Saturday. The hazy canyons and clogged horizontals of Los Angeles were gone, replaced by warm shadows and luxuriant greenery glimpsed intriguingly through slatted light in the listless air.

Bernie strained to tune in to what Josh was saying. Outside he could hear the sound of passing traffic and the shushing and heaving of the giant trees in the park, Port Jackson figs suffering slow death by brake dust.

The not-yet-thirty-something producer said he had some disappointing news. He was sorry to say that Bernie had been dropped from his next project.

Bernie emitted a foul combination of reflux and expletive. The caller did not quite know what he heard. The director loved Bernie's work in the past, Josh hastened to explain, but she wanted a different approach for this particular project. She had chosen an exciting new talent to work with. That was all.

Bernie told Josh that the director was a damage victim who didn't know technique from ordinary. Geez. *Terminal Care* was a sex comedy set in a geriatric hospice! A crappy movie that might be talked up on the art-house circuit if the director got very very lucky. 'Did you know this when we spoke in LA? You gutless wonder. You could have told me to my face.'

Time was when to act like an ape just down from the trees worked well with the Hollywood people. They recognised a kind of reality and respected it. But this new generation, insulated in their diapers from their dirty selves, wanted none of that.

'You're one of the great cinematographers, Bernie,' said the young producer, quite unperturbed. 'Your work has been a little uneven of late. That's all. Don't worry, you'll get your release fee.'

Bernie heard what Josh was saying. A year after winning the Oscar he was history, replaced by a kid from Seattle whose major achievement was ten minutes long.

'You, sir, are a pitiful specimen of humanity,' Bernie responded. He knew he was digging his own grave. He couldn't help it.

'There is no need to get cheap. Know thyself, *sir*,' said Josh insouciantly before switching to a tone of concern. 'Your friends are worried about you, Bernie. You might need to think about that. What were you doing in Arizona? I heard some stories about you out in the desert. It's not a good look at your age, man.'

'What are you talking about?'

But Josh had hung up, leaving Bernie to stew in his own juice in his daytime bed a hemisphere away.

'My *friends* are worried!' Bernie spluttered angrily into the silence as the bad news regurgitated itself. Award-winning cinematographer Bernie Mittel, with one of the best track records in the business, forced to negotiate a lousy release fee. Explain that!

Bernie propped himself up on the bed with a couple of pillows and stretched out his legs. He was still muscled under the flab. His chest, round and open, curved down into a gut that was brushed with a dark arrow of hair to his groin. Where his folded arms met his drooping pecs, more hair fanned out from the clefts of flesh. He felt prehistoric. He clenched his hands around his biceps in the folded arm position and flexed his toes. Then the old feller's head popped up. He put his hand down and fondled himself for a few seconds. That was no museum piece. Then he caught sight of white hairs among the brown down there and let it go. Every time you did it was one less from your lifetime quota. It was necessary to go carefully.

He would not pick up the phone if it rang again. Josh Blane could go to hell. The whole industry would know already that Bernie Mittel had been sacked from a major Hollywood project. That was bad enough. But there was worse. Bernie was filled with a sensation he could not name. It made him uncomfortable. Frustrated him even more. If it had a name, he could do something about it. Take a pill. Roll a joint. Call a number. He looked round for his cigarettes. He had given up smoking. Perhaps that was what unsettled him. You never really gave up. The craving for a cigarette, like any craving, was always there. And you did not want it to go away. It was life, asserting itself, stirring you into restless motion with unsatisfied desire.

Heave-ho, he told himself heartily as he swung his legs over to the floor and got vertical. He found his boxer shorts – silk, moon and stars pattern, gold on navy, fresh from Venice Beach – and pulled them on. The band was a little too tight. Know thyself, indeed, sir. What sort of swipe was that from a cub like Josh Blane to an old grizzly like himself?

Bernie was a master craftsman. He knew how to focus on the job in hand. The team was always happy to learn from him. Looking through the lens, he saw only what needed to be seen. The jacaranda from next door, for example, billowing across the balcony in a cloudy scatter of mauve as he opened the shutters and stepped out into the day. Not the sort of gorgeous image they would appreciate in *Terminal Care*, light graded from saturated shadow through flickering cobalt and fiery purple to feathery white radiance. The wind gusting, scattering flowers over the road, blue settling gently on the cars as if they were just married, or just dead. A few flowers drifting across the boards, tickling his bare feet. A woman with grey pageboy hair in one of the cars honked at him as he stood there in his boxer shorts. Someone he knew, or a stranger unable to restrain herself while she sat there in the traffic? He had no idea. It made him feel light and loose, a stranger on his own balcony, his feet scuffing the timbers while his spirit floated. He laughed out loud. In such moments he could look from outside at himself in the frame. That was the only way. As if he were not himself.

He tilted his neck from side to side, hearing it crack. Touch therapy. That's what he needed right now. Then he remembered Jasmine. Now *she* was good. Deep into the shoulder muscles and the neck, into the back of the head, between the eyes, up the thighs, front and back. He could feel her hands on his body. Release and adjustment. He should return her call. But when he dialled, he was told that the number had been discontinued. So if the phone rang, he would have to pick up, even risking Josh Blane, in case it was Jasmine trying to find him.

His osteopath had recommended Jasmine. Straight up and down therapeutic Chinese massage. She had come to the house a few times. Then Wanda found her card on the hall table and asked if she was a prostitute. If so, Bernie replied, he was yet to experience the full service. That was enough to make Wanda walk out on him. She said it was the last straw. And from what Bernie could see as he wandered round the house, Wanda had not been back during his absence. Her yoga room was empty of its paraphernalia. Mat, bolster and eyebag were gone. There were no papers or texts on the table. The wardrobe was empty of her clothes and shoes. Bernie concluded that Wanda was gone for good, and he realised he didn't really care.

The phone rang and this time it was his friend Andy, who was producing a long-running, high-rating television series about harbour police. At first Andy pretended that he hadn't heard the news. Then, unable to conceal his sympathy, he admitted that the whole town knew. Bernie Mittel had been dropped from the next big project. They were saying that Bernie was finished. Classic 'tall poppy' stuff. Envy and malice trashing a reputation.

'Do you want to go for a meal?' Andy offered.

Bernie almost hated Andy for the way he said it, but he was also grateful. That's what friends were for. 'No, thanks,' he grouched. 'I'm expecting someone.'

'Yeah,' said Andy, 'I heard that you and Wanda have split too.'

'You know everything, mate.'

'Look after yourself, buddy, that's all,' said Andy, preparing to end the conversation before it got any worse. 'Your friends are worried. You have to keep going.'

'Mate,' said Bernie, 'I'm keeping going. Okay? Fuck my friends. I'll see you sometime.' Then he hung up before Andy could do likewise.

At times like this Bernie hated everyone in his life, except maybe Andy who meant well and was a true mate. Most of all he hated Josh Blane, that smooth-talking know-nothing moralising kindergarten kid. In one turn of the wheel his career had dived and people were telling him to look after himself.

Then the phone rang again, after he thought it never would. Third time lucky, he told himself as he picked up. Yes, it was Jasmine. She said she could come right over. Bernie smiled as he went into the bathroom to sort himself out. Wanda had designed the bathroom in pure white marble and tiles of blackened silver. When you turned on the light you also turned on radiant heat and an extractor fan. He chose the bath tub in preference to the shower and turned both taps on full, cold and steamy hot. Imagining a long deep soak to soothe his limbs, he added a good squirt of green herbal gel to the gushing water. He sat heavily on the toilet, the new boxer shorts stretched from ankle to ankle, straining to expel the pills and the evil airline food from his body. Then he rinsed his hands and tramped downstairs to the kitchen to check the fridge.

There were olives in a plastic container that had white mould oozing from the slits in their sides. There was a squeezed tube of wasabe. There were oranges, blue with mould, and jars of chutney and jam. The milk, bread and apple juice were long past their use-by dates. A single egg remained from a carton of a dozen, and some dark yellow scrapings of non-dairy spread in an otherwise empty container. The best was the beer, five out of a six-pack, beautifully frosted. He reached for one of those bottles and closed the door on the rest.

As Nonie his first wife used to say, it wasn't that Bernie couldn't look after himself, it was that he didn't want to try, because sooner or later someone else would come along and do it for him.

Outside in the courtyard he saw the crowd of potted plants – gardenias, bright and fleshy ferns, bromeliads with lipstick flowers. That was all Wanda's work too, he acknowledged, as he unlocked the kitchen door and stepped out. The wind chimes tinkled lightly in the warm stirring breeze. Black and white butterflies flitted among the rouge bougainvillea that flounced along the rusty iron fence at the back. A whiff of frangipani came from next door. Voices, muffled, vanishing in the lane, and a cat screeching, a scrawny creature creeping as if invisible along the top of the fence. It was like entering a fecund, fanciful temple garden, Bernie thought, a garden that needed water now that Wanda, its resident goddess, had dematerialised. He looked round, checking what was alive and what was dead, sucking on his beer in his jet-lagged, disorientated state until, with a jolt of wakefulness, he remembered the bath. The taps were on full bore. He rushed inside with an image of fragrant, foaming water cascading down the stairs.

Jasmine was standing there when Bernie opened the door. She kept her finger on the buzzer when there was no answer the first few times, and pounded with the knocker with her other hand. She knew he was there.

He was pleased to see her. She put her head down in embarrassment when she saw that he was in a bathrobe with water dripping from his stubbly beard making a puddle on the floor.

'Excuse me,' she said, raising her head. 'I'm too early.' She brushed her long black hair from her face and her black Chinese eyes glistened. Bernie had forgotten how beautiful she was. She was tall and slender, with high cheekbones and powder-white skin. Her lips were full and glossy and her small nose crinkled as she let her head fall to one side, sighing and smiling at him with relief.

'You look great,' Bernie said crudely, shifting back in the open doorway for her to enter. 'Come on in.'

She brushed past him, bumping him with her large black leather shoulder bag. Bernie liked the tight blue jeans she wore with a gold belt, and the little pink high-collared shirt. She had gold bangles on her wrists to match the fine gold chain round her neck. He directed her into the kitchen.

'Take a seat,' he said. 'Can I get you a cold drink?' He was waking up.

'How was your trip?' she asked politely. Despite being so well presented, she looked strained. He noticed how her face drained of life when she looked away. When she turned back to him, she switched the light in her eyes on.

Jasmine laughed as Bernie downloaded the inconsequential stuff about the movie shoot. He kept on talking to hold her attention, to keep her gaze alight. The film in the Arizona desert was the story of a Hopi snake charmer who turns the chief's daughter into a snake. The girl can only be rescued by the love of a brave from the rival Navaho tribe. 'A period piece, all gloom and washed-out light,' said Bernie, declaiming with a twisted smile. 'The director was acting like a real bitch.'

Jasmine nodded, sipping her juice, just as the guy next to Bernie in business class on the flight from LAX had done before reaching for his headphones and sleeping mask.

'I'm glad you turned up,' said Bernie, dropping the tone of performance as he pulled up a chair beside her.

'So where's your wife?' Jasmine asked, as if the question were just more small talk.

'She's not my wife. She's my girlfriend,' Bernie said. 'And she's left me. As you can probably tell by looking at this place.' He waved his arms angrily at the ceiling. 'I have no idea where she is. She said she needed more space for her yoga.'

Jasmine turned her head from left to right and back again. The kitchen alone was large enough to live in, with its double sink and double refrigerator and double oven and high cupboards and large eating table and heavy chairs, and a sound system even now burbling with music. She wondered how anyone could need more space in such a large house.

'Wanda has shed one of her skins,' Bernie said with exasperated finality. 'She's slithered away.'

Jasmine looked at the creased, weathered skin lying in dark folds under the man's chestnut eyes. Curving smile lines swept up to join his sprouting eyebrows. His nose was ruddy, his lips cracked, his olive complexion glazed red by desert sun and skin cream, and overgrown round his mouth and chin with the makings of a tough salt-and-pepper beard. 'Your energy looks low,' she said.

Suddenly Bernie's smile turned sad. His eyes were like precious stones, a topaz facet of merriment in one light, a toffee-coloured depth of melancholy in another. He caught something of the woman's anxiety. Her skin was smooth and pale, in flawless condition, but her eyes were puffy, narrow, half curtained by the long black hair that kept falling forward and that she kept pushing back out of the way with nervous hands.

'Can we start?' she asked.

Jasmine worked on Bernie's feet with fragrant oil as he peered through the hole in the massage table at the grey corrugations of the carpet. The feet were a microcosm of the body, she told him. Each organ had a corresponding point on the soles of the feet. Today she found blockages there that anticipated failure. She pressed her thumbs into his flesh, hoping to start the process of release. That hurt. Then she started on his right leg, applying the oil in long steady strokes, upwards from the knee.

'Is something the matter?' she asked softly. 'You're very cold today.'

'Could be the travel. My body clock says it's the middle of the night.'

'No,' she said. 'Maybe my *chi* is too low.'

Bernie whimpered as she moved to his upper thigh. Her fingers were cold. He pressed his groin against the massage bed with a moan, making her ease off. She moved down to the ankle and calf.

'My new project has fallen over,' he said, answering her question. 'I'm not sure what I'll be doing next. It's an unusual situation for me.'

'Are you unhappy about that?' she asked.

'It would have been better if I'd chosen to quit myself. If it didn't just come out of the blue. One phone call.'

She showed no emotion as she pressed her weight against the back of his knee to open it up.

'Depends what happens next, I guess. It's like falling dominoes.'

Bernie's worry was that he might not get another project after this fiasco with *Terminal Care*. Never. Then how would he pay his bills? How would he live? He felt the fear of obsolescence in his body as Jasmine subtly adjusted her pressure, moving up now to his arms and upper torso.

'That feels better,' he said.

'Don't worry,' she pronounced as if it were an aphorism from a book of ancient wisdom. 'Your vitality is low. You need more energy.'

'That's right,' he said, exhaling from deep in his chest. 'Give me more energy. Do you know how to do that?'

'How's your money situation?' she asked. 'Is that a problem?'

'I'm okay,' he said. He knew he spent money on his own pleasures, but he had never lived extravagantly. He had money that he just sat on, a few small investments that he let accumulate over the years, and money he used to support his ex-wife Nonie and their daughter Cloud, who was nineteen now. Cloud – she was a great kid. Pity she was still in Adelaide. And he would need money for Wanda now too if she insisted on it. So that was a bit of a worry.

Jasmine was gouging the tight little muscles around his spine, working her fingers in between the vertebrae to separate them.

'I want acupuncture for you next time,' she said. 'Did you try that before?'

'Needles? Will it hurt?'

'That is what I studied in China. You need it to make your energy flow. To move the *chi*.'

The room smelled of the oil – eucalyptus, chilli, cedar – and the closeness of human heat. Bernie stared through the hole in the massage bed, conscious that he was naked but for a candy-striped towel across his arse.

Jasmine looked at the whorl of hair around the centre point of his scalp, the lanky tips of mane that licked his hairy neck, and the black hair curled down his broad back right into the pale crack that disappeared under the towel. He looked just like some shaggy animal cadaver as he lay there.

And that's how Bernie felt, suspended between consciousness and unconsciousness, as he contemplated the path his life had taken. He had produced good work. It was there on celluloid, no matter what happened, no matter what anyone said, cans full of realised dreams. He had fought for his career, focusing each step of the way, and he had won. But he shuddered, his pride crumbling again when he thought of how quickly oblivion could sweep even the best and seemingly most lasting things away.

'I dreamed of opening my own clinic in China,' Jasmine said, 'but it was impossible. Now I want to open a clinic here. Traditional Chinese medicine. That is my training. I can help you.'

Bernie grunted, emerging from his reverie to listen to Jasmine. 'Huh?' he asked, rolling over and reaching for the towel to keep himself covered. He was half aroused. 'What sort of help?'

'You need someone to help you look after your house and your business.'

'I need to get organised.'

'I can help you,' she said. '*You* can help *me*. You're a lucky man. You got that circle of hair on top of your head. That's special.'

Bernie observed the woman sharply, wondering what was pragmatic and what was fantasy. He distrusted omens. One thing he had learned in a lifetime of actualising the vexatious visions of producers and directors was to subdue the dream. Be realistic. No greater human capacity. And that way, no matter how incoherent the brief, he always came up with the problem-solving kind of work he was renowned for. The art, he liked to say, lay in delivering a solution on time.

'Run that past me again,' he said, propping himself on one elbow to assess her, to admire her.

'I'm looking for somewhere to live,' Jasmine explained. 'You have space. You need someone to help you. It can be me. I'll do it in exchange for the rent. You don't have to pay me.'

Bernie felt vulnerable and excited. He did not answer

straightaway, but he felt lighter, conceiving already how one thing might lead to another. The woman could be his partner in a threatening world, his at-home healer, the housekeeper he needed. She could arouse him with a touch. She knew how to read him. She was right. Her solution was his solution.

'I hardly know you,' he said, hesitating for one last moment before throwing himself forward into the rush of the situation.

'You're lonely,' she replied. Just like that. There was something so clean and matter-of-fact about it. 'I'm lonely too.'

'Okay,' he said, meaning it as a promise, but keeping it light. 'Why not?'

'Thank you.' She spoke solemnly as if to confirm their deal, then broke into a frowning smile that she managed to turn to laughter. He was relieved she didn't cry. 'Thank you.'

Bernie sat opposite Jasmine at a window table in the restaurant. Yellow oblong trains trundled below the escarpment on which they perched. The city lights buzzed at different heights, with different intensities, against a black sky that seemed to shudder in the night breeze.

'Like fireflies,' Bernie said.

Jasmine laughed in response, flashing her eyes and teeth as if to outdo the outside scene.

'There's just something about Sydney makes you feel good,' Bernie went on, 'even when you shouldn't. It's a comfort zone like anywhere that's home but it's something more than that gets under the skin about this place. It's the general looseness and the surprises. Things leaping from the shadows. Blasts from a pretty rough old past. It's the meeting place, the dealing place, just one big casino. We're ruining it, of course.'

The condensation ran down the bottle like surf as Bernie poured out the white wine. 'It's a mess, I admit. B-grade design, shonks, no vision. That's all part of it. The worst people are the winners.'

Bernie wanted to let the Chinese woman know that, as an Australian, he carried in his head a template of fairness and fundamental simplicity that he could call on from more complicated moral terrain. As a cinematographer, he saw himself as a tradesman who was lucky enough to be paid like a doctor or a lawyer.

'My parents are Chinese doctors,' Jasmine told him. 'They trained me to be a doctor. But I'm a girl. Their only daughter. Everything is hard for a girl in China.'

Bernie said he believed that his ancestors had blessed him. He was thinking of the tailor from Bremen a hundred and fifty years ago who set sail for Port Adelaide with his wife and kids and a bit of tough hope, and won blessings to pass on. Jasmine replied insisting that she had not done the right thing for her ancestors. Not yet. In this foreign land where time and space were distorted she had lost her bearings. North-south, east-west: the reference points were turned around and all she could do was to discard them, leaving nothing.

'Don't you have a boyfriend?' he asked.

'No,' she said. She hung her head in shame. When she looked

up again she was composed against the black window. Despite the shadows her eyes glinted, her hair shone, and the yellow light made her white skin like wax. Her long neck was turned, sinuously, and her face was half in darkness, as if she were negotiating a set of questions and answers with herself.

All that would play out, Bernie guessed with eager anticipation.

'I didn't know you won an Oscar,' she said. 'That's amazing.'

'It's just a lot of razzamatazz,' he said. 'I flew my daughter over for it. We had a lot of fun. She got to hang out with Keanu Reeves. Her mother didn't approve.'

'When did you grow the beard?' Jasmine asked. 'You didn't have that before you went away.'

'I was too lazy to shave out in the desert. Do you like it?'

'I don't know,' she said. 'Makes you look older. Where's your daughter now?'

'She's in Adelaide with her mother. Cloud,' said Bernie tenderly. 'Her name's Cloud.' He could still see the day Cloud was born, too small to find in the bundle of cloth. He could see the scowl she gave before settling to Nonie's breast. Perhaps that was what excluded him. He had walked out on his breast-feeding wife and their one-year-old daughter with no apology. The only work for a cameraman was in Sydney in those days and, anyway, the woman who had his child had discovered that she no longer loved him. He paid for them, money transferred from his account every month, but they were over as a family. He set out on his own, starting again in Sydney with an attitude of no encumbrances.

'Wanda redecorated the studio at the back of the house so my daughter could come and stay,' Bernie said. 'Cloud's finished school now. Wanda did the studio, the courtyard and the garage. It's all Wanda. She likes spending money. She's a very creative person. But then Cloud said she didn't want to come and Wanda didn't have any more projects. Maybe that's why she left.'

Wanda had stopped accompanying Bernie on shoots because in luxury hotels – in Prague, Mexico, Santa Monica – the only interest she could find was to turn inward and deny herself the luxury being pushed at her. Bernie would come back at all hours and find a Do Not Disturb sign on the door: Wanda would be inside in a shoulder stand. A yoga obsession, Bernie called it. She did the same back in Sydney. Before she walked out on him she was in yoga poses day and night, counting every breath. On the rare occasion she let him touch her, he was amazed to discover what she had become. Her skin was held taut by control from within. She could turn her body into a serpentine knot. Even as he held her, Bernie could feel her sliding out of his grasp. Through yoga Wanda had learned to satisfy herself by herself, without need of anyone else.

'Then she disappeared on me altogether,' he said with a smirk. 'Sorry to bore you with all this.'

'It's interesting,' Jasmine said, reaching out to touch Bernie's hand. She had a way of dipping her face so she could look up at him with side-on eyes. 'What happened to your daughter?'

'She never wanted to come to Sydney in the first place. It was

Wanda's fantasy. Happy Families. Cloud just decided to stay in Adelaide where her friends are.'

'You miss her,' said Jasmine. Her face was oval, tapering. Her expression was clear in dealing with emotional truths. 'Why don't you invite her again?'

'She'll come when she's ready,' Bernie answered, not sure if he was ready for her.

'If she doesn't come,' Jasmine ventured. 'Maybe her studio can be my clinic.'

'Now that's a good idea,' said Bernie. But Jasmine was moving *too* fast. 'I was very young when I got married,' he sidestepped. 'It was a way of finding out things. We were glued together until it all broke up. Nonie's with a woman now. We've been divorced for eighteen years. But I still love her in a way.'

Jasmine's straightforward expression emptied as she continued to look at him. She was no longer listening to what he said. It was all old rubbish as far as she was concerned, stuff to sweep out the door. What mattered for her, what put the excitement into their proximity, was what they might be for each other in future, if things could be so arranged.

Bernie did not feel the same pressure. He felt after-dinner desire. He knew that he would always go on loving all the women in his life. Nonie and Cloud. Wanda. That was part of being a good man. And right at the moment he wondered if he would love Jasmine too. Meaning attachment. Beyond all her charm, she had a sharp intelligence that really hooked him. But that's not what he was saying.

'Can I take you home somewhere?' he asked when they were in the car.

'It's really too far,' Jasmine replied. 'It would be more convenient if I could stay in your house tonight.'

'Okay,' said Bernie, not putting any further obstacles in their path. 'Sure. Nothing better.' He was grinning like a boy. 'There's plenty of room. Just the two of us, hey?'

# Chapter IV

Bits of hair, bits of skin, bits of crushed bone. First thing Monday morning the preliminary report from Forensic came through to the Pleasant Vale police. Detective Sergeant Ginger Rogers dug his fingertips into his scalp as he read, feeling for the skull beneath. He chewed his cud at the same time, as was his habit, behaving like the cows he had grown up with on the family farm on the South Coast in the days before dairy farmers went broke. He used to have milk-white skin then, covered with orange freckles, and carrot-coloured hair. That's where his nickname came from. Strangers might call him Blue, but he was Ginger to friends. Ginger Rogers. And he recognised his bovine behaviour, like his name, as the legacy of a cherished past.

The report identified the deceased as an Asian man between the ages of sixteen and forty. The Homicide Squad at Sydney Police Centre was calling for witnesses to come forward. Ginger Rogers didn't like to think about the number of young Asian male identifications in the area in recent years that had gone no further than a forensic report. Just too much trouble. If information was passed on, well and good, the police would follow up. Problem was you could never be sure. Chinese. Vietnamese. Names changed, Asian one minute, Anglo the next, first names and last names swapping round, inconsistent spellings, nicknames, gang names. The names alone were too much for the police computer. People slipped through the net.

The police officer thought these thoughts with no ill will. He was a relaxed bloke, professional, with a cheery view of life apart from his work. His assessment of the different varieties of motley humanity was cool and steady, containing no prejudice. Newcomers from everywhere were welcome in his part of the world, he maintained, with no discrimination according to colour, creed or culture, as long as they behaved. He and his kind didn't have a monopoly on this good life. Other people deserved as much. But Ginger liked to chew over the implications of things before he took action. He called it facing the facts. Not bad behaviour for a man of the law, he thought. He may not have been as smooth on his feet as his namesake, the real, gorgeous, silver-screen Ginger Rogers, dancing partner of the fleet-footed Fred Astaire, but he had earned his colleagues' respect for the effortless way he could glide across the surface of his professional duties. The facts of this case, Ginger had concluded already, suggested a matter that would not surface for long before sinking under its own opacity.

The forensic report provided some additional information that was not for the press release. They had identified the wheelie bin the body was dumped in and confirmed that death had taken place inside twenty-four hours of the body's discovery. The pelvic bones, helpful in establishing that the body was an Asian male, had been crushed. Forensic queried whether the garbage compactor truck could have done that as efficiently as a human boot. They made the observation that the skin of the face had been sliced off expertly. It was a known gang practice to attempt to erase the identity of the deceased: ritual humiliation. Probable cause of death was loss of blood through multiple knife wounds.

Ginger Rogers groaned. The Homicide Squad would take responsibility for the case. Those at the Pleasant Vale station would be given the routine tasks. Detective Superintendent Ronnie Silverton from Sydney Police Centre had already asked them to make inquiries as to whether a young Asian man had gone missing in the local area. Of course. And they were also requested to interview householders who lived in the vicinity of the Pleasant Vale Recycling and Waste Depot. Which of them had put out garbage that day? It was shit work, almost literally.

He decided to take Shelley Swert along. Constable Swert was a good talker, a good questioner. The guy at front desk said the detective sergeant needed her to soften his image. Not that Shelley was soft. She prided herself on not having an ounce of fat and her muscle tone, especially in the blue police uniform, gave extraordinary definition to the compact golden package that was her body.

'Any softer and I'd be yoghurt,' Ginger retorted. 'Don't be taken in. She's peanut brittle by comparison.'

Tall and rounded, with a receding line of fine deep red hair and an oversized head, Ginger considered himself a gentle giant. He would share the joke about his name with folks on a first encounter and they liked that. Ginger – for the bloodnut hair – Rogers. Irresistible. It disguised how cluey he really was.

Shelley Swert was new to Pleasant Vale. She looked good in a police uniform, preferring stretch pants to the skirt. She was lean and fast with a tight cut of white-blonde hair that suited her Slavic cheekbones. She liked to drive an operation. Every cell in her body contained the mutant gene of suspicion. Shelley wanted to know what was going on and never took no for an answer. So Ginger had discovered.

'Are you really that good on the dance floor,' Shelley asked him. 'Leading with you would be like trying to push an elephant round backwards.'

'Try me,' he chuckled. 'You can lead any time. I'm good at passive resistance.'

'I'd say you can be distant,' Shelley said.

'You have to be. Especially with a dancing partner. Anyway,' he said, putting her right. 'It's not about body weight, it's about poise.' Ginger knew he carried too much condition.

A woman had rung in, a nosy parker who was out walking her whippets on the road to the dump at dusk when she saw a couple of blokes unload a sofa from the back of a truck. They left it on the road beside someone else's wheelie bin. 'Furtively,' she said when questioned. 'Strangers to the area.'

By dumping the unwanted sofa on the roadside the men were

avoiding the fee at the council dump. Everyone the police spoke to knew whether they had seen the sofa or not. All those who saw it had taken a second look to see if it was worth grabbing. They had all decided against. The springs were bursting through the velvet and the foam innards were chewed up. It just stayed there until someone else dumped blackberry canes on top. The black-berry clippings were dumped after dark. That was illegal too. As a noxious weed, blackberry should have been burned. The thorns were vicious enough to tear the black plastic garbage bag that must have landed on top at some stage. That caused blood to drip through to the sofa. The blood was fresh and matched the dead man's. After catching on the blackberries the plastic bag containing the body had been lifted into the wheelie bin. The owner of that bin said it was not full. He only ever had one small bag of household rubbish a week. The council insisted he use the jumbo-size wheelie bin anyway.

Stopping for his collection down the road next morning, Jimmy had left the sofa and the blackberry canes sitting where they were. For health and safety reasons the drivers were instructed not to touch anything that was not in a bin. Then the busybody woman with the whippets was out walking again and found the blood. Her dogs had gone wild over it. Later in the day, after her call to the police, the forensic team removed the sofa. The bag containing the mutilated body must have been dumped there between the time the blackberry canes arrived after dark and the time the bin was emptied. Between nine at night and eight in the morning.

'I'll buy you lunch,' Ginger offered Shelley as they drove back along the country road from the interview with the whippet lady. 'Chinese okay?'

Patricia, the owner of the Green Dragon, was an old mate of Ginger's. She was a petite, friendly woman with waved hair and a tendency to wring her hands. Ginger ordered his usual bean curd and mushroom hotpot. Shelley went for the honey prawns.

During the meal, Patricia came to check that everything was all right. 'Enough ginger for you today?' she grinned. She liked to joke about the policeman's name too.

Ginger asked if she knew of anyone who had gone missing.

'Chinese or Vietnamese?' she tossed back, knowing the Aussie police could not tell the difference. She had seen the papers like everyone else.

'Asian,' said Ginger. 'Chinese for starters.'

Patricia looked around. She was neat in her tailored linen suit, watchful, self-contained, proud of the place she ran. 'We're all here,' she said. 'Nothing like that happen here. Better try over at the housing.'

Ginger noted what she said. 'Thanks, Patricia. Great lunch. My colleague here is new to Pleasant Vale. Constable Shelley Swert.'

'Pleased to meet you,' said Patricia with a bow, extending her hand.

Shelley reciprocated, not quite getting it.

Ginger explained as they walked to the car. 'It's the public housing development she's talking about. Those new blocks of units up by the freeway. Patricia reckons they're bad for the area.

All people on welfare. She doesn't approve of government hand-outs. Thinks people should look after themselves. Thinks welfare attracts no-goods. Crims, migrants, folk in community care that no community wants to know about. Patricia's got her prejudices.'

'Is she just fobbing us off?'

'She doesn't want any trouble. She runs an honest business. She's been here for years, seven days a week, all year round.'

'Does she really know what she's talking about?'

'If she doesn't know, she's pretty good at reading the tea-leaves,' Ginger said.

'I always feel hungry after Chinese,' said Shelley, still puzzled.

From the torn bits of bloodstained clothing that were mixed up with the body Forensic had made a list of what the dead man was wearing. A white cotton T-shirt, a crimson cotton gym shirt, black nylon running pants with GT stripes and, probably, the size eight trainers found among the garbage. Made in China. The apparel of a frugal person, Ginger observed, which made him more likely to be Mainland Chinese.

'The Vietnamese are the old boat people,' he explained to Shelley. 'They have prospered by now. A lot of the Chinese are fresh off the plane with only the clothes they're wearing.'

A group of young mothers were in the yard outside the housing block watching their kids play on the equipment provided by the junk food company, red and yellow swings, slippery dip and roundabout. There were no Asians among them.

'Who ya gonna do today, guys?' called one of the women as the police got out of the car. Her tone had the aggressive familiarity she reserved for her own kind. The redhead cop might have been her brother. She had a heart-shaped face and golden highlights through her own wispy orange hair.

Ginger asked if anyone had noticed an Asian person missing from the block of flats.

The woman laughed derisively. 'You're joking! The Asians are never the same from one day to the next. Coming and going all the time. No way you'd ever know if one of them was missing.'

'It's the second time this week we been asked that question,' said her beak-nosed friend, butting in as she pushed her dark twins back and forth in the stroller. 'Must be something up, Nicole.'

'Who else has been here?' asked Ginger, hoping he wasn't duplicating what Homicide had done.

'That wasn't the cops, stupid,' said Nicole, her heart face twisting into a lemon. 'That was Immigration last time. Telling the Chinese girl on the ninth floor that her time was up. She was shouting and screaming so bad after they'd gone that I went and thumped on her door. She told me they were sending her back to China. Seventy-two hours notice. Haven't seen her since.'

The woman leaned back with her hand resting on her swelling belly.

'How long have you got to go?' asked Shelley, indicating Nicole's pregnant condition with a look of sympathy.

'Too long,' replied the young mother with pride. 'Just hope it's not twins like Bec's got. My one-year-old is trouble enough.'

Shelley nodded, then she asked her how long the Chinese girl had been living there.

'I dunno. Not long. I never seen her before.'

'Do you know which flat?'

'909,' said the woman, tossing her straggly blonde tips. 'I remember that one because mine's 990.'

'Could you say how old she was?'

'You can never tell how old they are,' said Nicole, voicing it as a grievance. 'Same sort of age as you and me, I suppose. Twenty-something, and pretty.'

The long corridor of the ninth floor was cool despite the afternoon sun. The paint was new. People had different things hanging on their doors. Golden bells, red paper cut-outs, football transfers – Bulldogs, Panthers and Sharks. Shelley found 909 and pressed the buzzer.

When no one answered, she buzzed again. An old man opened up, Chinese she assumed. He wore baggy grey trousers and a sleeveless white vest. 'Police,' said Shelley, as if it were not already obvious, two strangers at the door in blue uniforms with their caps on. 'Can we come in?'

The man peered at them through scratched glasses, crinkling his face. His legs were bowed, his hands lifting. He shuffled aside to make way, nodding his head without saying anything, and when Shelley asked if someone else was living there, he replied, 'No speak English.'

'Great,' said Shelley, rolling her eyes at Ginger who was

amused at his colleague's frustration. Nothing would stop her anyway. Her jaw was set. 'We might as well take a look around,' she said impetuously, stepping round the old man and heading for the kitchen. Ginger didn't mind standing back, watching as the old man muttered something to Shelley that sounded grumpy. Ginger nodded at him amiably and said, '*Ni hao!*'

'*Ni hao, ni hao,*' the old man repeated in mocking singsong, as if that version of the greeting were as strange on his own tongue as on the policeman's.

Constable Swert moved through the flat, skimming things with her eyes. It was tidy and empty. The kitchen had an electric kettle, a wok resting on the gas stove, some pans and chopsticks and cooking oil and salt, and a few jars in the fridge. Some half-used toiletries sat on the bathroom shelves. Chinese newspapers were in a pile by the television. The beds were made with crumpled linen. One bedroom had two single beds, the other bedroom had two double bunks. There was another bed in the living room with a suitcase open on it. The old man came up to Shelley as she was examining the case. He went to stop her, but held back. It was packed with his clothes. After the policewoman had looked through it, he snapped it shut.

'He's the last one to go,' said Ginger. 'What time?' he asked, pointing at his watch. The man shook his head, raising his hands in ignorance. 'He probably doesn't know himself.'

'I wonder how many others there were?' asked Shelley. She was keen to make sense of the situation for herself. 'The place sleeps at least seven. Do you want to stick around?'

'Not now,' said Ginger. 'If it's a missing person we're after, we've already missed them.' He gave the old man a card with the telephone number of the Pleasant Vale police station. 'We should have these made up in Chinese,' he apologised facetiously. 'Thanks for your cooperation.'

The old man stood at the door and waved them goodbye. He called out something, then he frowned in confusion as he watched them walk towards the lift.

'Did anything strike you as weird about that?' Shelley asked Ginger as they went down. 'It was almost as if he expected to come with us. Did he look worried to you?'

'He went into defence posture when he first opened the door.' Ginger bent his knees and flexed his hands to show how it was done.

'Where did you get that from?' she asked. 'Are you into martial arts too?'

'No thanks. I'll leave that to you. You're the tae kwon do champ, aren't you? No, I've got some videos at home. Kung-fu movies. That's my idea of keeping fit.' He scratched his head. 'If that old bloke was nervous opening the door, maybe someone else has been round lately. We better find out the names of the people who have been living here. Mr Wang, I suppose. Mrs Wang, Miss Wang, Master Wang.'

'Happy Families,' Shelley laughed, adjusting her cap on her head as they crossed to the car in the fierce western sun.

'You got it.'

'How can they expect us to get anywhere with a case like this when we don't speak the language?' Shelley felt she had made a fool of herself invading the harmless old man in his flat.

'Good old-fashioned Aussie police methods,' responded Ginger with some sarcasm. 'That's all we've got to help us.'

Shelley slammed the car door, flushing. 'I don't think that's enough.'

On the drive back to the police station through a landscape of pale brick bungalows arcing over the grassy dales of new estates, Ginger ruminated aloud. 'We're waiting for a message. That's all we can do. It seems there's nowhere to start in a case like this, then something happens. If we're open to it. Without that message, we've got nothing. But for now the file just stays open.'

'I don't feel comfortable being as passive as that,' said Shelley, blasting off. 'That's not why I'm here. A man is skinned to death down the road and we just sit round waiting for a sign to drop on us. No way.'

Ginger watched her from the corner of his eyes. Her arms were tightly crossed and she was digging her sharp pink fingernails into the bare tanned skin of her upper arms, as if to punish herself for being so ineffectual. She pouted, flashing her icy eyes from side to side.

'Hey there,' said Ginger. 'Let it go. As long as you're ready when the message comes, champ.'

He put his foot down, exceeding the speed limit by just enough to feel good, crouching over the wheel like a tiger ready to pounce.

# Chapter V

'Lewis Lin? Thanks for calling back, mate. I didn't know if you'd get the message. The bloke said he didn't take messages for drivers. I said I left something in your cab. Which in a way I did. You know who I am, don't you? The geezer from the dump. I'm back in the city where you picked me up.'

'Reg?' said Lewis, recognising the raspy overdone enunciation at once. 'Where are you?'

'I'm back at my daughter's. In Surry Hills. The dump's closed today. Because of…you know. Can I buy you a cappuccino if you're passing this way? Then I'll be catching the train back to Pleasant Vale.'

'I'm on the road now,' said Lewis. 'I can meet you in half an hour. Where?'

'How about Central? At the top of the ramp, Country Trains entrance.' The man's voice sounded tentative, anxious to avoid trouble. Lewis felt his gut tighten.

'That's good,' said Lewis. 'Plenty of space to park. What's up?'

'Tell you when I see you,' said Reg, ending the call.

The old man was waiting under the awning by the luggage deposit when Lewis drove up. It was a warm, gusting afternoon, approaching three o'clock when many drivers changed shift and taxis were hard to find. Lewis could have picked up a dozen fares outside the station. People swore at him when he wouldn't stop for them. He cursed the money he was losing when he should have been driving, just to meet up with Reg, the man who brought him trouble in the first place. Against the dirty sandstone walls of the station building, Reg looked self-contained in his pressed trousers and a wind jacket. He was smoking a cigarette out of the wind. His backpack, neatly buckled, hung from his hand. He was unrecognisable as the harried figure that had been caught on television, dashing across the yard. Lewis flashed his lights before looping round to park.

'Look, there's a place inside,' said Reg, coming over to the car and shaking Lewis's hand with a conspiratorial air. They would be invisible among all the comings and goings of the dusty concourse beneath the cavernous dome and the old clock that was slow when you were late for a train but could never stop it gliding out a fraction of a second ahead of you. 'Unless you'd like to go somewhere else. Thanks for coming, mate. I hope it wasn't out of your way.'

'That's fine,' said Lewis. 'What's up?'

'Can I get you a coffee?' asked Reg. 'I owe you one. I got you into this.'

They got cappuccinos from the cart and found a bench to sit on.

The coffee cups oozed where the plastic lid was not on properly and the coffee was too hot to drink.

'I hate these cups,' said Reg. 'Rubbish before you even start. You know what they found out there?'

'I saw it on television,' said Lewis.

'So the police haven't been on to you yet?'

Lewis shook his head. 'No.'

'And you haven't contacted them?'

'No.'

'You see they interviewed me. I mean they came back. They found me at home. I didn't tell them anything the first time, but they said Jimmy, the truckie, had told them there was a taxi out there, and an Asian driver. I told them I'd been running late for work. It was my daughter's birthday, a special occasion, and I stayed over in town. I had to get a taxi back. I'd only just been dropped off when Jimmy arrived. Just before eight. Now they want to check with you. I said I couldn't remember anything about the cab or the driver. I just hailed it on the street.'

Lewis listened. 'I gave you a receipt,' he said.

'I suppose I forgot about that at the time,' said Reg. He paused. 'You know what they're saying. The dead man was Chinese. That's why they're interested in you. They see a connection.'

'Because I'm Chinese? Did you tell them that?' Lewis stared at Reg accusingly, wanting to know what box the old man's mind put him in.

'That's how their minds work,' said Reg apologetically. 'Look, I don't want things to get worse than they already are. Someone told them I used to work at the abattoirs. Well, that's right, I did, long ago. It was good money. We all eat meat, don't we? Most people, at any rate. I was apprenticed to a butcher when I was a kid. My father was a butcher back in Belgrade. It was the only work he could get when we came out here and he got me into it too. I left school for that. The police are saying the dead man was *skinned*. It was done by someone who knew how to do it. They're looking for butchers and surgeons. "Don't forget fishermen," I told them. There are too many fishermen. Everyone's a bloody fisherman.'

Reg was talking too much, Lewis felt. He was under suspicion because he had worked at the abattoirs and had not told the police about the taxi ride and the Chinese driver. Too many stereotypes fusing together. Deep down in the man, layered over by the fat of the years, Lewis sensed a terror of authority that he understood, a fear of power when it was backed up by brute force blind to fairness or justice. China instilled such fears, and no doubt Yugoslavia had. It was part of life under that sort of communism.

Reg raised his bristling white eyebrows at Lewis, not in ironical friendship this time, but sharply questioning him. 'You believe me, don't you? I had nothing to do with it. I couldn't even invent something like that. I'm about recycling. I'm not about creating garbage for myself. Just like I know you had nothing to do with it, no matter what people might think. One Chinese, two Chinese. Doesn't make a Yellow Peril. That's why I didn't tell them about you. Not even that you're Asian. I don't want trouble for you either.'

Lewis blinked as Reg stared at him frantically.

Then Reg said, 'I gave you the number. Do you remember? I wrote it down. That runaway black Beamer that nearly killed us both. Do you still have that card?'

'Did you see the driver of the car?' asked Lewis. He saw that Reg's line of thought was the same as his own. The black car, racing away from the dump at just that time, was the clue. They were both almost among its victims.

Reg shook his head. 'I didn't tell the cops about that car or the number. You're Chinese and the dead man's Chinese and suddenly they're wondering about the connection between you and me. The more they know, the more complicated it gets for everyone.'

Reg had gone round the mental block a few times to reach the conclusion that Lewis had reached the moment he saw the news on television, the conjunction between the car and the dead man. They were both at the mercy of the trouble that conjunction could cause.

'We've got nothing to hide,' said Lewis.

'They might think it's strange that I've got such a bad memory,' said Reg.

'No one has contacted me about it except you. No one knows it was me who drove the taxi unless we tell them.'

'There's a reward for information,' said Reg. 'Doesn't the taxi company keep a record of journeys? It was quite a long one.'

Reg fiddled to get the lid off his coffee. He sipped it apprec-iatively. Lewis and the old man were joined by the same desire to protect themselves, to forget whatever they knew in order to remain invisible. They were like partners in a card game who must signal what they know while keeping part of the truth hidden, even from each other. On the bench in the concourse their voices were drowned by the announcements of departing trains. Passengers strode decisively ahead with newspapers and bottled water and luggage, tourists and commuters and patients who had come to the city to see a specialist doctor, going home, while another group, mostly students, funnelled from the Blue Mountains train, screwing up their eyes as hot gritty wind whipped in off the tracks. The crowd flowed past Reg and Lewis, islanded in the middle, ignoring them.

They drank their coffees. 'I enjoyed the ride out with you that day,' said Reg. 'You're a human being. This horrible thing – it's a revenge killing. It'll be someone taking the law into their own hands. It's got nothing to do with us.'

Lewis recognised the old man's anxious, roundabout way of approaching things. It was a defence ploy. He was just like Lewis's father.

'Don't worry, Reg,' said Lewis. 'No one's going to find the card with the rego number of that car on it. I hid it. It doesn't exist. No one's going to come after you.'

'Yeah, well, that receipt with your signature on it is out of the way too. It's not hard to dispose of something at a rubbish dump.'

'Why was that Beamer in such a hurry out there?' Lewis asked.

'You and I know why,' said Reg. 'Bastards.'

They looked at each other intently. The black Beamer hurtling towards them, speeding away, a man at the wheel, another man in the passenger seat, someone in the back, turning – and a murdered man at the dump. Lewis felt the wind rush as it came close. The back of his neck bristled.

'We shouldn't jump to conclusions,' said Lewis nervously.

'No one needs to know what we know,' said Reg. 'Better leave it to the police to put names on faces, and keep our mouths shut before we end up skinned alive too.'

'Skinned *alive*?' repeated Lewis, feeling his heart tighten with disgust. That was a detail not spelled out in the reports he had seen.

Reg nodded, with mute respect for what the dead man had suffered. 'That's what the cop from the city let slip.'

Between them Reg and Lewis held a few clues. But it was not their business. It was not their law. Not their birthplace. They could not trust the way things would unfold. Justice was not theirs to deliver. They could only, awkwardly, trust each other, and only as far as was needed. 'My train's at the platform,' Reg said, heaving on his backpack. 'Better get moving. No taxi this time, eh? Finished with the coffee?' He stuffed one empty cup into the other. 'Well, you know where to find me, mate. Toodle-loo.' He gave a fruity articulation to this favourite farewell phrase of his, picked up somewhere along the way in a lifetime of scavenging words. Lewis had no idea what it meant.

He watched Reg cross the concourse. The old man didn't turn. He dropped the used cups into a bin and punched his ticket through the turnstile that led to the train. He held himself upright, shoulders at ease, as if for the moment his task was accomplished, as if he had cleared some space around himself and felt safer.

Lewis felt relieved too. To say nothing was the only way of keeping themselves out of it. And keeping out of it was the only way.

# Chapter VI

On Tuesday morning a message came. An anonymous caller to the *United Australian-Chinese Times* said that the corpse at the garbage dump was a Chinese man by the name of Zhou Huang. The caller identified the two Chinese characters for the name and hung up. The editor, William Mak, discussed the call with the newspaper's owner, then rang the police. He believed that the anonymous call came from the killers. They wanted people to know.

'I want a scoop,' said Mak.

'Okay,' said Detective Superintendent Silverton at Homicide. 'Can you wait twenty-four hours?' He wrote down the exact spelling of the name to be checked against information on police files.

'Oh, another thing,' said the editor. 'That voice on the phone said the dead man was a dog.'

'What does that mean? He's double-crossed somebody?'

'He's double-crossed his own people.'

'Good stuff, William. We appreciate it. You'll be the first to hear if we get anything. I promise.'

Ronnie Silverton groaned as he put down the phone. Another promise he wouldn't keep. And a Chinese gangland killing after all, just as he had predicted. In a way that made it easier to close the case, even if, like all the others, it would never be solved. He called the boys at Pleasant Vale to give them the news. Shelley Swert answered the phone and passed him to Ginger Rogers.

'Zhou Huang?' said Ginger, repeating the spelling. 'Just a minute. We've already got that name on our list of Asian men missing in the area.'

But Silverton wasn't listening. He just went on talking. 'They got this guy as a warning to others. He'll be a drug dealer who kept back some of the money. They want people to know who's in charge. We'll never get to the bottom of it.'

'We can go ahead and follow up this report without much trouble, Superintendent.'

Silverton ignored him. He had got to the top of Homicide by crashing through and covering his tracks. 'I've seen it before, Sergeant. You'll be wasting your time. It's a Chinese matter. Let the Chinese sort it out.'

'But Ronnie, it's a serious crime that has happened in our patch. People out here want it solved. How would you like a dead body in your rubbish dump?'

The superintendent could hear the man's disappointment. It was territorial more than anything. The suburban boys were always like that. Rogers was a good man. He was doing his job. But he would never solve the case without expert help and extra resources. 'Okay then, see what you can do for starters,' said

Silverton. 'Do you want me to repeat the name? Remember, it's last names first, so just make sure it's Zhou Huang you're chasing and not Huang Zhou.'

'With your pronunciation, sir, no one would know the difference.' Ginger chuckled to himself after the superintendent hung up. He had a video at home on Chinese Mandarin pronunciation. Those Homicide guys thought they knew everything. Ronnie Silverton hadn't even asked what Ginger knew. So Ginger didn't tell him. And Ginger knew a few things already.

'Homicide are letting us go with the case,' he said, leaning across to Shelley.

'Big of them,' she said.

'They've confirmed the deceased's name.'

'And we have his telephone number,' she trumped.

Gerard Ciccolini, director of Kangaloon Native Garden, had left a voice message for the Pleasant Vale police late on the previous day. Shelley had called him back while Ginger was taking the call from Silverton. The director told her that one of the garden staff was missing from work, a young Chinese man who had been absolutely reliable up to this point. His name was Zhou Huang. He had phoned in to say he was taking the day off. That was the day before the body was found at the dump and the call for information went out. Zhou was a quiet sort of chap, a good worker and a gifted gardener, in the director's opinion, and they had not heard from him again.

'I don't want to jump to conclusions,' Ciccolini said, 'but I'm quite worried.'

He told the policewoman that the only contact details he had were a telephone number and a post box address. From the telephone company Shelley got the street address of a house at Fairway Heights.

'That's the sort of message you mean,' Shelley said to Ginger. She was at the wheel of the car today. 'We're on our way.'

A face peered through the lace curtains when the police car stopped outside the brick veneer dwelling. The bare garden was well looked after. The lawn was close cropped, the standard rose bushes pruned and flourishing. New tiles had been laid on the porch in a recent renovation. It was all very neat. The door chime played 'Greensleeves' when Shelley pressed the buzzer.

A jumpy young Chinese man opened the door and looked at the pair of police through thick glasses. He had unbrushed black hair and his sunken chest showed through his thin nylon shirt. He was curious rather than afraid, and wanted to know how he could help. The policewoman explained that they were trying to get in touch with a Mr Zhou Huang.

'Ah,' said the man, his expression livening, 'come in, please. You can say we are also trying to get in touch with Mr Zhou Huang. He has not been home for a couple of days and his food is wasting in the fridge.' The man grinned as he shuffled into the house in his slip-ons, assuming the two officers would follow.

A sallow Chinese woman in a pale-green dress emerged from one room and a plump, baby-faced woman in a sports shirt and white pants from another. The man introduced them as students from China who rented the house with him. Then he announced loudly and with an out-of-key formality that he was the designated head of the group. His name was Fu Shaohua and he was a physics researcher. He had the look, thought Ginger: head like a bean and a high brainy brow. 'You can call me Fu to make it easy for you,' the man added ingratiatingly.

'Will you have some tea?' asked the woman in green. Her name was Hong and she wore her hair in a tight bun. 'Chinese tea?'

'Mm, thank you,' said Shelley hesitantly. She turned to Ginger who nodded in agreement. They were going to be there for some time and Ginger was approaching the whole thing as a cultural experience. The other woman, Mei, who had a mole on her dimpled chin, sat on the couch, watching the proceedings keenly.

Shelley looked at the tiles that continued from the porch through the living room and hallway and into the kitchen. She guessed that the house had been purposely renovated as no-frills student accommodation. The lease on the house was in the name of someone else again, also Chinese, she had ascertained from the agent, and the owner was Chinese. The current residents had lived there for varying lengths of time. Zhou Huang had apparently lived in the house for eighteen months.

'So Zhou Huang is a student too?' asked Ginger. Fu nodded vaguely. 'Whereabouts?'

'He's work experience at Kangaloon Native Garden.'

'Please,' said Shelley, 'I want you to tell us everything you know about him. I'm sorry we can't speak Mandarin, but your English is very good.'

Her parents still spoke Ukrainian in the home, and she was conscious of parroting the kind of thing she had heard unwanted visitors say as a child.

The man began. 'Zhou Huang's home town was Hangzhou, Zhejiang province, China,' he said. 'Zhou was proud of his birthplace.'

'Hangzhou is one of the great cultural cities in China,' declared the woman in green, who was more like a teacher than a student, as she brought the tea.

The man said something to her in Chinese, as if to silence her, then resumed his account in English. Shelley stiffened, taking against him. She wondered what the relationships were between the three Chinese, wondered how she could ask. There was a sense of solidarity among them, but also distance.

Fu explained that Zhou Huang came originally to study English, then he switched to a course in horticulture. He was quiet and kept to himself. In the house they usually shared the dishes they cooked but Zhou Huang, because he was vegetarian, tended to eat by himself.

Ginger looked up with interest. 'Why was he a vegetarian?' he asked.

The man shrugged. There was a pause. Then Hong, the woman who had brought the tea, seized the opportunity to join the conversation. 'He was quite strange, really,' she said in a tone of authority.

Then Shelley asked, looking at Ginger, 'Why is anyone a vegetarian?'

That set them off. The dumpy woman, Mei, revealed that Zhou Huang spent most of his time locked in his room working on the computer. They heard him tapping the keyboard for hour after hour. Mei smiled, enjoying the gossip. They could not imagine what he was doing. It was certainly not part of his horticulture course. When they asked him he said he was writing letters home.

'But he never printed them out,' said Hong.

'He didn't have a printer,' added Mei. 'He said he used the printer at work.'

The rest of the time he looked after the garden. He never invited friends to the house. They didn't know whether he had a girlfriend or anyone else. Sometimes phone calls came for him from a Chinese woman. Recently his most regular calls were from an Australian man, with an old-sounding voice who could not pronounce his name correctly. He was often away at the weekend without saying where he went.

'More tea?' asked Hong.

'No, thank you. You've been very helpful,' said Ginger. He had the impression that the household had few visitors. 'Do you mind if we take a look around? Could you show us his room?'

The occupants were a little put out by this request. They knew they had no choice but to comply, yet wondered whether it was right to do so.

'We've got a warrant,' said Shelley. 'Show them, Sergeant.'

Fu glanced at the document before passing it to the two women, who examined it carefully and handed it back. Fu pointed out the door to Zhou Huang's room. 'It's locked,' he said. 'He's the only one with a key.'

Each of the four bedrooms in the house had its own lock. It was a rental situation in which each of them lived on their own, independently.

'How did you meet?' asked Shelley.

'We belong to the Chinese Students Association,' offered Hong. 'They help us. I'm doing a Masters in Educational Psychology.'

Shelley nodded wisely. She guessed that Hong was really the one in charge. Later she would check the Chinese Students Association. It was probably funded by the Chinese government.

Ginger rattled the door of Zhou Huang's room and told Shelley to check the window. 'There's definitely no key,' he concluded.

'And the only way in through the window is to smash the glass,' she reported.

'That's a pity,' he signed, gesturing at the door. 'Would you mind, Constable?'

Then Shelley stepped back and with one sturdy kick she broke the lock and opened the door.

'Nice one,' said Ginger as he walked in through the open door. He enjoyed martial arts videos, but Shelley Swert was a real live master. 'Sorry,' he said to the perturbed householders. 'We'll cover the cost of any repairs.'

In the room was a single bed with a brown cover. A dirty white pillow sat at the head of the bed and a padded quilt of brightly patterned cotton was crumpled at the foot. The mattress retained the indentations of the last person who had lain there. A suitcase of clothes was open in one corner of the room. Shelley rifled through and Ginger made some notes. The clothes were neatly arranged. There was a rack hung with trousers, shirts and a jacket and tie on wire coathangers. On a shelf were Chinese and English books, a couple of dictionaries and a tome called *Australian Native Plants*, along with magazines, a mug and a toothbrush and other toiletries. The desk was bare but for the computer monitor and keyboard. No printer, Shelley confirmed. The window to the back garden was covered with a closed venetian blind. On the floor were leather shoes and a black briefcase propped out of sight. Ginger leaned down and pulled the briefcase towards him. There was something clunky inside but it was locked and, without forcing it, he passed it to Shelley. He opened the slats of the venetian so they could see better and the room filled with bands of light that revealed a slurry of dust drifting through the air.

Shelley turned on the computer, going straight to the documents on the hard disk. She clicked open an assignment for an English language course. Student: Huang Zhou, names reversed in the standard Anglo order. She clicked open another file and found it blank, and another, also blank. She checked what else was installed on the system. Chinese software. His housemates said that Zhou Huang spent hours working at the computer, but he seemed to have removed all trace of what he was working on.

Shelley packed up the computer, pulling it to bits briskly.

'Isn't there a box in the back of the car?' she asked. 'Jesus, we're organised.' As she stood there, Ginger just went on piling things into her open arms. 'Shouldn't we make an inventory?'

The householders, watching through the open door, might have protested if they had not been relieved to see the room emptied out.

'Let's just get it all back to the station and sort it out there,' said Ginger, pulling rank in his laconic way. Sensing his colleague's annoyance, he turned his back on her. He knew the damage her well-aimed kicks could do. Instead he assessed the room. Apart from the computer, there was nothing of value and little of any personal significance. They were things that could have belonged to anyone. The room was faceless, just like the body at the dump. The imprint of his reclining weight on the bed seemed to be the only mark Zhou Huang had left on the world.

Balancing everything else, Shelley stooped to pick up the round black cushion from the floor. She tossed it at Ginger's head. 'Do we want this thing?' she asked.

'Hey, what are you doing?' protested Ginger, turning on his toes. 'It's a *zafu*. A Buddhist meditation cushion. Better write a receipt for it.'

'You're full of information, Sergeant.' Shelley squeezed the cushion playfully. 'And full of shit.'

Out the back in an expanse of lawn a Hills hoist fluttered with drying towels. There was a line of old fruit trees – a lemon, a fig and a peach – that must have been put in when Fairway Heights was first subdivided, back in the sixties. Italians and Greeks first, then Lebanese, Vietnamese and Turks. Now Chinese. And Iranians. And Russians. From wherever in the world there was hardship, turmoil and some stubborn residue of hope. A concrete path led to the garage, ropes of grass pushing through the cracks. Apart from some stored boxes and a couple of bicycles the main thing in the garage was a 1970 Volvo sedan, silver.

'Classic motor,' said Ginger.

'It's my car,' said Fu proudly.

Mei tugged at Shelley's sleeve, indicating that she should pay special attention to the row of young native trees down the fence line. The saplings were newly planted, thoroughly staked, weeded and doing well. Zhou Huang had planted them, she said. They came from the botanical garden where he worked. He had put them in only a few weeks earlier, tending them with great care, wanting them to live.

Her implication was that he expected to be around to see them grow. *He* wanted to live too.

Shelley got out her video camera and proceeded to photograph the trees, individually and together. The householders grinned vacantly, making sure they were not caught in the frame, approving of this casual ceremony nonetheless. It was all the commemoration Zhou Huang would get at his last home.

Police instructions were that nothing should be touched for seven days. Shelley gave Fu a list of the objects they were taking away, property of the missing man. They would be back later for a follow-up interview with each of those who had been acquainted with Zhou Huang. Fu wanted to know, on behalf of the group, how soon the room could be let to someone else. Zhou Huang's rent was paid to the end of the month but, if there was no problem, they would get someone else to move in straightaway.

'Leave it for seven days,' Ginger said. 'Now I'll need one of you to identify the body. Not a nice job.' He picked out Fu. 'I'd like you to come with us now, Mr Fu, if that's possible. We'll bring you back when we're through.'

As self-proclaimed household head, Fu had no choice but to agree. The two women looked on in commiseration, glad it wasn't them.

'I need a couple of minutes,' said Fu. 'Please.'

While they waited for him in the car, Shelley and Ginger heard Fu and the two women talking at the top of their voices in Chinese. It sounded urgent, alarmed, as if Hong was giving Fu instructions.

'Do you have any idea what's going on here?' Shelley asked. 'We can't come back without an interpreter.'

'That means going to Ronnie Silverton for help,' said Ginger, who was in the driver's seat this time. 'I don't want to do that.'

'We can't interview them, not properly,' Shelley complained.

'We'll use what we've got. Our six senses.'

'Unfortunately I've only got five,' retorted Shelley, going into a sulk.

The two Chinese women stood on the porch and waved Fu off in the car. Maybe they hoped to see the last of him, Shelley surmised. When they reached the freeway, she asked Fu what Zhou Huang had been wearing that last morning. As Ginger drove, she noted down his answer. Black nylon training pants with a white stripe. He had only just bought them. Training shoes. A Harvard University sweatshirt.

'What colour is that?' she wanted to know.

The man laughed. 'Crimson. That's the Harvard colour.'

Fu's confidence was ebbing away by the time they reached the Forensic morgue at Sydney Police Centre in Surry Hills. Surely ill fate had brought him there. Shelley put a hand on his elbow as the Director of Forensic walked them down the corridor together. The Director was a short Indian man with a high-pitched voice and great enthusiasm for his work. His eyes receded into his skull almost to disappearing point. He was a keen amateur poet in his spare time, he told them. His first love was literature.

The reassembled body was lying ready for them. Shelley did not particularly relish the thought of viewing it. An autopsy had already taken place. The Director removed the plastic sheet to uncover the head, back in place on the neck. The face, if that's what it was, had features and its own defiant, still human expression. Fu looked at it for longer than was necessary to make up his mind before the Director respectfully covered it over.

'*From out our bourne of Time and Place, the flood bears our friend far,*' quoted the Director in his fine Indian voice, not for the first time, conscious of the incongruity of the Tennyson with the grisly doctored remains.

But Fu did not say anything until they were outside. When Ginger and the two police quietly asked him if it was Zhou Huang, he gave a silent affirmative nod.

Among the personal papers the police had removed from Zhou Huang's room was a photograph taken against the background of the Sydney Opera House on an overcast day. It showed Zhou Huang with his stray hair blowing back in the breeze and his eyes half closed. He was looking somewhere far away. His nose was small, his face wide. His head was tilted up, slightly in profile, as if he were the hero of a struggle. With a tentative smile for whoever was taking the shot he gazed toward the light of a distant glory that might one day be his.

Ginger attached the photograph with a paperclip to the piece of paper that Fu signed to confirm the identification. On the long drive back home, the man sat in silence, staring out the window at the endless houses and yards. He might have been contemplating a difficult problem in physics. Neither Ginger nor Shelley knew what to say to him. Shelley turned on talkback radio and, with those inflamed voices, she and Ginger sat in silence too.

The photograph reproduced well enough for it to go out with a press release identifying the deceased as Zhou Huang, twenty-four, of Fairway Heights.

'Why would anyone want to kill this guy?' Shelley asked Ginger when the day's work was done. Shirts unbuttoned, they were sitting on the cop shop's baking verandah, sucking light beers. To the west the dividing range was clear against the sunset sky, purple trimmed with gold.

'Why in such an ugly way?' was Ginger's pensive reply. 'He's clearly not what he seems. I wonder how many people knew that.'

# Chapter VII

Bernie slept late in the morning in his jet-lag routine. Jasmine rose early. She put her bag in the yoga room, like Bernie said, across the stairs from his bedroom, but she had only the things she used for massage and a few spare clothes, nothing else. She stayed in the courtyard enjoying the fragrance of the gardenias in the thick summery air. The cat from the lane came to visit, jumping down from the fence, prowling warily at first but then becoming bold enough to brush against her. Jasmine knew the cat was hungry.

The second morning she decided to go out. With her blue jeans she wore the green top with a heart outlined in sequins, plastic sandals, dark glasses and a cloth hat. Deep in her pocket was the key to Bernie's house, and the key to the locker where she had left her case. She felt the keys flat to her groin as she slipped out the door by the garage to the back lane.

At ten o'clock the day was already getting hot. As she strode the pavement she kept to the shade cast by overhanging balconies and the trees that strewed the ground with their dusty leaves and scrolling bark. She hated the way people here let their skin go the colour of roast duck and would not let it happen to her soft bean-curd complexion. Like the trees, the houses and shops she passed also seemed unkempt and askew, she noticed. People drifted by giving her a split second's assessment, people somewhere between bouncing and sagging, too young, still young, once young, bursting out of themselves to become some-one noticeable, someone definite, for that day. She stopped to admire a grand display of strelitzia, orange cartoon birds, in a florist's window and looked at the party dresses in a vintage clothing shop. Tube skirts of tiny metallic silk pleats. Slashed tents of opalescent chiffon. She wondered how people could wear the clothes of unknown people who might be dead, clothes with the smell of old bodies, clothes of ghost dancers from a party long past. The thought made her shudder. She needed new clothes.

She passed three hairdressers before she found a supermarket where she could buy milk and bread for Bernie and orange juice for herself. They had cat food too, though the prices were ridiculously higher than she was used to paying and she did not feel comfortable. Like an animal, she must retain the scent of the way back. She did not want to be noticed either, passing café tables where people were hissing into phones or creeping by the old sandstone courthouse where criminals came before the law.

At the traffic lights the cars were jumpy and metal creaked in the glare. Along the street there were pubs, restaurants, bars, galleries, sex rooms, and people splitting and regrouping, eyes concealed, flesh exposed, without faces, laughing, turning down

ORIGINAL FACE

a lane, through a door, into a hidden space. Peeling its surface back, Jasmine imagined, from bottom up, the rock and sand beneath, and the brackish water sluicing endlessly into Sydney Harbour. She was relieved when she was back in Bernie's house with the door safely locked behind her.

Bernie was still asleep upstairs, sprawled across the bed, his naked butt like two boiled eggs on his brown body. He snuffled while she was watching him, as if he sensed her. She tiptoed down to the kitchen, opened the tin of cat food and put some in a bowl on the step. Immediately the cat was there, brindle tabby, purring and mewing with satisfaction as it ate.

Like the cat, Jasmine had food waiting for her today. She could either go or not go. But when she remembered the way the invitation had been given, she knew she had no choice but to go. If she did not go, maybe they would never find her. But if she went, she would arouse no suspicion, draw no attention to herself, and afterwards perhaps she would be out of their reach, safe in her new haven. She was expected at the meeting as confirmation that she acknowledged her obligation. The invitation to eat lobster in Chinatown could not be refused. There would be lobster sashimi and stir-fried lobster and lobster claws to be eaten clean. The lobster would be alive to begin with, scratching on the plate ready to have its brains spooned out. And after that it would be over.

Having made up her mind that she must go, Jasmine went upstairs and shook Bernie awake. 'I'm going out,' she said. 'I have a meeting in Chinatown.'

'I could drive you,' he offered groggily.

'You're not even dressed. I don't want to be late. I'll call a taxi,' she said. 'What's the best number?'

'There's a card on the hall table,' he remembered. When he came in from the airport he had left it lying there. A helpful driver was something to hold on to.

Jasmine called the taxi, then made some coffee and Bernie staggered downstairs in his monogrammed robe, Four Seasons Hotel, Santa Monica. When the doorbell rang, it was Bernie who went to the door.

'Hey, there's a familiar face!' he exclaimed. Actually he had forgotten what the helpful driver looked like. Forgotten he was Chinese. And a DOP aficionado. Or maybe he made the connection without thinking about it. 'Lewis Lin,' said Bernie, surprising himself with his recall. 'Hey, that's not bad.'

'I remembered the house,' said Lewis Lin, standing at the top of the steps in his blue uniform. He looked doubtfully at the man in his robe. 'Are you ready?'

Bernie laughed. 'No, it's not for me. It's for a friend of mine. Jasmine!' he called. 'Your taxi's waiting.'

A Chinese woman appeared in the hallway. Lewis registered the look on her face when she saw him there, a Chinese man, before she realised he was the taxi-driver she had called. In one movement she turned to the mirror above the hall table, checked her reflection and turned back with her gaze pleasantly set. She had narrow, fine eyes, Lewis noted. She was taller than he, elegant and well-groomed, with her long black hair parted on one side and brushed to fall over her shoulders.

'See you later,' she said, passing Bernie in the hallway with a tilt of her slender hips and her flat, willowy body. She did not touch him or kiss him in front of the watching taxi-driver.

'Have fun,' Bernie responded, reaching out after her, wanting to feel her against him. But she was out the door. 'Home before dark, eh?' he called after her. 'See you again,' he added for Lewis. 'Have a good day.'

Bernie wondered whether the taxi-driver was surprised to find he had a Chinese girlfriend. Pleased or disapproving? If that's what Jasmine was. A live-in.

The traffic was congested around Centennial Park, cars banked up in two lanes that grew longer and tighter as more cars cut in. A sign warned of delays where the new tunnel was under construction. Victorian-era houses stood bravely by with their red tiles and rusty iron roofs, their flaking faces and curling ironwork, dwarfed and tired by progress. Leaves rattled to the ground from grand old figtrees that were also marked for eradication.

'We'll be here for hours,' said Lewis by way of apology. He stuck his arm out the window and nudged his way across the outer lane of traffic and up onto the concrete median strip, ready to scoop round in a U-turn when the moment came. 'I know a better way,' he said.

Jasmine smiled gratefully. He wondered if she was from Shanghai, or somewhere round there, the part of China where the famous beauties come from. Looking at her in the mirror, he saw something in the turn of her neck. He decided to be direct. 'Where you from?' he asked.

'Hangzhou,' she replied.

'That was my guess,' he said. She was indeed a southern beauty. He told her he was from Beijing. She couldn't help screwing up her nose. But they switched language from English to Mandarin, which for him was mother tongue and for her a marker of education, fricative and stiff.

She sat in the back seat, diagonally behind him with her head erect. She was haughty and composed, but Lewis sensed something else about her. She was holding her agitation under control. Her fear. How long had he been in Australia, she asked him. When he said 'Since 1989', she could place him immediately. He was one of those who had taken advantage of the opportunity to leave China in the wake of the violence at Tiananmen that year. The Bob Hawke visa, it came to be called, after the Prime Minister who wept in parliament for the slaughtered youth of his favourite foreign country. Lewis asked the same question back, to which Jasmine replied, 'Not so long as that.'

'You're doing well,' he said. 'Your English is good.'

'My mouth is full with it,' she joked. 'It's tough. It's indigestible. Same as *putonghua*.'

Her velvety skin and full lips gave her class, and she talked to him as if he might be a friend. But he could tell that something was bothering her.

'I drove your friend from the airport a few nights ago,' Lewis said. 'He's a famous cinematographer. He got an Oscar for one movie.' Lewis wanted to ask how long she had known him. Instead he asked if she was working in Sydney.

'I do Chinese medicine,' she said. By then they had reached the ceremonial arch at the end of Dixon Street in Chinatown where she wanted to be dropped off. There was nowhere to stop. It was lunchtime and cars were circling, looking for places to park on the street in order to avoid the exorbitant cost of a parking station. Office workers were heading for yumcha restaurants in packs, cutting through the cars, making the congestion worse.

The woman reached into her bag for some money.

'No, no,' he said.

'Don't be polite,' she insisted. 'It's your job.'

'It doesn't matter,' he said.

She pushed some money into his hand and opened the door. They were in the middle of the traffic and cars were backed up behind. He was fumbling for change.

'Thanks,' she said, getting out. 'Don't worry.'

'Your name's Jasmine?' he asked. That was the name of the taxi booking.

'My name's Lihua,' she replied. 'Bye-bye!' And she was gone into the lunchtime crowd that jostled and elbowed its way along the street, down past the painted *pailou* to the rows of cloth-covered tables outside and the cooler restaurant tables within.

Cars were veering round Lewis from behind. One impatient car honked now as Lewis nosed out, blocking its way. When he glanced in the mirror, he saw it was a black Beamer. The same car that had nearly killed him. Was his mind playing tricks? He glanced at the registration number. It was the same. He tried to see the driver but the view was blocked so he pulled in and let the Beamer go ahead. Then he followed it, around the back of Chinatown to an underground car park. The car drove in and Lewis waited outside.

In that moment he could have let it all go. But he felt an invitation being put to him, by chance or some other connection. He could not ignore it. He parked the taxi in a loading zone and got out. Feeling less conspicuous on foot, he walked into the car park and crossed to the lift that went up from the lower floors to street level. He took it all the way to the top floor where there was a big restaurant. The Emperor's Palace, Lewis knew. The place was popular with Mainland Chinese. That was where the two men in the car were headed, the driver and the front-seat passenger.

The restaurant was a vast hall of red and gold with paintings of dragons and horses in gilded cartouches and placards down the walls announcing special dishes in black calligraphy on scarlet. And it was packed. Noise surfed through the place as patrons ate and drank under chandeliers of crystal and ruby. Waiters and waitresses in black-and-white uniforms rushed steaming dishes through crowded tables under the direction of a skin-and-bones maitre d' in a floppy bow tie. In his taxi-driver's clothes Lewis looked as if he had come to find a passenger. No one took any notice of him as he walked through the place. Suddenly Lewis felt hungry too. It was a long time since breakfast.

He saw the two men from the black Beamer being ushered to a private room at the far end. One was soft and portly, with a duck's waddle and a superior air. The other, the driver, had a crew-cut head and a lithe body with a boxer's swagger. Lewis wanted to catch their faces. Once he had seen them, he knew he would recognise them anywhere, always, as if he had taken their photographs.

He hovered by the reception desk while a short round man in a mustard jacket and a bejewelled lady in black were ushered towards the same private room by the head waiter. They looked like Taiwanese. Important people. A junior waiter followed with a pot of tea. Lewis came up behind them until he could pass by the door to the inner room. He saw the driver of the car, the man built like a boxer, rubbing his pencil moustache and looking down. As the waiter poured tea, the maitre d' came to display the writhing lobster that they would consume. It clawed the air in vain, as if performing for their attention. In that moment Lewis was able to get a look at the group around the table. The older Taiwanese couple. Another three men, Beijing types, their eyes agape at the delicacy they would feast on. And the soft-looking man, sitting with his back to Lewis, a charcoal suit coat stretched across his shoulders. He was the host, judging from the way he approved the lobster. At close range the man was younger than Lewis first thought, for all his formal appearance. Next to him was the woman Lewis had just dropped off. Lihua. Jasmine.

He moved away quickly in case she turned and saw him. Still he wanted to get a proper look at the man beside her, the host, judging from his position at the table. Was the woman his girl-friend? Lewis surmised from the way they sat together that she was not. There was a defined space between them. She was there for another reason that seemed to weigh heavily on her.

Lewis headed for the bathroom to give himself time to

think. While he relieved himself, he could hear his father's worn-out voice giving the advice he had given all his life, in China, in Australia. Mind your own business. It was his wise, timid formula for keeping out of trouble. The world's affairs were best left for others to entangle themselves in. Curiosity was stupid. He should get out of the place immediately. But he was there. It was already his business, whether he liked it or not. So he dried his hands under the hot air blower and swung out through the door.

The man whose face he had still not seen squarely was standing at the reception desk talking into a phone. His charcoal suit was double-breasted with turned-up cuffs on the trousers. He wore a creamy white shirt and a crimson tie picked with silver chrysanthemums, and his shoes were shiny black, Lewis noticed, passing close. The man was absorbed in talk on the phone. Then he raised an eyebrow in a casual sign of greeting. Lewis blinked. A sudden puff of breath passed through his nostrils. An amused double take was the best he could manage under the circumstances. There was no doubting the mutual recognition, for all that the two of them had changed since the last time they saw each other

Sydney's Chinatown was so small, after all. Like a single flower pot in all the vast land of Australia. And the flashy, crowded, popular restaurants could be counted on the fingers of one hand. The man from the black car was Ah Mo, the violinist. Lewis gave a hesitant smile and made his exit.

# Chapter VIII

Lewis drove off without even looking for a fare. He almost ran over the woman who waved him down outside the Powerhouse Museum. Swerving to the kerb to let her in, he was pleased when she directed him down the hill to Wattle Street, past the carpet warehouses and the fish market, out west. He flew over the Glebe Island Bridge, high above the water, as if escaping on his magic carpet from what he had seen in Chinatown. The distance cleared his head, allowing him to think. The Hangzhou woman. Jasmine, Lihua. The dead man. Ah Mo and his banqueting friends. He felt the web sticking to his skin. He felt faint. He felt his hunger, not having eaten a thing since morning and being amongst all that food.

Talkback was on the radio, snarling and accusatory. The passenger asked him to turn it down. He switched to the classical music station, on low volume.

'Is that okay?' he checked with a smile.

'Thank you, that's fine,' she said, offering no further conversation. The music happened to be Beethoven, the Pastoral

Symphony, a piece that was played all the time in China. It made Lewis remember the first time he heard Ah Mo play his violin in person. Ah Mo, who had been the star of the New Year Gala on Chinese Central Television at the start of 1989, then playing Beethoven's Spring Sonata in a benefit concert at the Sydney Town Hall, with all that promise of a new beginning. Ah Mo in a borrowed tuxedo with a red rosebud in the lapel, his violin tucked under his chubby chin as if it were part of his body. How the audience had loved him!

They were newcomers then, refugees of Tiananmen banding together in a strange land to organise self-help events. Ah Mo, with his charisma and courage, had quickly become the leader of the Chinese Democracy League in Australia. He gave interviews to the media fearless of reprisals back in China. He chanted human rights slogans outside the Chinese Consulate each year when the anniversary of the June 4th massacre came round. He was a hero. How long ago it all seemed.

Lewis remembered the cramped office of the Chinese Democracy League above a video hire shop in Dixon Street. They wanted to do everything for their supporters: Public Relations, Media Consultancy, English Language Training, Legal Advice, Immigration, Business and Computing Services, as well as Human Rights. When his two-year temporary visa expired, Lewis had gone to seek their help. That was how he met Ah Mo. Both being from Beijing, there was immediate rapport. And Lewis had demonstrated in Tiananmen Square too, like Ah Mo, in those last days before the tanks were sent in to end the peaceful, straggling protests in a final savage onslaught. In the small hours of June 4th Lewis had roamed the streets of Beijing with his camera, recording what he could. Those negatives, smuggled out to Australia in his hollowed-out Chinese-English dictionary, would form the basis of his refugee claim.

Ah Mo beamed when Lewis explained his case. He came round from behind his desk and shook Lewis's hand.

'Of course there's no charge for today's meeting,' Ah Mo insisted. 'Only if it goes any further naturally the lawyers will have to cover their costs.'

'Does your organisation provide any financial assistance?' asked Lewis.

'You mean the donations we receive? That money is reserved for our campaigns.'

Lewis nodded. 'Let me show you something.' He pulled out a black-and-white print that showed Ah Mo in front of a group of School of Music colleagues as they marched through the cheering crowds in the capital in the days of May 1989.

Ah Mo could not help flushing with pride. 'It's an extremely important photograph,' he commented. 'A piece of history. Have you got any more?'

Lewis pulled out two others. One showed a woman shot in the leg. The other showed a man's face gaping in terror as a tank rolled towards him. Ah Mo passed his eyes over the photograph of the wounded woman with respect. But when he looked at the photograph of the man, he grimaced.

'I was pushed from behind and fell forwards,' said Lewis.

'I didn't see what happened next. When I looked the tank had moved on and I couldn't see the guy anymore. It wasn't safe to stop for another shot. I scrambled away.'

'I know him,' said Ah Mo with tears in his eyes. 'He was my colleague. A brilliant zither player at the School of Music. He was rehearsing in the Concert Hall that night. He left his instrument in the rehearsal room and went out to check what was happening in the Square. He was never seen again.' Ah Mo's hand was shaking as he held the photograph. 'This is proof of his tragic end. You must have been the last person to see him.'

'I always hoped someone would recognise him,' said Lewis. 'I wanted him to have a name.'

'Can you leave these photographs here with us?'

'They are my only prints,' Lewis lied.

'We can make copies for you,' said Ah Mo.

'I can do that myself and bring them to you,' countered Lewis. 'I've got a darkroom at home. It's simple.'

'We can help you,' said Ah Mo. 'If *you* will help *us* bring true democracy to China. We're brothers in exile.'

Lewis smiled. He wasn't entirely convinced. He wondered what sort of outfit Ah Mo was fronting for. But he would not let the violinist lose face by raising questions. 'How long would an application take?' he asked.

'With those photos,' said Ah Mo, 'it's easy. The lawyer won't have to spend much time. That's a promise.'

Lewis had heard what he needed to know. If it was so easy, he could do it himself. He shook Ah Mo's hand when they parted and did not contact him again, except to mail him copies of the photographs he wanted. Lewis, his brother Alan and his sister-in-law Nancy had applied for permanent residency with a lawyer they found for themselves. They preferred to keep a distance from Chinatown with its gangs and support groups and mesh of obligations.

Yet Lewis retained a degree of respect for Ah Mo who had, after all, been an artist of the first rank. Ah Mo was refined, courtly, the product of a good background in the upper echelons of Chinese political life. All doors had been open to him. But as an artist of the first rank, Ah Mo needed special permission to leave the country. That meant sucking up to the powerbrokers in the School of Music. He refused to grovel and permission was consequently denied. It was then that he threw himself angrily into the protest demonstrations that erupted that year against the whole rotten system.

After the turmoil was suppressed, the authorities ordered nationwide investigations of the so-called troublemakers. There was nowhere to hide. The School of Music demanded that Ah Mo write a self-criticism. Instead he sent them a letter saying he was quitting music altogether. He grabbed at the first exit from China he could procure, which was a temporary visa to study English in Australia.

The last time Lewis had spoken to Ah Mo was the day they ran into each other in the streets of Chinatown. The Chinese Democracy League had been wound up and there were rumours that Ah Mo and his mates had cleaned out the account. Lewis half believed the reports in the local Chinese press, as he used to half believe the rumours that circulated all the time back in Beijing when there was no other reliable news. Ah Mo wanted Lewis to know he had sent a copy of the photograph to the zither player's family in China. Their son would have been a great traditional master of the instrument. Now that hope was ended. Thanks to Lewis's photograph one more name could be added to the list of glorious Tiananmen martyrs. Ah Mo's eyes filled with tears as he relived the tragic story.

'Do you still have time to play the violin?' asked Lewis

'At weddings,' Ah Mo confessed, 'on Saturday nights. That's how I make ends meet.'

'Like I'm driving taxis,' Lewis groaned in reply.

The Spring Sonata! All those joyous trilling quavers of the violin. All those buds bursting. Lewis was preoccupied with the image of Ah Mo in the restaurant, and the Hangzhou woman beside him, and the other man, with the boxer's body, the driver of the black Beamer, who had to be Ah Mo's sidekick, his bodyguard. He saw the angle of the woman's neck, turning as the car flashed past in a moment of near collision, little more than an afterimage registered in shock that came to him now for the first time. Jasmine or Lihua had been in that black Beamer too, sitting in the back. Or was he imagining it?

'Right here,' the passenger said. She pointed out the house in the quiet street that was her destination. 'Thanks,' she said, accepting the change of twenty cents with a pleasant smile.

Lewis had learnt not to expect tips from nice people. The

ritual of not tipping was a sign of respect for the contract between driver and passenger. Unless the fare was being charged to someone else's account. Then both sides were happy to round it up.

# Chapter IX

Detective Sergeant Ginger Rogers dropped his only son at school on the way to work each morning. It was one of the favours a policeman father could do for a kid, letting the bullies in the schoolyard see that he existed. Not that he was in uniform. He wore loud shapeless clothes straight from the dryer when he was off duty, knowing that his neatly pressed outfit was waiting for him at the station. He drove an old orange Ford Falcon that he would not give up because it was so roomy. His wife Toni took the bus to and from work. They were a one-car family and did one shop together on the weekend. They were paying off a hefty mortgage on their home and didn't like spending money otherwise. Shelley Swert's flash Mazda sports was waiting in the police car park when Ginger arrived. Shelley had a sponsor for her tae kwon do. She was Olympic grade. She had no other expenses in her life, Ginger thought with wry envy. And she was at work early, ready to make a fresh start on the investigation, while he was late as usual.

'Solved the missing Chinese yet?' he asked her.

'Owch,' she said, approaching him like a robot from the other side of his desk. 'I've done my neck. Can't move left or right. Had to skip training this morning. So I'm warning you.' She screwed up her nose. 'Here.'

She presented him with the locked black plastic briefcase they had retrieved from the house in Fairway Heights the previous afternoon.

'Feels empty,' he said.

'Shake it.'

'Cha-cha-cha,' he said as he shook it from side to side in his big hands. There was something rattling round inside. He prodded at the lock to no avail.

'Give it here,' she said. She pulled a Swiss Army knife from her pants pocket and prised the lock loose. It bent, but did not come free.

Ginger took over, wrenching the lid of the case between his hands, twisting until it burst open.

'Made in China,' he quipped.

Inside the briefcase was a thick little notebook with a creased brown cover. Ginger went to pick it up.

'Careful,' said Shelley, slapping him away. 'Fingerprints, mind.'

She found a clean handkerchief in her pocket and used it to pick up the notebook and flick through the pages. They were filled with small blue handwriting, dark then fading to indentations on the page as one pen after another ran out.

'Looks like a diary,' he said.

'How's that? Can you read Chinese?' Her eyes were wide with disbelief. 'How multi-skilled are you, Sergeant?'

He pointed to the numbers on the tops of the pages. 'Don't they look like dates. Let me see,' he said.

'You should put your gloves on.'

'What's the last date?'

Using the handkerchief between her fingers, Shelley found the last page. The date was the day before the body was found.

'That fits nicely,' he said. 'Pages of Chinese. Wonder what the hell it says.'

'How are we supposed to know?' complained Shelley. 'I keep saying we need expert help. We need some Chinese police.'

'That would mean handing the whole thing over to the Asian Crime Squad at Police Centre,' Ginger acknowledged. 'Is that what we want to do?'

'Can they translate this for us?'

'Maybe,' said Ginger, ruminating. 'I reckon it's one we can pass on to Ronnie Silverton, eh? I'll give him a call. Tell him we need it urgently.'

'What's this?' asked Shelley. A black-and-white photograph had fallen out of the notebook. It showed a young man and woman leaning together against a stone balustrade surrounded by willow fronds with water in the background. It looked long ago and far away, a little indistinct and framed by a white scalloped border, a foreign place. 'Must be China,' she guessed. 'By a lake somewhere.'

'Is that Zhou Huang?' Ginger asked. 'He looks different.'

'Younger,' she said. 'It's him. And the woman?'

'Could be his sister.'

'She's not his sister,' Shelley said. 'Why would he have a photograph of his sister hidden in his diary? Do you have a sister, Sergeant? Do you have her photo in your wallet?'

'It's getting hot in here,' Ginger replied, flustered by Shelley's cheekiness. 'Are you sure the aircon's working?'

'This place is a dump. Architect-designed state-of-the-art cop shop dump,' declared Shelley. She looked at the photo again, nipping it between thumb and forefinger in a tissue. 'But they don't look like lovers either,' she said, looking for Ginger's reaction. 'Their smiles are too forced. More like two people marking a special occasion with a photo. Maybe the day he left China. What do you think?'

'Dunno,' Ginger muttered. 'The guy was a bit of a writer. All that scribbling in the diary and all those hours tapping away at the computer keyboard.'

'There's nothing at all on the hard disk,' Shelley informed him. 'The techies checked. Not even any automatic backup. He didn't bother to save any of it.'

'What a waste,' Ginger said.

'Weird behaviour,' Shelley said, still holding the corner of the photograph and staring at the woman's face. 'I wonder where *she* is now. We should get it blown up and show it around. There's apparently an old lady who called in with a sighting of our boy in the Macarthur Park Shopping Mall. She says she saw him meet an Asian woman at four o'clock in the afternoon on the Saturday.

The same date as the last diary entry. He was waiting for her at the entrance to the mall. A woman with long black hair. The caller said they were sweethearts. We should show her the photo.'

Ginger agreed. 'He got a call the night before according to Fu, remember. From a woman. What else have we got?'

'The block of flats. We're still waiting to hear from Immigration about who they called on there. A woman there too. A bit of a looker, like this one.'

'You're travelling too fast.'

'Our boy was working for Immigration. Isn't that the story?'

'That's one of the stories,' Ginger said, heaving himself back in the chair. 'I hope Immigration are not doctoring their information for us.'

'There's Kangaloon Native Garden too,' Shelley reminded him.

'His boss said he never spoke to anyone.'

'He said visitors liked the Chinese gardener. I wonder why he would say that?' Shelley had found Gerard Ciccolini a bit too prim.

'Maybe our boy had a life after all,' Ginger speculated. 'We're just having trouble getting inside it.'

Shelley spoke more positively. 'We're not doing too badly. For westie cops with no special skills.' She had a heavy line in irony. 'It's less than a week. We have an identification and a time and a place and a possible motive. Once we know who the guy dobbed in to the Immigration Department that should take us straight there.'

'There's something missing. No money. No documents. There was nothing in his room.'

'Why did he leave his diary?'

'Everyone makes a mistake, Detective.'


Shelley drove out to the housing estate by herself and went looking for the two young mothers she had met in the playground. She remembered that the pregnant one with the blonde tips said she lived in unit 990. She knocked there first and the woman answered the door.

'Hi,' said Shelley. 'Nicole, isn't it?'

'What a memory,' replied Nicole, looking the policewoman up and down. 'I suppose you expect that from a cop.'

The one-year-old, crawling on the floor behind, called out to let his mother know he was there. Shelley laughed and asked if she could trouble the woman just for a moment for help with a photograph. She produced a blown-up photocopy of the shot of Zhou Huang and the woman by the balustrade. Nicole tilted her head from one side to the other before saying, 'Yep.' It was black-and-white and fuzzy, but she was prepared to swear that the girl in the photograph was the same Asian girl the Immigration Department had threatened when they called a few days before.

Then Shelley went along the corridor to the flat where she and Ginger had encountered the old Chinese man. This time no one opened the door. She knocked again and waited. Then she tried the handle. The door was unlocked. 'Anyone at home?' she called, walking in cautiously. There was no answer. She looked in the living room. Nothing there except the pile of newspapers. Not even the television set. She walked through the flat on her guard. There was nothing left at all except the bare furniture. No sign of the old man who had been waiting last time. The place had been abandoned, reverting to its raw state as unoccupied public housing.

Shelley shrugged her shoulders. Nothing to fear. It was a vacant concrete box now, an empty shell. She recalled what Nicole and her friend in the playground had said about all the comings and goings. A week later and there was no sign of a Happy Family left at all. The game had been packed away.

The old lady was pleased when the detective sergeant rang to make an appointment. She was keen to cooperate with the police about what she had seen at the shopping mall. For someone who minded everyone else's business, Joyce Nobes led a barricaded existence, blinds down in the middle of the day, doors and windows barred. She had pale papery skin and mauve hair that she curled herself. Once stately, she was now bent with arthritis and felt vulnerable. The officer had specified the precise time at which he would arrive and even then she hesitated before letting him in. She sat him down in a front room filled with ornate furniture, frilly cushions and figurines on display, smothering in its fussiness. She would not let him get any further. That would not be proper or wise.

'Well, Mrs Nobes, I appreciate your help,' Ginger began, preparing to charm.

'You can't be too careful these days,' the old woman observed. She lived on her own. She said that Asian people coming into the area were making life impossible. The old corner shop was gone, replaced by an Asian grocery. Her church had more services in Chinese and Korean than in English. It was dangerous to go out because of the youth gangs. Thursdays were pension days and she went to the bank and the post office to pay her bills and trundled up to the shops with her trolley to buy things for the week. She kept her eyes sharp about her in case she was mugged and raped on the way home and left for dead. That was how she came to notice the poor man who ended up in the dump, she said. She was an avid reader of the *Telegraph* where she had seen the story.

Ginger showed her the photograph and she adjusted her glasses, considering it from different angles. 'Yes, that could be her,' she concluded. 'Yes, that's her. Just last week it was. Last Thursday afternoon. There are more and more of them. Slinky young women like that one. You never know what they're up to.'

At least it was a positive identification, Ginger sighed, even as he wondered whether to believe her. The scrawny old thing evidently had her prejudices and her fixed ideas. Nevertheless he thanked her for being a good citizen.

Mrs Nobes looked back at him with beady eyes from the over-stuffed couch. 'I hope you can do something about it, sonny,' she said through mauve lips, pursed to match her tight curls.

The response from the Immigration Department arrived in the form of a confidential document delivered to the Pleasant

Vale police station by special courier. It confirmed that the Department's Compliance officers had called on a flat in the public housing complex on the Wednesday before the alleged killing to investigate the case of an illegal immigrant, a female national of the People's Republic of China called Guo Lihua. Acting on information received, the officers found the woman at the flat and advised her that her temporary entry visa had expired and no new application had been received. She was in breach of the terms and conditions of her original entry to Australia and had seventy-two hours in which to leave the country voluntarily or she would face deportation.

On checking the records they found that she had come to Australia as the fiancée of Zhou Huang, a PRC national who had gained permanent residency status as a refugee. Since there was no record that she and Zhou Huang had ever lived together, the Department concluded that the relationship was a sham or had broken down before marriage. Therefore Ms Guo no longer had any basis for staying in Australia.

The document included a not very clear photocopy of Ms Guo's photograph from her original visa application. Despite the speckle of black, she was recognisably the woman in the photograph from Zhou Huang's briefcase. She had the same prominent cheekbones, narrow angled eyes, small nose, full upturned mouth and disappearing chin, the same delicate, confident beauty.

'The question is,' said Ginger, 'who dobbed her in? She's been living here as an illegal all this time and no one has taken any notice of her till now.'

'It must be Zhou Huang,' suggested Shelley. 'She dumped him and he gets his revenge. And she gets back by murdering him.'

Ginger scratched his head. 'Why did they meet that afternoon? The day before he was killed. They were on friendly terms. The Immigration Department hasn't told us he put her in. It could have been anyone. For any reason. Have they given us anything about Zhou Huang?'

Shelley read out the paragraph point by point. He arrived in Australia. He applied for refugee status. He was granted permanent residency. He invited Guo Lihua to join him as his fiancée. When the time came he took out Australian citizenship and got a passport.

'What about the woman?'

'No record of her leaving the country.'

'So she's still here,' said Ginger. 'Wonder where she's hiding.'

On these late summer afternoons the light blazed from the west. The louvres of the police station windows were wide open, but still the heat was suffocating. Shelley stepped out on to the verandah and did some stretches, diagonally across her body, touching left and right toes in the full glare of the sun. She was in good shape. She could kick the pants off anyone in tae kwon do. But with her neck frozen by the pinched nerve she only hurt herself as she tried to get some movement going.

She went back inside and found a cigarette. She was not supposed to smoke but right now it felt like a better way to oxygenate her lungs. She said to Ginger, 'You don't think she did it herself? Skinned him alive?'

'Some people get their kicks from that,' he replied dryly.

Shelley was startled by the concept that had floated to the surface of her trusty colleague's brain. 'You mean it could have been consensual?' she quipped. 'I don't think so.'

# Chapter X

The needles quivered as Jasmine slid each one from its sheath and twirled it into Bernie's flesh at the precise point where she had rubbed the surface numb. He murmured at the tiny pricks of pain.

'Is it okay?' she asked.

A sensation of burning spread along his nerves. The right elbow ached more than the rest, where he hoped it was doing him most good. His camera-toting arm.

'Is that too strong?' she asked, twiddling the needles a bit deeper. 'I'll leave you now. Just rest. I'll check you in a few minutes.'

Jasmine was trying to cure Bernie's sluggishness – what neither of them was calling his depression. She had always intended to follow in the footsteps of her parents in the noble, humble profession of traditional medicine. But in Australia, she discovered, therapeutic massage was the only part of Chinese medicine for which there was any real demand – and not strictly Chinese-style massage at that. What they called Swedish massage.

It humiliated Jasmine that this had become her line of work, when her healing skills were so much greater. She was pleased to add acupuncture to Bernie's treatment, aiming to channel and revive his energy. The needles quivered like fine wands in his ankles and knees and hands and elbows and neck.

She covered him with a towel for warmth and went downstairs in search of an armchair in a sunny corner where she could coil up while the time elapsed. She closed her eyes, wanting to doze. Yet she shifted restlessly in the chair as the fragrance of the gardenias wafted in from outside, reminding her of Zhou Huang.

Ever since they were kids he had hung around her. Little Huangzi. They lived in the same district of Hangzhou and she used to call him when she wanted to go walking by West Lake. They would go to view the camellias and the peonies, and smell the osmanthus and the gardenias, season by season. If she walked alone, people harassed her. Huangzi was useful. But she never dreamed he would fall in love with her. *Suanmiao*, she called him, Garlic Shoot, so young and raw. Nothing like the fine flowers she admired. Huangzi idolised his big brother too, the musician, that weird guy who played the zither day and night. 'Cassia Fragrance in the Autumn Moon' was the melancholy tune from an old opera that he played over and over again. It drove her crazy. Garlic Shoot dreamed that she would marry his brother and be serenaded in the most famous concert halls in the land.

'But your brother's not normal, Garlic Shoot,' she laughed furiously. 'He's only interested in playing his zither.'

She was in love with Mengzi, a tough-talking army man who

had come back from his term on the Vietnam border and was using his contacts to establish businesses in town. 'Get-rich-quick-schemes,' he called his ventures with the naïve optimism of those days, when the economy was just starting to move. To prove things were going his way, he splashed money around. She liked that. When she quit her training in the traditional medicine school, she told her parents that Mengzi had promised to set her up in a clinic of her own. She really believed him. She shuddered, thinking about it now. She had been jelly in his hands...

Huangzi looked so forlorn whenever she went out with Mengzi. 'Garlic Shoot, you're jealous,' she teased. Any object associated with Mengzi, any silly gift, made him frown. Mengzi satisifed her needs...she was too easily satisfied...and Garlic Shoot was no more than a smelly green tip that she could tread underfoot.

Huangzi worked in a factory that produced eggshell porcelain for tourists. When the factory went on strike in support of the democracy demonstrations that broke out in Beijing, Huangzi ran around passing on reports from his big brother. His brother telephoned from the capital every day. Rumours were flying about and everyone wanted to know more. The people were stirred up by what was happening, daring to hope. Then the news came from Beijing of the suppression of what the television called the counter-revolutionary turmoil and there were no more phone calls from Huangzi's brother. Eventually the parents heard from his classmates that their son had not returned to the School of Music after he ventured into the streets leading to

Tiananmen Square on the eve of June 4th...There was gunfire and the grinding of tanks all that night and in the morning as dawn came up over acrid smoke and wreckage their son was gone.

Their elder son! Their first-born! A curse from heaven! Mengzi warned Lihua to keep away from the Zhou family. He was on the side of the army and the Communist Party against the protesters. Army and people were one, like fish and water. The students wanted to reduce the country to chaos, Mengzi argued, so no one could make money. But she went straight to the old couple's house to offer condolences and stood with tears in her eyes as she wrung their hands. They must put all their hope in Garlic Shoot now, she said. They must send him out of the country to somewhere safe. It was not good to be the brother of a protester who disappeared at Tiananmen. The authorities would come after the family. She had heard of a scheme for young people to go to Australia to study English. If you paid enough money and had the right connections and were lucky, you could make it happen. Maybe old Mr Zhou's work unit could help, to avoid trouble all round.

The old couple nodded. Their first son had been taken from them, they said, but since she was special to their second son, they would welcome her into the family as their second son's fiancée. Zhou Huang and Guo Lihua. Garlic Shoot and Jasmine.

Mengzi cackled when she told him. He put his hands up under her fluffy angora jumper and in behind her tight bra and squeezed her breasts until she yelped. She was as soft and sweet as sugar dumplings, he said. No good with smelly garlic.

The old couple paid all their money to an agent that someone at Mr Zhou's workplace introduced and Huangzi's visa
came through. Huangzi smiled painfully. He was doing what
they wanted him to do. Mengzi took a photograph of Garlic
Shoot with Lihua the day before he left for Australia. They were
standing by the white stone balustrade at their favourite lookout spot on the famous Nine-Arched Bridge over West Lake,
where they used to go walking.

'Closer,' she could hear Mengzi saying. 'Smile!'


The gardenia petals were turning from white to the colour of
toffee in the sun. Jasmine stirred herself from the chair and
climbed the stairs to check on Bernie.

'How long have I been here?' he moaned, opening his eyes as
she twiddled the needles.

'Only a few minutes actually,' she said. 'You're doing fine.'

She turned each needle, making them go a little deeper. He
felt tingles, nothing more. He wriggled his toes. She told him to
lie there without moving until she returned.

She had forgotten to close the garden door and went back
down to lock it. Once again the fragrance of the gardenias assailed
her. Even inside the house she did not feel safe.


With the needles adjusted Bernie felt the pain intensify at each
of the points until it was like being skewered by sharp pressing
weights. Not the needles so much as his own heaviness paralysed

him, as if his body was nailed to the bed and his mind had disconnected. He felt pinned down like a butterfly, unable to lift his limbs from the massage table.

Then his mouth opened wide, his lips stretched and his jaw started to work. The only way to overcome the pain that radiated from the acupoints was to let his head explode and scream. But he emitted no noise. He was laughing as mutely as a mime artist, panting for air. And as his nervous system raced, his groin stirred, his penis moving, uncurling slowly. There was no other movement in his body, only this, his penis bobbing under the towel, becoming bigger and bigger, and his wide open mouth laughing silently with pleasure. He wondered what was happening to him. Where was Jasmine? Had she forgotten and left the needles too long? What had she done to him? He tried to shout, but was incapable of making any sound as he felt himself sink, only to rise and ride with a surge of burning light in his eyes, red, green and oceanic blue. He tried to clench his jaw, to exert control over what was happening, to drive the energy up his spine. He did not know how long before he would lose it. He felt the pulsing of his blood. Then a bright white light burst in his inner vision and he saw a pair of hooded eyes.

He was beaded with sweat when Jasmine found him. She noticed the tension in his neck, his hands, his feet, the mound under the towel across his groin, his shaking.

'Bernie, what is it?'

Breath hissed between his teeth. He could not speak.

'Hold it,' she said. 'Hold tight. Don't let it go.'

His grin stretched even wider as the fiery light travelled up his spine, flooding him to the extremities of his body. Jasmine moved around the massage table deftly removing the needles. His breathing steadied. His arousal subsided. 'There,' she said, watching how he settled.

'Is that normal?' he asked, overwhelmed. 'What happened?'

'Sometimes,' she said, 'a needle will touch a very special point. It can happen by accident. Certain lines intersect and release your fundamental energy. From the base of your spine to the crown of your head. The snake rises. In India they call it *kundalini*. The same. Maybe you know.'

'Does it cause damage?'

'It's a gift. But when it happens by accident like this, with no preparation, it can be too much. It can make people crazy.'

Bernie gathered the towel around himself and rolled to one side, reaching for her. 'I feel a little crazy,' he said, all fired up.

'Please, Bernie, just rest. No activity for at least an hour.'

'Oh,' he sulked. His eyes were blazing now, black set in red, and her black eyes seemed to burn back at him.

She took his hand and laid it by his side on the bed. 'Just lie here and let your body settle,' she said, giving him a light pat. 'I'll be downstairs.'

Bernie lay there and remembered how out in the Arizona desert a snake had crossed his path while he was walking by himself on the trail one day at dawn. By pure luck he did not tread on it. The Navaho woman who doled out his breakfast beans in the canteen was wide-eyed when he told her. It was a powerful omen, she warned him. Spiders he didn't mind. There was often a big huntsman in the corner of his bedroom ceiling, growing fat on mosquitoes. But snakes were different. A snake meant trans-formation and the shedding of skin.

# Chapter XI

'All personal stuff. The birds and the bees,' Silverton had scrawled across the copy of the translation of Zhou Huang's diary that reached Pleasant Vale from Sydney Police Centre next morning.

Sometimes the force could pull its finger out, Ginger noted. Perhaps the superintendent was regarding this case as a competition. Ginger pictured a freelance translator working through the night on triple pay and was impressed by the prompt work as he sat down to read.

The diary entries had not been made on a daily basis, but weeks apart, sometimes months. The style was lyrical, even vaguely pornographic, Ginger felt, tilting back in his ergonomic chair with his large legs planted wide apart on the floor.

*Frost covered the bed last night and in the morning the wild orchids were budding in the winter cold. I dug the bed, pulling out weeds, and manured it with chicken shit. The smell of those flowers reminds me of her, of her smile, bitter, only half-fragrant. She needs the warmth of real deep love to make her smile fully fragrant. That is what can come from me, but she rejects it now.*

*How strange the flowers are in this country. So many different forms, spiky and bright, like spiders. They jump from the bushes into my eyes. I trimmed the wattles today, cutting their golden-yellow tails all over the hillside. The artist sketches them in crayons and coloured pencil. They are like a painting anyway.*

*She came into the garden to find me. She needs my help. I am the only one here who truly knows her. We are meant to be together. But she resists, like an unopened bud, looks away and goes cold when I ask her. She is ashamed. My only love. My only connection in this place, all this lonely time. Her skin, her half-closed eyes, her long raven hair. My one desire. She doesn't think of me. I telephoned her tonight and HE answered. He knew it was me and said nothing. He put her on and she asked me what I wanted. She was angry. She told me to leave her alone. She didn't want me bothering her.*

Ginger highlighted the last phrase in yellow, and the word 'HE', and put a question mark in the margin.

*I am learning to know the trees. At first they all look the same, like one big tree, then they start to look different and I can tell them apart by shape and colour. I prefer the trees to the people. I accept their money gladly and live an orderly life. My mind is empty most of the time, except when I think of her. But she empties my mind too. How can I explain that to anyone else? When they ask, do you have a girlfriend? I say yes.*

Ginger yawned. On and on it went. No wonder Zhou Huang had left his diary behind. There was nothing in it. Just a lot of wanking. Ginger scarcely had the patience to read on. He marked the word money and skipped forward to the last entry.

*She is willing to accept my help. She wants a lot this time. She said my hands were rough from gardening. She said I had become a peasant. In China I was a worker. I ran the machines that glazed the eggshell porcelain in a factory. In Australia I work with my hands, with nature. It's a healthy life. She is scared. She is escaping back to China. It's winter there now but spring is not far away. She will fly back to China and I will meet her there soon. She needs money for the ticket. HE has betrayed her.*

Ginger put a pink question mark in the margin. Who?

*Leaves fall in autumn, buds come in spring. Even rock is only a thought. Currents vanish underground, release their flow elsewhere. Danger turns to flight. She cares for me. She is willing to risk her own safety for my sake. I am not afraid. She is gone. For this time I am gone too.*

Ginger highlighted the last short sentence and wrote on his pad. 'A muzzy love triangle. Maybe the deceased expected his end.'

Then he got on the phone to the Immigration Department and battled to be put through to the person who had penned the answer to the police request. Des O'Neill. Community Relations.

'Now, this woman, Guo Lihua,' said Ginger, once the preliminaries were over. He mangled the pronunciation. 'Who put her in?'

There was an embarrassed silence, a clearing of the throat. 'Well, in our work we rely on help from outside,' said the Immigration Department voice. 'I'm sure you understand. We don't like to make a big thing of it.'

'Sure,' said Ginger curtly. 'Understood. Do you pay for information?'

'Sometimes we engage a consultant. It's above board,' came the reply. Ginger wondered if the voice was put through a computer. It was flat, without dynamics, the vowels squashed and the consonants squeezed together.

'What was it in this case?'

'The information came from someone we've been working with for a while now.'

'Anyone I might know?'

'It was Zhou Huang.' Remarkably this faceless voice – Des O'Neill, Community Relations spokesperson – was able to pronounce the name in correct tutored Mandarin, while presenting no other distinguishing features. The two syllables leapt out from the featureless vocal terrain, as if inserted from elsewhere.

'Tell me more,' asked Ginger coolly, hiding his excitement.

'That's all we're prepared to say at this stage,' came the formulaic reply.

It was as flat as the desktop on which Ginger imagined Des O'Neill leaning. 'Come on, pal. Aren't we working together on this one?' he suggested as humanly as he could.

'I'm sorry,' said the voice, breathing asthmatically into the phone, giving nothing more, as if the energy required to respirate had now been exhausted. After a further pause, the call rang off.

'Fuck you,' said Ginger, then commenced a tuneless whistle.

'Why are you whistling?' Shelley asked.

'Because I've got a headache,' Ginger answered. He rubbed his temples while he whistled. It was more like hissing.

'Does that song have a name?' she asked, winding him up.

'It's meant to be an old Beatles song called "In My Life",' he confessed. He pushed the telephone to the edge of his desk. 'I don't get it, Shelley. He loved her and he squealed on her. He was helping her get back to China but she's disappeared into the noodles. He knew he was in trouble but they got him anyway.'

'Don't get yourself in knots about it. There's more coming in all the time,' Shelley said consolingly. She was reading a fax from Homicide. 'The guy's parents back in China have been contacted by the Australian Consulate in Shanghai. Says here they've got his medical records. They're coming out to claim the body. Soon we'll know a lot more about our man. It says here that his older brother was killed in Tiananmen Square back in 1989.'

'An unlucky family,' said Ginger. His head was pounding. 'Why don't you read the diary, mate. I'd welcome your perspective. It's like something out of Mills and Boon.'

'Just the thing for me,' Shelley smiled, leaning forward eagerly. 'I love true-life romance.'

'Don't look at me,' said Ginger, blushing as only a fair-skinned man with ginger freckles and a receding hairline can blush. 'I'm a married man.'

'And I'm a busy woman,' Shelley replied, rolling her shoulders back as if preparing for a fight. 'Are you ready? We have an appointment at the botanical garden, remember.'

Gerard Ciccolini, director of Kangaloon Native Garden, had picked up the phone at once when Zhou Huang did not turn up to work and the Pleasant Vale police put out its call for information on missing Asian men. It was his duty as a senior administrator. Later the director called Jerome Hampton to inform him. Hampton, heir to the Hamptons retailing fortune, was a member of the garden's board and its most generous benefactor.

When the valet passed the phone to Jerome, however, and the director conveyed the news, the man's reaction was strange. 'He can't be missing,' Jerome said. 'There must be some mistake. He can't be *dead*. What do the police say?'

'It's a Homicide investigation,' Ciccolini replied carefully. 'The body of an Asian man was found at the Pleasant Vale Recycling and Waste Depot.'

Jerome was silent. Ciccolini could hear his breathing. 'It's a dreadful business, Gerard,' he said at last. 'We don't want the Garden involved. Thank you for getting in touch with me so promptly. You'll keep me abreast of things, won't you?'

Ciccolini knew he had made a mistake, although he couldn't put his finger on why. The rich are certainly different, he thought, and hard to predict.

Jerome Hampton, who lived nearby in the leafy highlands of Bong Bong, liked to paint in Kangaloon Native Garden. The way he explained it to the director was that he loved nature and painting was his passion. By setting up his easel in a quiet corner of the garden and working from life, he could combine the two. Always restricting himself to weekdays, of course, to avoid the madding crowd.

Sometimes on his rounds the director would see the artist at work. He praised Jerome's practice to the skies, calculating the value of a board member and major patron having such a personal involvement with the garden.

One day, passing by on a tour of inspection, Ciccolini had discovered Hampton in an out-of-the-way grove of grevilleas – a favourite spot – busy at his easel. The millionaire was a dapper man with silver hair and an unlined face. He had kept his figure, but for a gently swelling midriff. And here he was excitedly brandishing a brush at the subject in front of him. The director was startled to see it was the Chinese gardener, standing motionlessly amongst the flowering bushes, eyes closed in a posture of prayer, seemingly unaware of anyone else's presence.

'I'm glad you find the garden so inspiring, Jerome,' said Gerard, his lilting tenor breaking the artist's reverie.

Zhou Huang opened his eyes. 'Hi, sir,' he said with a broad grin. Gerard turned his gaze from the living figure of the Chinese to the disturbingly abstract canvas.

Hampton looked up slowly. 'I've borrowed one of your workers,

Gerard. I hope you don't mind, he said with pre-emptive urbanity. 'The boy fits, don't you think?'

It was a new development and the director, although something of a pedant, knew he must try for a broad and lofty approach. 'Sure. No problem,' he said uncomfortably. 'Just pretend to be doing some work while you're standing there, Zhou. Don't want the other staff to get ideas, do we?'

Zhou Huang smiled sweetly. The director didn't know whether he had understood.

'I've been meaning to mention it,' said Jerome. 'Would you like me to do *you* next, Gerard,' he added in a fruity tone.

Ciccolini felt spindly and pedantic in response. 'If you need me, I'm always available,' he bantered. 'But where would *I* fit in? Your style is rather…non-representational.'

'You would go with the bad old banksia men, Gerard,' laughed Jerome, easily impatient with the thyroidal director.

'Well, I'll leave you to it then,' Ciccolini said. 'Good luck!' He put his hands in his pockets and strode away down the path, rankling from being made the butt of Hampton's wit. He frowned at this unwelcome precedent. It was wrong for a board member to use a member of the garden staff that way. But there was nothing Gerard could do about it.

And then, the day after he called the police about Zhou Huang's disappearance and alerted Hampton, the director had the man's vintage Jaguar stopping right at the door of the administration block before he could finish the latte and the muffin he had picked up for breakfast.

Jerome walked in without even knocking, as was his privilege. He was dressed to deal with affairs of the world in a collegiate tie with a buttoned down pink shirt, buff blazer and sharply creased black slacks. Not his painting clothes. Gerard Ciccolini rose with concern while discreetly disposing of the coffee cup and half-eaten muffin.

Jerome took a seat and crossed his legs. 'Gerard,' he began, 'you do such a good job here, following up every little thing. So it must alarm you when something untoward happens. I refer to the disappearance of the Chinese boy.'

'Zhou was such a reliable guy,' commented the director as naturally as he could. 'I was worried when he didn't turn up and there was no explanation.'

Jerome smiled sympathetically. 'I daresay he had some personal plans of his own. I seem to remember him mentioning something like that to me. I expect he felt too embarrassed to tell you he wasn't coming to work anymore, considering how good you've been to him.'

The office was hung with botanical watercolour prints and through the wide windows were matching shrubs, chosen with an educational purpose in mind, luminous green in the clear morning light. The director strutted away from his desk to be near the window, like a lyrebird in his bower, ready to mimic any sound. 'Perhaps you're right,' Gerard replied vaguely. 'But I'd have expected him to call.'

'I'm sure you'll hear from him in good time,' Jerome said soothingly. 'It's simply drawing too long a bow to link our gentle

Zhou with this awful business of the body at the dump. And we don't want anything that will bring adverse associations to Kanga- loon Native Garden in the public mind.' Jerome gave a manly chuckle, to be shared with Gerard, as if he were distributing some of his largesse. 'I don't know that we want the police sniffing round either. Families will be scared to bring their children here. Let's stick to the botanica, my friend. What we do best.'

Gerard did not return the chuckle. 'How would you like me to handle the situation if anyone makes enquiries?' he asked.

'I don't know that you need to handle anything,' advised Jerome. He was already rising to go. 'Don't go out of your way. We don't want trouble. Less said the better.'

'I see,' said Ciccolini, exaggeratedly obsequious as he followed the man to the door. 'Thank you for your support. At a time like this it's greatly appreciated.' The director found himself giving the benefactor a lanky bow. Eventually a hill at Kangaloon Native Garden would be named for Jerome Hampton and a lookout built on top. Some folly or other...Mount Jerome.

When the police came to interview the director about his miss- ing Chinese workman, Gerard Ciccolini said he had noticed nothing unusual, nothing apart from the information he had communicated already by phone.

They asked if he had any reason to believe that Zhou Huang was an Immigration Department informer. The director said he knew nothing about that. Then Detective Sergeant Rogers asked if Zhou Huang could have been getting money from anyone, apart from his wages. The director looked thoughtfully into the distance, wondering if Jerome Hampton paid the Chinese man for sitting, or standing, or whatever it was. But those things were out of bounds for him now, on Hampton's instructions, and he drew a veil over them in his own mind. Not that he knew of, the director honestly replied. The young man kept to himself. He hardly talked to anyone. He was mute as a tree.

Just like you, thought Shelley, not entirely convinced by the lean and academic director's performance.

The walk back to the car park was flanked by verdant ferns and flowering tea-trees that were swarming with bees, and there was only room for one on the concrete path. Ginger pushed ahead and Shelley was flicked by fronds as she weaved along after him.

'Listen to the buzz,' said Ginger. 'Don't you like that sound?'

'It's all right as long as you don't get stung,' Shelley replied.

'It's the sound of honey-making,' he said.

Shelley snorted. 'You're at home with all this greenery, aren't you? Vegetarian heaven, eh? I don't think it goes with my skin.'

He smirked back. 'Your cool blonde complexion reflects the green.'

'Yuk. How long have you been a vego?' She was teasing him and testing him all at once.

'My last flesh-eating meal was ten years ago,' Ginger said. 'I remember it well. A big platter of prawns and oysters. I hung on to seafood for a while after I gave up meat. It was expensive and it was garbage. That's what seafood tastes like, once your palate loses its adjustment. Crustaceans are an organism for processing decayed matter.'

'So you don't miss it?' she asked, genuinely curious. 'You can just pick a few leaves and munch on them to be happy? Like a koala.'

'Occasionally I hanker after a bit of dead cow. Just as a reminder. The living feeding off the slaughtered.'

'Sounds like police work,' Shelley quipped.

'I started by trying to simplify things,' Ginger went on. 'Get back to basics. I was lean and young and wanted to live my life with maximum efficiency. Now it's an ingrained habit.'

'Yeah, a grain habit.'

He chuckled. 'I know I'm not lean and young anymore. And there's no way you can manage maximum efficiency in the work we do.'

'Do you think Ciccolini gave us everything?' asked Shelley, changing the subject. 'I wasn't satisfied with the way the meeting ended.'

'For example,' said Ginger, gesturing with open hands. 'He called us the first time, when the bloke went missing. What would he be hiding now?'

'He was pretty quick about recognising the photograph,' Shelley said. 'Given that Zhou was a lot younger when the photo was taken. His mind is made up that Zhou's a loner, a good worker who never talked to anyone. Then suddenly he's a problem.' Shelley was trying to unravel the knot of her suspicion.

'You're not being very systematic, Detective.'

ORIGINAL FACE

They reached the car and got in and sat there talking with the doors open to the fresh mild air.

'We already know that Zhou did talk to someone,' said Shelley, trying to justify her intuition that something was missing. 'A woman and a man phoned him at Fairway Heights. If this is the woman,' she asked, holding out the photograph they had shown the director, 'who's the man? The people in the house said it was a man he met at work. A man who couldn't say his name properly. An Aussie.'

'Maybe it was Ciccolini,' conceded Ginger

'Maybe Ciccolini knows,' corrected Shelley, 'and is keeping it quiet.'

'It's time to give the woman's photo to the press, anyway,' said Ginger. 'There are no other leads. Put in the release that the guy worked at Kangaloon Native Garden. See what that flushes out.'

'You're disappearing on me, mate. Not reading what you're seeing.'

'I'm not seeing anything. It hasn't pushed up into the light yet,' Ginger continued despondently.

'You're reading too much of that flowery diary. You and our Zhou – both vego. That's the trouble with vegos. Too much chewing. No meat to get your fangs into.' Shelley was baring her teeth in the mirror to check for nicotine stains. She was back behind the wheel today and ready to drive fast along the freeway. 'Anyway, Sarge, don't worry, a good work-out and I'll get it.'

It was Shelley's tae kwon do night and she needed a well-aimed left foot to kickstart her mind.

131

# Chapter XII

The light at Kangaloon Native Garden was marvellous more days than not and Jerome Hampton took his painting there seriously in the plein air tradition. He was not a mere amateur setting up outside. Carefully evolved practices structured his life more than most people's. Wealthy and in advancing years, he proceeded with uncompromising precision. The manner in which a thing was done, no matter large or small, constituted for Jerome a form of devotion to the higher beauty of spirit latent within the lower beauties of this world. He could afford for it to be that way.

When his family's department store chain was turned into an endlessly profitable public company, Jerome held on to his portion of shares. Never married nor partnered, he lived in a mansion within a garden within a formal park within bushland and pasture well outside sprawling Sydney and ordered his life in part for the benefit of his loyal staff and associates. If you had money, he realised early, life could be spent in a welter of misdirected whims. The noble alternative was to cleave to a self-determined mode of being. Thus he had placed art at the centre of his life, building his fine collection, and in later years adding his own work. And the golden expanse of Kangaloon Native Garden, the pungent vigour of the native plants, the commanding landscaped space, became his regular site of artistic inspiration.

Jerome favoured landscapes, stylised and inward, or flowers and foliage that burst with their own life from an envelope of light. He shared the philosophy of the old unfettered Chinese masters for whom the world was merely an expression of their own mind at its most exalted. So he was flattered when the young Chinese gardener appeared, apologetic about disturbing the artist, and responded to his work with a luminous smile. 'Like Chinese painting,' the boy said.

Jerome liked such polite attentiveness and was pleased when the boy came back. When Jerome asked what he did in the garden, Zhou Huang said he tended each plant for itself. 'Everyone different,' he said.

Jerome approved. But when he asked if he could put him in a painting, the young man was coy. He had not done such a thing before. Jerome said he needed his face. It could only be done from life. Zhou Huang said he was worried about not doing his work. Jerome said he would speak to his friend the director and have the boy relieved of his gardening duties. So Jerome charmed Zhou, as he called him, and made promises, until the young man agreed to stand among the flowering shrubbery for the preliminary sketches. Jerome asked him to shut his eyes like a Buddha. Among the sprays of crimson and grey-green the subject stood in his khaki gardener's uniform. The thick black hair disappeared in shadow. Light shone on the settled lips, on the golden skin. The artist grew more and more absorbed.

After those first outdoor studies Jerome worked up a large oil painting of Zhou among the grevilleas. The theme of a spirit becoming manifest within the foliage, an expression in the light itself, made for immediacy and abstraction in the paint. But to depict a human face took effort and Jerome was painstaking. When he had finished one painting, he was immediately dissatisfied and wanted to do another.

All the time, however, Jerome was careful to keep his relationship with the Chinese boy on an aesthetic plane. The gilded quality of the boy's skin was a warm version of bronze or stone, offset by the dusky shadows of his neck, the sooty eyebrows and the soft, serene mouth. Zhou told Jerome he worked in a porcelain factory in China. He understood shape and translucency. Jerome said that was why the young man's presence gave the picture spirit and dialogue. He was greatly pleased.

Eventually Mr Hampton asked Zhou to come to his house on the weekend and sit for him there. The young man nodded his head with a smile. On Saturday morning the driver picked him up from the Macarthur Park train station and drove him in a direction he did not recognise until they reached a set of automatic gates that opened into an avenue of heart-shaped leaves and dappled light that swept up to the grand house.

That afternoon Jerome painted Zhou in the open by a round

pond covered with waterlilies and surrounded with the hanging purple shafts of butterfly flowers. He asked Zhou to take off his shirt so he could paint the planes of gold and tarnished shadow on his bare chest. Reluctantly Zhou complied. After dinner that evening he slept at the house in a small room with lace curtains that was like a monk's cell. In the morning the driver gave him money and took him back to the station.

Next time Jerome gave him a book of Buddhist sculpture to look at. In the garden, in the afternoon sun, as Jerome instructed, Zhou removed his shoes, his shirt and his trousers, and with an orange cloth across his groin, he tried to adopt the poses from the book. He held a pose as long as he could while the light turned his body to another substance. Fragrant flowers steamed in the air and breezes danced from the shrubbery to his shivering skin.

'I don't want to catch cold,' he protested.

But they worked for hours, until a bell from the house rang to announce a break. Then Jerome asked questions that Zhou did not know how to answer.

'Who are you, Zhou? Who are you really?'

The sessions became regular. Before and after each one Jerome made Zhou join him in meditation in a special room where a statue of the Buddha sat on a bare wooden table among flowers and burning incense. After making three prostrations Jerome would descend with creaking joints to a round black cushion, encouraging Zhou to follow, clumsily at first, then with suppleness. How much suppler was the boy than his instructor.

After half an hour Jerome would release a moan from the

cavity of his belly, freed from excessive emotional attachment and one hundred per cent refreshed. He had suffered in the past, in the blind enthusiasm of youth, in the panic of middle age, and he was not going there again. The intimacy of the one awareness circulating between himself and his subject was enough. Finally he rose and bowed to Zhou, ready for the next stage of their road together.

And then Zhou Huang was gone. Jerome struggled to maintain his inspiration but he was bereft. He returned to the grove of grevilleas at Kangaloon Native Garden, attempting to recapture the living image from memory in that original place. But the expression on Zhou Huang's face in the bliss of repose eluded the utmost effort of his hand and eye.

# Chapter XIII

Bernie stretched out on the old cane chair in a sunny spot on the balcony. The cappuccino he had made with the new machine in the kitchen rested in an out-size cup on his chest where the towelling robe from the Four Seasons in Santa Monica fell open. Bernie had the knack of operating gadgets. A local producer, hearing he was out of work, had approached him for a low-budget documentary project. Not a good sign. Documentaries were stepping stones to feature films. But he realised, taking a slurp of his coffee, that stones could step backward as well as forward. Before he had even swallowed the warm milky liquid, he set the cup down on the boards and swayed toward the dusty corner where the rolled-up newspaper had landed, as if to show he was still capable of moving forward. The newsagent threw the paper up on to the balcony to stop it from being stolen. Not that there was anything in the paper worth stealing it for. Usually it lay there unopened, yellowing in the dust, until the dead news was piled like little logs and could be bundled up in an armload and carted to the

recycling bin. But on a lazy morning like this Bernie was prepared to unfurl it and spend half an hour absorbing its gossip
and opinions and occasional nuggets of weirdness.

On page three he found the photograph that the police had
released for information. It showed a Chinese couple. The man
was named as Zhou Huang, the mutilated victim from the
dump. The woman without a name, overexposed in grey mist in
China long ago, was Jasmine. Undeniably Jasmine. Wanted for
questioning.

Bernie took a long breath. He folded the paper over at the
page and laid it at his feet with the photo face up. He picked up
his coffee and sucked it to the dregs. What's in a picture, he asked
himself, crossing his arms. Could be many things.

He could hear the woman stirring behind him in the bed. He
could smell her, sweet and tangy on his skin. 'Jasmine,' he called.

Drowsily she came out onto the balcony in her T-shirt, keeping
her hair over her face like a curtain. His arm hooked her bare
thigh. She bent her head and kissed his shoulder as a way of saying hello, too sleepy to talk. Then she grunted as her eyes saw the
photo in the newspaper at her feet. With an indecipherable
sound she stooped down and grabbed it. She peered at it close-
up, hiding her face with the paper as well as her hair.

'Looks like you,' said Bernie.

'Ah-ha,' she said. 'It's Huangzi and me in Hangzhou. How did
they get it?'

'Did you see what happened to the guy?' Bernie asked. 'Do
you know about this, baby? Is that why you're hiding out here?'

Jasmine retreated inside to the edge of the bed. She sat with her head in her hands.

'I want to know,' said Bernie, coming to sit beside her.

Jasmine started sobbing. He put his arm around her, holding her until her heaving ceased. 'I'm so afraid,' she said, shaking her head from side to side to make her tears fall to the ground. 'I'm afraid now.'

'Who is this guy?' asked Bernie. 'The dead guy?'

'I'm really afraid to see that. He's my old friend. Same town, same neighbourhood. We grew up together. He helped me come to Australia. I can't believe he would get himself into anything like this. I don't know why anyone would kill him.'

'When did you last see him?' Bernie asked, putting on the weightless voice he used for dickhead directors and lumpen lighting guys.

'Bernie, I have to tell you one thing. Don't think bad of me. He wanted to marry me. He brought me to Australia as his fiancée. I was so desperate to leave China that I went along with it. But I could never go through with marrying him. He was like a kid brother. He would never give up on the idea, even here. I had to stop seeing him.'

'Is that the truth?'

She wiped her eyes on the back of her hand. 'I just didn't want to get involved. When this happened they were already looking for me. My visa had run out. I knew they would throw me out of this country. That's why I came to you.'

'Your friend has been murdered. Do you know who did it?

Surely you should go to the police.'

'He's dead,' she said. 'It's too late. I can't help.'

'Who is he?' Bernie was alarmed by her decisiveness. Was her weeping for the dead man or for herself? It was the first time he had seen her so upset, and he didn't know how to read her. Yet she touched him, and he couldn't resist opening his heart to her predicament.

'He came here to make a new life. It's pitiful, isn't it?'

'Why did they kill him?' he asked.

'I don't know.' She hung her head. 'Just let me stay, Bernie. I'll look after you. I can't get involved in this.'

'People will recognise you from the photo.'

'It's an old photo.'

'*I* recognised you. I'd recognise you anywhere, baby.'

'I'll stay in the house. Till people forget. I'll wear dark glasses. Okay?'

Bernie bit his lip. This was serious protection she was asking for. 'Okay, but if anything happens, *tell me*.' He could let himself be angry now as he disentangled himself and stomped into the shower. He needed to think it through. 'Just tell me, okay?'

Jasmine came into the shower cubicle after him. He saw her through the streaming water as she soaped him. He pulled her towards him, struggling to get the slippery T-shirt over her head so he could feel her breasts. She resisted him, her hair over her face, her hands folded in front of her breasts, protecting herself.

'Come on,' he said. 'It's okay.'

'I'm afraid,' she pleaded. 'I don't want to lose you, Bernie.'

'I don't want to lose you either, baby. What if they find you?'

He took her hands and unfolded her arms and gently guided them behind her back so he could feel the skin of her breasts against him, small flat breasts smooth against his rough flabby chest. She was in his power now, more than ever. It turned him on more than he could resist, but he wondered what he was getting into. He was used to disposable pleasures, to walking away when it got messy, before crossing the threshold into people's difficult lives. And this was like the worst sort of plot from all the bad movies he'd ever had to try to make look good. A murder, a defacement, an ex-boyfriend, a migration scam, if he even believed her. But at the level of skin to skin he couldn't not believe her. They held each other and, for reasons of need and want and the shape of the moment, whatever else may have been true, their bond seemed real and strong enough to act on.

'Thank you for helping me, Bernie. I can help you too, if you let me. I can fix your neck and your back and all those things.'

'Does anyone know you're here?' he asked, pressing her against him.

'No one knows,' she said.

'Can you make that *kundalini* thing happen again?'

She laughed for him, spitting the running shower water from her mouth. 'I can try.' He was awed by her vulnerability. Yet it scared him, to succumb to the temptation, to possess her so completely. Such a beautiful woman, too much of a fantasy even for him who was a tailor of fantasies. He felt almost ashamed to be so aroused when he could take advantage of her in any way he wanted. Steadily her resistance had yielded to holding, to clinging, to grasping.

'If they find me and you're here, they can't touch me,' she said, pleading with him. How fast she moved. She was trouble, he knew, clear as day. Yet she was saving him as much as he was saving her. And at his age how glorious the experience felt. The abyss of his own emptiness if he sent her away was more terrifying than he could bear. He hung suspended by a thread above that dark gulf of failure and recrimination. She held him from that, warm and close. Cradled him, as the shower jets flooded their clasping bodies, hers pale, smooth and concave against his tanned, matted, sagging mass. He could not turn away.

# Chapter XIV

Lewis saw the photo when he opened the *Telegraph* that a passenger had left on the back seat of his taxi. It was so formal that it almost looked staged. In the blurry background he recognised Hangzhou's famous West Lake, though he had only ever seen it in photographs. The man and woman looked like ghosts, he thought, in the overexposed grey. Lewis recognised the woman straightaway as Jasmine or Lihua, the woman he had driven from Centennial Park to Chinatown. And the man too, from the other photo, with the Sydney Opera House behind him, though his face was less strained in this one. There was something about his youthful face that moved Lewis. He was identified as Zhou Huang, the man found dead at the dump. An informer on his own people. But he just didn't look the type. Was the woman his girlfriend? Lewis wondered. Clasping the stone balustrade, she was smiling not for the man who stood with his arm around her but for the invisible person who held the camera. He thought about the woman's involvement with Bernie Mittel, the Director of Photography.

He knew the house where he had picked her up. Again Lewis had information he could give the police. He recognised that his curiosity was aroused by his own connection to the case. What did it mean? Did his information matter, or was it just the vapour trail that must follow any case like this? A student from China who had a job as a gardener and whose corpse was found skinned. 'Mutilated' was the newspaper word. When Lewis looked at the indistinct face in the paper, it was as if the man were trying to speak to him, as if there were a shadow of familiarity. And then there was Ah Mo, and the driver of the black Beamer. Was Lewis protecting them by not telling the police what he knew? Was he endangering others? Was he incriminating himself, though he had done nothing wrong? If he waited, would more information come his way?

He tore the article from the paper and bought a copy of the *United Australian-Chinese Times* to see if the more freewheeling Chinese press had anything else to add. Sometimes, with their own idiomatic way of sidestepping the defamation laws, the Chinese papers had less compunction about publishing un-substantiated rumours than the English language press. With a certain innuendo the paper described the woman the police were seeking as the fiancée of the dead man and a massage therapist. When he got home Lewis showed the photo to his old father who said that the woman was beautiful and that the poor young man would still be alive if he had stayed in China and never known her.

The old man repeated his advice to his son. 'Mind your own business.'

Then Lewis took the newspaper stories out to his darkroom and filed them away.

The release of the photograph brought a good response. A number of people recognised the woman as Jasmine. She was someone they called for therapeutic massage. They were wondering why she had stopped returning their calls. But all they had was a card with a phone number that went through to an answering service. For someone who spent professional time so close to her clients, Jasmine had given very little of herself away.

'To run a massage business, you need protection,' claimed Detective Heidi Lee, the Asian Crime Squad representative at the Homicide summit at Sydney Police Centre.

'There's nothing to suggest she worked with anyone else,' snapped Detective Superintendent Silverton. 'Or that she gave any service other than honest therapeutic massage, Chinese-style. All that hammering with the fists.'

Those around the table laughed at this, with the exception of Detective Lee, prepared to accept that it was true. Ronnie Silverton did not want the Asian Crime Squad brought in just yet. Wisely, thought Ginger, who was sitting on the sidelines of the meeting with Shelley. Once a case went to the Asian Crime Squad it disappeared behind a hedge of specialists to be used as material for commissions, taskforces, international operations into syndicates, corruption, organised crime. In the end there were no boundaries and arrests were never made. Silverton at Homicide had more resources at his disposal than the suburban police at Pleasant Vale yet he was still liable to be squeezed by the Asian Crime people. That was why he insisted it was a Homicide matter first and foremost. That was why he kept the Pleasant Vale pair in the loop, even though his expectations of them were pretty low. He insisted that all cards be laid on the table.'

What about the Immigration Department?' Ginger asked, unimpressed so far. 'What have they provided?'

'Bloody little,' Silverton replied. 'They're running their own law enforcement nowadays, so it seems. They don't need to co-operate with us.'

'Any news on the parents?' Shelley asked.

The parents of the dead man were due in Sydney at the end of the week. 'This will cheer you up,' said Silverton. 'We sent the photo by the lake to Shanghai for the parents to have a look at. The Consulate has come back to us already. The old folks named the girl at once: Miss Guo Lihua. They confirmed that she came to Australia as our boy's fiancée. Then she dumped him.'

'She's the woman in the diary,' said Ginger.

'Could be,' said the superintendent, not in a mood to share his conclusions.

'The love of his life,' added Ginger, feeling like a yokel.

'Could be.'

'The woman that Immigration are on to,' said Ginger, gauchely showing how the pieces fitted together.

'So that's her name when she's not Jasmine,' said Shelley. 'Guo Lihua. Guo's the family name, right. Given name Lihua. Miss Guo Lihua.'

'Lihua means Jasmine in Chinese,' said Heidi Lee.

'Ronnie, are you sure Immigration are giving us everything they've got?' asked Ginger. 'Is there anyone else there I can talk to?'

'With my blessing, Sergeant, if you can find someone who will talk back.'

It rained all the way back to Pleasant Vale, plashing steamy summer rain that made visibility low. 'The wipers aren't working,' Ginger observed.

'This car's shit,' said Shelley behind the wheel. 'We need to call on your friend at the restaurant, don't you think, to ask about the woman.'

'Hunger pangs, Detective? My wife's expecting me home.' Ginger was weary, but the prospect of Chinese food appealed to him and his excuse for Toni was that he and Shelley Swert had constabulary duty. He'd ask his wife to join them, knowing she had to stay home with the kid.

'It's not like I'm suggesting a date or anything. It's raining,' said Shelley, as if that had anything to do with it. 'We're on the job. When did rain ever stop play, Sarge? We don't rest till this thing's solved.'

He looked at her sideways and yawned. 'That's the spirit.'

The wet night made business dismally slow at the Green Dragon. There was a dating Chinese couple in one corner and a pink-faced man with a white beard and a bottle of wine to himself at a table by the wall. 'Hey, the joint is jumping,' said Shelley as she followed Ginger to the same table as last time, though they could have sat anywhere. The place was cavernous.

'Nice to see you,' said Patricia, frowning as she came forward with the menus. She bent her head between the shoulders of the two police officers and lowered her voice. 'Those flats are all empty,' she said, as if that explained why no one was in the restaurant either. 'The Chinese families have all gone, every one. I don't know where. I don't know why. They leave the furniture. They leave the pots and pans. They take all their personal effects.'

She signalled to a waiter. He brought tea and poured it out.

'That's a big move,' said Ginger, blowing on the soup in the little china spoon. 'Did a truck come?'

'No one saw it. They go one by one. At night maybe.'

'*Why*, Patricia?'

The waiter was back with two bowls of soup. Shelley took a sip of the scalding hot soup and put the spoon back in the bowl. She had burned her mouth.

'Everything all right?' Patricia smiled.

'Sure, it's great,' Ginger said. 'Thank you.'

'My kitchen staff gone too,' said Patricia. 'Some of them live out there. Wash dishes for me. What can I do? They're gone so suddenly I can't find new ones.'

Ginger looked at her sympathetically, waiting.

'I think maybe someone tell them to go,' she said. 'I guess they move elsewhere.'

'Who tells them, Patricia?'

But she was not saying. The waiter presented the stir-fried baby corn and bokchoy with mushrooms, a vegetarian dish for Ginger.

'Was it Immigration?' asked Ginger.

'You cannot say that,' said Patricia.

He waited, but she was doling out rice and said no more.

Shelley broke the pause, pronouncing the name. 'Miss Guo Lihua. What about *her*?'

Patricia scowled, brushing an imaginary fly away from her eyes. 'That woman – she was the first. I saw her picture in the paper with that other one. They're in it together. I know.'

Ginger pushed a piece of pork rib away from the vegetables and struggled with his chopsticks to pick up a squishy mushroom.

'Your food all right?' Patricia smiled. 'Everything all right?'

'Mm,' said Ginger. 'Excellent.'

Patricia gave her little bow. In the near-empty restaurant she counted them as honoured guests. 'So, enjoy your meal!'

'You want a beer,' Ginger asked Shelley. The rain outside made the restaurant seem damp inside and made the white table linen seem not quite dry either, smelling of bleach.

'I do,' she said. But when, a few minutes later, he asked Shelley if she wanted a second beer, she said no, she was driving. A flush coloured her cheeks.

# Chapter XV

'Haven't seen you for ages,' Lewis said to Ah Mo over the phone. 'I want to invite you to eat mutton hotpot.' It was an old Beijing favourite. Lewis wanted to imply that the call was for old time's sake and that he had a favour to ask. The video hire shop in the Chinatown arcade where Ah Mo used to have his office gave him the contact number. Lewis's curiosity had got the better of him and he had decided to investigate. 'You don't have to bring your violin,' he joked.

He named a family-run restaurant in suburban Ashfield where they were less likely to be recognised than in Chinatown. Recent migrants from Shanghai had settled there and their enterprises were turning the old red-brick suburb, with its competing churches and pubs, gracious gardens and fine civic architecture, into a bustling hub of small business. Lewis suggested they meet outside the Ashfield Town Hall.

He was taken by surprise when Ah Mo climbed down from the shiny green Forester that pulled up right on twelve noon. He had been expecting the black Beamer. This brand-new Subaru AWD had tinted glass that screened the driver. As soon as Ah Mo slammed the door, the vehicle pulled away.

Without a glance over his shoulder Ah Mo strode across the footpath with a wide grin and outstretched hand. He clasped Lewis's hand with his left as well as the right to signal that they were brothers. Ah Mo wore dark glasses, his face was white and his hair thickly waxed as if he were about to go on stage. Lewis in his blue jeans and ponytail felt poor by comparison.

Ah Mo told Lewis he looked too thin. He chuckled to see his hometown buddy and glossed over the fact that there had been no contact between them for so long. Ah Mo had the manner of a high-ranking Communist Party cadre whose every nod counts. He told Lewis to lead the way. When they reached the restaurant, Lewis ushered Ah Mo ahead through the door in a gesture of deference. They were the first guests this lunchtime.

The restaurant was one room in what used to be a hardware store. It had been painted white and a Chinese calendar hung on the wall. The kitchen was improvised around the sink out the back. Compared to the palatial establishments in Chinatown, it was a basic operation serving the food that people ate at home in Beijing. No lobsters or abalone, but all the salty, vinegary little snacks that they missed. The table reserved for Lewis was already laid with side dishes of pickled garlic and fresh coriander and peanuts. Ah Mo took off his jacket, hanging it over an adjacent chair. His snowy white sleeves billowed, revealing a gold Rolex on his wrist.

'Real one,' he joked. 'Not fake.'

Lewis noticed the flashy tie and the chubby jowls making folds of flesh around Ah Mo's collar. 'You've got fat,' he said. 'You've got rich.'

'I'm a fat white pig,' beamed his compatriot.

The restaurant proprietor brought the hotpot to the table and lit the gas burner under it. The man was pale from long hours of work for his business-minded wife. He had been an office clerk back in China, anticipating early retirement on health grounds, but his wife, who stayed guarding the counter, was determined to see their money grow, dollar by dollar. '*Qian zhuanbuwan!*' she insisted heroically. 'You could never make enough money!' So she had turned her old man into a shuffling, abstracted waiter.

He brought a frozen slab of mutton next, sliced into marbled pink shavings, and a tray of cut cabbage, rice noodles and bean curd. As the broth began to steam, they prepared their bowls of oil, sesame paste and chili. Lewis ordered the *erguotou* and poured out two little cups for Ah Mo and himself. They drained their first cups in a toast and the fiery alcohol went straight to their heads.

One whiff of the rough sorghum spirits was enough to take them back to the old Beijing world they had left behind. They recalled frozen sooty days in the capital and smothering indoor gatherings of mates, eating around crowded tables, the savour of fat and salt on the tongue, and the strong liquor making faces red or white in the bonding of upended drinking cups.

'*Ganbei*,' Lewis toasted, letting the clear spirits trickle over his hands.

'*Ganbei*,' echoed Ah Mo.

Into the bubbling soup went the first curls of meat. Half a minute later the swirling grey mutton was sieved out and doused in sauce for eating. Steam rose from the pot, condensing on their flushed faces as they chewed and laughed.

'It's delicious,' nodded Ah Mo, approving. 'I'd forgotten how good it is.'

'It's not as good as Beijing,' said Lewis, 'but it's not bad. Australian lamb. Not as good as Mongolian mutton.'

'It was export Australian mutton in Beijing,' Ah Mo corrected him, chewing with relish. 'How are things going for you anyway?' he asked. 'Here in this labour camp known as Australia?'

'Endure suffering and strive to move forward,' replied Lewis. 'That's what I do. Struggle to stay in the same place.'

'Still driving the taxi?' Ah Mo asked.

'Still driving the taxi,' Lewis confessed.

'Bought your own place yet?' Ah Mo asked.

'Still renting with my brother,' Lewis admitted.

Ah Mo nodded. 'Sending all your money back home, is it?' His glasses misted up in the steam and he removed them. He had well-shaped eyebrows that curved above his shining eyes. Even as he stared at Lewis he reserved his concentration for fishing out morsels of meat or vegetable from the hotpot and dunking them in his bowl of tangy brown sauce.

'My mother died last year,' said Lewis. 'From cancer. We needed money for the funeral. Now my father has come from Beijing to stay with us.'

Ah Mo nodded solemnly.

'And you?' asked Lewis. 'How about you? Still playing the violin?'

'I don't get any time to practise,' replied Ah Mo.

'That's a pity,' said Lewis. 'You're a great musician.'

'It's a different life. Culture doesn't get you anywhere here. The consultancy takes up all my time.'

'What do you actually do?'

'I run a Chinese community support group for migrants. People from China who want to come here. We fix them up with housing and schooling and employment and other things. Help them get going on their dreams.'

Lewis swallowed a piece of gristly mutton. 'That's important work. More important than driving a taxi.'

'We Chinese have to look after each other,' said Ah Mo. 'Foreigners are not going to help us. The Australians think this place is theirs but by what right? They've done nothing to develop it, except for the beach maybe. Beach culture is what they know. They don't know how to do business. They have no real civilisation of their own. Beer and sport and fuck you. They stole the land from the Aborigines.'

'Right,' agreed Lewis.

'They should give it back,' said Ah Mo.

'But the Aboriginal people don't want *us* here necessarily either,' said Lewis.

'That depends,' insisted Ah Mo. 'We Chinese amount to one-fifth of the world's population so we are entitled to one-fifth of the world's land and sea and one-fifth of its wealth. We have never been given that. It's unfair, don't you think?'

'History hasn't worked out that way,' Lewis agreed.

'We Chinese have the longest history of any people today. By the rights of history we are entitled to even more than one-fifth. We should be number one.'

Lewis laughed. Ah Mo had raised his voice and there was no arguing with him. It was just like the heated drunken debates around those meal tables in Beijing, when all positions were up for dispute.

'If the Communist Party hadn't corrupted the Revolution we would be there by now. That's why I'm continuing the revolution here in the south. I'm bringing my own people here so they can continue the victorious struggle of the Chinese people,' said Ah Mo, talking through a mouth full of food, his head thrown back at the extravagance of his claim.

'You're bringing them here?' asked Lewis. 'How do you do that?'

'If they want to come, I help them,' said Ah Mo with the earnestness of a revolutionary hero.

'Do you cooperate with the Immigration Department?'

'We've got good contacts there,' Ah Mo said. 'And back in China, in the Consulates. In Hong Kong. Everywhere.'

'You're prospering,' observed Lewis.

'China is prospering,' Ah Mo responded. 'People are free to spend their money on the chance to realise their dreams. It's their right. It's no one's right to stop them, is it?'

'What about the Australian bureaucracy?'

'It's racist. It's discriminatory. Obstacles in our path only make us struggle harder.'

'You mean – ?'

'I mean our brotherhood works together.' Ah Mo had finished eating. His belly was full. He started using a toothpick to clean his teeth. 'You said you had something to talk about.'

Lewis poured some fresh tea. 'Like I said I'm sick of driving the taxi. It's taking me nowhere. I thought you could help me find a new job. Maybe we could work together.'

Ah Mo looked warily at Lewis. 'You always kept your distance before. Why the change of heart?'

'You get a lot of hostility as a Chinese,' said Lewis, feeling his way. 'It's hard to deal with on your own. I get shit all the time in the taxi.'

'That's why I have my own driver,' Ah Mo boasted. 'It's more convenient.'

'The driver of the Forester? Where's he gone?' asked Lewis. 'He could have joined us to eat.'

'I'll call him when we're ready.'

'Maybe *I* could drive you?' suggested Lewis, offering himself.

'I already have Daozi,' Ah Mo shot back dismissively. 'He's a good man. But there might be something else for you. We lost one of our guys recently. He was disloyal. He betrayed us. This is serious business.'

'What happened to him?'

'He's gone,' said Ah Mo more dismissively still, toothpick hand over his mouth. 'Why don't we call you when there's something we want you to do for us. A bit of running around at first, most likely.'

'Thank you, brother,' Lewis said submissively.

'Don't thank me,' said Ah Mo, sweeping away Lewis's thanks as mere formality in the grander scheme of mutual obligation among brothers. 'Anything else?'

'One thing. Maybe you saw in the paper. There's a Chinese man who was murdered. His body was found in a dump.' Ah Mo's face remained impassive as he listened. His breath was steady. Yet the angle of his head changed slightly, causing the flesh of his neck to tighten. 'Did you see that?' asked Lewis.

Ah Mo put down the splintered toothpick and nodded, then he put on his glasses and looked at Lewis with a stern unflinching gaze. 'Why are you telling me this?'

'Ah Mo, you have powerful connections. Maybe you can do something about it. The Australian police will never be able to solve this crime. They don't care. I saw his photo in the newspaper and I felt that he was one of us. A simple guy with a dream of a better life. His name was Zhou Huang.'

Ah Mo peered at Lewis, trying to evaluate the situation, then screwed up his eyes. 'Did you know him? Are you a friend of Zhou Huang?'

'No. But it's about protecting all of us Chinese. Maybe we have to take justice into our own hands.' Lewis hesitated, knowing he was on thin ice, then he turned that fear to a plea of emotional self-concern. 'It could be me, driving the taxi late at night in those remote places. Who is going to protect me?'

NICHOLAS JOSE

Ah Mo emptied his strong cold tea into the empty sauce bowl and signalled to the proprietor to refill the pot. The wife snapped the order in case her husband hadn't understood. With hot tea in his hands, Ah Mo responded. 'I saw the newspaper report too.' He clenched his teeth. 'You remember the zither player from Hangzhou – crushed to death by a tank at Tiananmen and incinerated without trace *except for your photo*? That Zhou Huang you're so worried about was his kid brother. He should have stayed at home.'

'He was skinned alive,' said Lewis.

'Don't waste your tears on him,' said Ah Mo. 'A pitiful rabbit.'

They were both afloat on the filling food and the spirits, the tastes of mutton, garlic, cabbage and *erguotou* in their mouths. They were carried along on a sensation of oceanic Chinese brotherhood, their bellies satisfied to the point where they could believe in an ideal of mutuality that caused their heads to lift and their shoulders to be thrown back. But there was always the disbelief too, the play-acting, the mistrust…

Ah Mo checked his watch. 'I better call my driver. Thank you for your concern, and your support.'

'I'll get the bill,' said Lewis. '*Jie zhang*,' he called in Mandarin. The proprietor relayed the request to his wife who had it ready, needing only to tear off a page from her pad.

'No, no,' said Ah Mo in polite protest. 'Let me.' But Lewis had the cash in his hand.

'Next time I invite you,' insisted Ah Mo. 'When we're working together. You'll get a call.'

They waited in the street as the green Forester approached. 'You used to drive a 320 series BMW, didn't you?' asked Lewis. 'Black-coloured.'

Ah Mo frowned a little. He couldn't remember when Lewis might have seen the black Beamer. He didn't answer the question. All he said was, 'Do you want a ride?'

'My car's in the car park.' Lewis shrugged.

'The taxi?'

'That's right.'

They said farewell, shaking hands like old friends, and Ah Mo climbed into the dark interior of the Subaru. Lewis bent forward to look at the driver. Daozi paid him no attention. But already Ah Mo's face had switched from the ardent grin of friendship to a narrow furrow of suspicion. He took the phone from Daozi, the door closed and all Lewis could see was his own reflection in the tinted glass.

'How would he have known about the black Beamer?' Ah Mo asked Daozi. 'He hasn't been in touch with me for such a long time and suddenly this.'

'Who is he?' asked Daozi.

'A taxi-driver,' said Ah Mo. 'A brother from Beijing.'

'Taxi-driver?' repeated Daozi, letting the fact enter his mind. It had been a taxi a few days earlier, careering along a country road headlong towards him.

The traffic heading into the city along Parramatta Road was jammed: cars, vans, trucks, cranes, tankers, queuing across intersections, locked into a tightening grid. The cooling had broken down in Lewis's vehicle and the afternoon sun glared. He hung his arm out the open window and the hot wind pummelled his face and flicked his hair. Drivers in other cars, in cool bubbles of music, peered back blankly. The traffic inched forward, down the hollow, under a train line, up the hill past old brick factories and glassy new car yards and *Just do it* billboards that inflamed the stalled motorists in their frustrated machines.

Yet even with the fumes and growling engines that surrounded him, Lewis was back in Beijing, his belly churning as it digested the mutton hotpot lunch. The growl of tanks was what he heard, moving forward impatient of all obstacles, unlike the standstill traffic that surrounded him. The popping of gunfire came back to him, the screaming of sirens, the smell of burning flesh in the hot dark smoke. The sensation of that toxic air in his nose and mouth was all there, vivid and real. The night his camera drew him on until there was no escape, only luck. He had been cornered as the tank ground forward. He jumped away. He crawled through a hole in a broken wall and came out the other side. The fear that coiled around him now was the same fear, tightening in his gut. Was this the bitter grief of the survivor? The same inescapable bitterness that sharpened Ah Mo's lack of pity for Zhou Huang, a dead compatriot? Surely Ah Mo would have wanted vengeance for the sake of his heroic Tiananmen friend. For his younger brother, slaughtered like an animal. Lewis could not see past Ah Mo's shining eyes yet even here in this bright hot sunlight he felt himself coated by the juices of a constrictor. So Ah Mo's money comes from migrants, he thought, and the newspapers say that Zhou Huang was an Immigration Department informer. But that didn't prove anything.

Lewis felt the heat frying his brain. There was the photograph of the zither player, his face turned with uncomprehending terror at the violence bearing down on him. And there were the photographs of the younger brother in the newspaper, blankly unaware of the violence that awaited him. Lewis could see the family resemblance. He was the third point of that triangle, the one who connected the lines, the point of view. He flashed his indicator light and butted into the next lane in front of a woman who was busy talking into her mobile phone. She blasted him with the horn.

'Cool it, lady,' he said to himself, smiling. He was cheeky on the road, but he had done nothing wrong.

# Chapter XVI

The first time Ginger Rogers lost his temper working on the Zhou Huang case was when the Immigration Department put out its own press release. He had a nagging sense that the case might never be solved. But when an agency on your own side concealed information and then used it to big-note itself at the expense of the police, Ginger saw red.

In the press release Des O'Neill, Community Relations spokesperson for Immigration, announced that investigations had exposed a series of abuses in which low-cost public housing in the Pleasant Vale area was being provided to newly arrived migrants with false identity documents. Compliance officers had raided the housing complex and advised a twenty-eight year old female from the People's Republic of China to depart Australia within seventy-two hours. The Immigration Department's Rockdale office had since sought to verify the documents of other residents at the Pleasant Vale complex. The Department was acting on information supplied by Zhou

Huang, deceased, whose body had subsequently been found at the Pleasant Vale Recycling and Waste Depot.

Police investigating the case had so far failed to make any arrests, the press release concluded.

Ginger waved the piece of paper at Shelley as they sat in the armchairs of the meeting room at Pleasant Vale police station at the start of a new day. Outside, the magpies were indulging in their full repertoire of song, a waterfall of sound from high to low.

'That slimy bastard,' Ginger fumed. 'Des O'Neill. That squashed-flat voice on the end of the phone. I asked him straight out and he never told me any of this.'

The message was clear. Immigration was doing a great job ferreting out illegals and other migration scams while the bumbling cops could do nothing to touch the organised networks behind it all, the evil masterminds who thought nothing of skinning one of their own kind alive if he ventured to cooperate with Australian authorities.

'They want the glory for themselves,' said Shelley. 'Dump shit on us and they don't look so bad. You'll notice,' she said, reading the press release with a calmer mind than Ginger, 'it doesn't actually say they've got any of the other residents on fake documents.' She shifted on the prickly orange fabric of her chair. They called these the thinking chairs. In the impersonal space of the meeting room, away from the desk, in those uncomfortable chairs, things sometimes looked different. 'Those happy families all got away, like your friend at the restaurant said,' figured Shelley. 'That old man we saw was packed and ready to go. The only one they're on to is the woman – it's Miss Guo Lihua, isn't it? – and we know they haven't got her either.'

'*We're* interested in finding her, *they're* only interested in seeing the back of her. That's why the bastards didn't say anything before now. I'm going to call him up.'

Ginger stood up, marched through to his office and dialled. 'Yeah, give me Des O'Neill. Community Relations. Right.' He waited. 'O'Neill? Rogers. Pleasant Vale police. We spoke before. That's right. Your little press release finally came our way. You could have briefed us first. A bit of courtesy.'

Shelley was watching over Ginger's shoulder. He turned and, for her benefit, shook his head in contemptuous disbelief at the noises coming out of the phone.

'Running your own investigation, are you?' Ginger interrupted. 'Well, just one question for now. You say you've got a woman. She's Miss Guo Lihua, I presume. Can you produce her?' Ginger waited. 'You don't know where she is? Then you haven't got her? Has she left the country? Not as far as you know. You deported her but she hasn't gone?'

Click.

Ginger looked into the silent phone with disgust.

'Her friend's body is found the day after she is seen with him. Her photo is in the paper. Why *wouldn't* she leave?' Shelley asked, squaring her hip as the logical inference pressed home.

'Rockdale, Rockdale? Something's stirring.' Ginger scratched his scalp, screwing his fingernail into his brain until he remembered. 'Janis! Janis works there. Or used to.'

'Janis?'

'Sue was Toni's bridesmaid when we got married. Sue and Toni went to school together. Janis is Sue's partner. Or used to be.'

'You mean girlfriend?'

'Yeah.'

'Your wife's best friend is a lesbian? Did you know that at the time?'

'Sure. That's why she was happy to be the bridesmaid. She said it was as close to being a bride as she ever wanted to get. Then Janis came along.' He picked up the phone and dialled. 'Hi, it's me,' he said.

'Hi,' Toni said. Ginger could hear his wife's smile. He could hear the computer keys she was tapping, filling prescriptions in the pharmacy, her head tilted to the phone as she typed a label.

'You know Sue and Janis?' Ginger asked his wife. 'Janis used to work at Immigration. Rockdale, wasn't it?'

'She's on leave with RSI.'

'But she's still with the Department.'

'Why do you want to know?'

'Would it be okay if I had a coffee with her?'

Toni laughed. 'They've always admired you, those girls.'

'What's her number?'

'Another thing,' said Toni, after giving him the number. 'Mangoes are $9 a case at the fruit market.'

The fruit market was on Ginger's route home. Huge, ripe, engorged: the mangoes were their shared intimacy. 'I'll get them,' he promised.

'I'd like to meet Janis,' said Shelley.

'I'm sure she'd like to meet you,' said Ginger, 'but not this time.'

'When were you thinking of?' asked Janis Moroni with a chortle when Ginger called. 'I'm not sure I'm available.' They got together once a year, Janis and Sue and Toni and Ginger, for drinks at Christmas with the old school gang. That was enough. She could never believe Ginger was a copper. She only ever saw him in plain clothes, his big freckled limbs sticking out of a Hawaiian shirt and shorts and his face as soft as a Smile balloon. He always told her to stop smoking and get back to her swimming. But she said she could smoke and swim at the same time. In fact she could smoke and scuba dive. 'I'm having my physio this afternoon. I'm free after that,' Janis said.

'Where can we meet?' asked Ginger.

'Only if you wear your uniform,' Janis laughed. 'There's a dyke bar we can meet at.'

'I was hoping for something more private.'

They met in the beer garden of the Macarthur Park Tavern. It was a sprawling place by the major roundabout where the four-lane road to the Mountains came off the freeway. It had a huge sign and a blind drunk driver could find it. Regular customers were inside at the bar and the pokie machines, watching horse-racing and downhill skiing and European football on the sports channel. The beer garden was deserted in mid-afternoon. Janis and Ginger could talk without being overheard.

'The stress of that bloody place gave me RSI,' Janis Moroni

began. She was a good-looking woman, rounded by flesh that stretched her stylish clothes. Her skin never saw sun, her short hair was waxed into place, her fingernails matched her dark lips. 'So much work, so much personal pressure, such inadequate systems.' Her face became mobile as she prepared to dish the dirt on the Rockdale office of Immigration. 'Talk about Repetition Strain Injury.'

Ginger told her about the Zhou Huang case and the public housing scam. He showed her a copy of the Immigration Department's press release.

'It's through Rockdale they were sprung,' she explained. 'We do an audit of passports reported missing. It's all analysed in Canberra, takes quite a while to come back. This one showed a huge jump on the graph for Rockdale over the period. We had issued dozens of replacement passports, all to Chinese, sometimes more than one to the same person over a couple of months. That suggests someone on the staff was putting them through without asking questions. A superior somewhere must have let them go past. Someone's got access through the back door.'

'Could be,' Ginger agreed.

'It's easy to jump to conclusions,' said Janis. 'It may just be statistics. It's a Chinese area so why wouldn't there be a lot of Chinese with lost passports? The whole visa and passport thing with Chinese has been a great big stuff-up ever since the influx that Hawkie let in after Tiananmen. But it's no accident, Ginge. Pressure is brought to bear through members of parliament, local council officials, community leaders. People inside

Immigration who are sympathetic to the Chinese. Some are got at through emotional pressure. Others are reached with money, the promise of business opportunities. A pretty girl or a pretty boy coming in with a request. Sometimes our system is so rigid and clumsy it's almost honourable to subvert it. There's enough racism around that place to make you sick.'

'You mean the whole Department in a generalised sort of way – or are there specific individuals?'

'It's individuals. But it's rare for anyone to get caught. Point a finger at the wrong person and their life can be ruined. There was a Chinese girl came round the staff at Rockdale giving us acupuncture and massage. Now she was something. She knew where to put her needle. Then you think what does it matter if one slips through the net?' Janis took out another cigarette, defying Ginger's health warning. 'Can you light this?' she asked, tossing him the lighter. 'I get shooting pains from the RSI when I do it. Is it worth it? Thanks.' She inhaled, enjoying the smoke. 'We're paid to do a job. We're not paid to be inhuman.'

'Police are no different,' said Ginger. 'The massage lady wasn't called Jasmine, I don't suppose?'

Janis whistled. 'Not bad. Did you meet her? Quite a number, that one.'

'Anyway, Rockdale, okay the whole place is a bit loose, but was there anything specific?'

She narrowed her eyes. 'There was a young guy doing the lost passport interviews. He was smart. He'd been doing some bloody dissertation for years. Working to pay for it. Ancient History was his thing. He had all these theories about slave culture. I don't know what his particular vulnerable spot was. Anyway I'd say he was putting the claims through and someone higher up was passing them on – there was an obese cow who was always bludging cigarettes off me, it could have been her – and then someone in Canberra was authorising them or at least not drawing it to anyone's attention. Those two in Rockdale both took redundancy packages before the shit hit the fan. You see what happens when they get a new passport in someone else's name is they're getting a whole new valid identity. Someone who's here illegally can just walk into it. Get a driving licence. A telephone account. It's the end of the journey for someone wanting a safe haven in this country. They climb into the new shell and that's it.'

Ginger adjusted his empty glass on the beer mat so that it exactly covered the wet ring. 'And whoever they were originally, that person ceases to exist.'

'Absolutely untraceable. The only problem is you've got two of some people walking around. Snap. Like pairs in a game of cards.'

Ginger's eyes crinkled sympathetically. 'We've all got a double, they say. We're all looking in the mirror. That's what the shrinks reckon.'

'One of me's bad enough,' Janis laughed. She felt good getting the Rockdale situation off her chest. 'What else can I help you law enforcers with?'

'Des O'Neill. Community Relations. What's his story?'

'I don't know the man.'

'Is he corrupt?'

'His job would be damage control. Look, Ginger, Immigration is not a happy place. But then not everyone's a rat. There are some who want to keep people out on any pretext. They're just as capable of perverting the system and feeling proud that they're doing a good job.'

'O'Neill told me Zhou Huang tipped Immigration off about the Pleasant Vale housing. Told them where to look for Guo Lihua. Jasmine. She's not on one of the Rockdale replacement passports. She's a long-term overstayer.'

'O'Neill was probably trying to get in first,' said Janis. 'Heading you off at the pass. Immigration never wanted a police investigation over Rockdale.'

'Whoever is behind the passport scam wants to cover their tracks too,' said Ginger. 'That's why people were moved out of the housing complex in a hurry.'

Janis pursed her lips. 'Immigration and the people-trafficking gangs are in it together. There's more in identity theft than in drugs.'

'Identity theft,' said Ginger, creasing his jowls along his collar in concentration. 'That's what you call it. By dobbing in Jasmine, Zhou Huang was threatening the whole thing.'

'Maybe more than he knew. Like I said, Ginge, I don't know Des O'Neill. He's just a name. Damage control.'

'He certainly gives nothing away and he sure doesn't want to cooperate. How would they have got Zhou Huang to work for them in the first place?'

'Immigration is desperate for information. They've got no idea what's going on. The Chinese know how to cover themselves. If someone can substantiate something with even an iota of truth, they'll go with them. They're complete klutzes. Zhou Huang delivered on Jasmine.'

'O'Neill made it sound like it had been going on for a while.'

'Let them all rot. I just want my compensation to come through.' She rubbed her right wrist. 'I get numbness all up my arm. Maybe blackmail would help. Let O'Neill know you're onto the racket out of Rockdale. I'm surprised that Jasmine didn't look after herself better, though. She was a smart little thing. I hope she wasn't counting on some bloody man to help her out.'

'Always a fatal mistake,' said Ginger with a twinkle. He rumbled with beer as he got to his feet. 'Janis, I appreciate it. All off the record, of course. You're a pal.'

'It's been good for me too, love. Therapy. Spilling the beans. Give Toni a hug for me.'

'Love to Sue,' he responded. They were parked at opposite ends of the Macarthur Park Tavern. As he walked to his car Ginger decided he had a case for asking the Federal Police to search the Immigration Department's records regarding its dealings with Zhou Huang. Time to move into offensive posture. Ginger Rogers taking the lead for a change, pushing his partner back across the dance floor in a traverse foxtrot. One drink too many, he realised.

# Chapter XVII

At midnight Daozi walked jauntily away from Circular Quay station to the Rocks against the flow of people heading for the last ride home after their night out. A summer storm had passed out to sea, releasing the air of humidity, and the night was mild. Fit and strong, Daozi climbed without slowing through the cutting in the hill, a dark moist tunnel hewn by the first shackled convicts, and down the stone steps to where the old wharves jutted in long finger-like extensions into the harbour, heavy with timber warehouses that were being reclaimed for theatres and fancy restaurants. He walked on to the fourth pier, swinging the bag with his fishing tackle, and slipped through a gap in a mesh fence. The rotting piles stood aslant the black water like old bones. He could feel the tipping and tilting beneath his feet as he walked lightly to the end. He could smell the decay of timber and the rank tidal odour as he inhaled the tangy air that came from the sea, the east.

He dropped his line in, felt it go slack as he reeled, pulling back against the tug of the current. That was all he needed as he huddled in his coat, fumbling for his cigarettes and his flask of lukewarm tea, as if he too were settling to a point of suspension in the cold black depths. The bodily pleasure of night fishing was ages old, an emptiness he shared with generations before him, a timeless way of slowing time. He was content to be alone, and pulled his cap down over his head as the night cooled the moisture on his skin.

Like a fan from Sydney Cove, the place where it had started, the city radiated out over huge distances, yet still contracted to that point where cruise ships docked and container ships passed and people stepped on and off trains, buses and ferries, beginning and ending their days. That tough old heart was still the place that visitors saw first, viewing the Opera House and the Harbour Bridge, the place on that munificent shore where the original people could always be felt alive.

Daozi rubbed the line of his thin moustache, rough as the scales of a fish rubbed the wrong way. He crouched in the darkness, dark and low to the worn timbers. The lights on the opposite shore were a speckle of gold and jade and as the night deepened the stars flung across the sky grew brighter. People came to this southern country following the strange brightness of its stars, seeking its silver and gold. Like himself, who had gone further south than anyone in his family, escaping China, seizing opportunity, travelling to the outer limits of the world.

It was not a bad place. As Daozi sat there invisible in the darkness, the underwater life played with his line. Ah Mo, his boss,

173

was at the Casino and would stay there gambling all night.
Sometimes his boss needed him, as protection or luck. Other
times, especially when they had been driving together all day,
Ah Mo let him go. Then Daozi liked to leave the car and come
down to the Quay on foot. He liked to fish, sharpening his
vision in the void as the night waned and the water became
light, reflecting the moon in broken ribs, and the land emerged
again from its contour of light. Engines chugged and horns
sounded as boats streaked through the huge nocturne with the
dawn approaching. Black became grey, green and silvery pink.
At a certain point the sky grew luminous. Perched on the edge
of the world, a solitary fisherman, dangling his legs from the
wharf in two inky strokes. A young man, a point of red glowing
from his cigarette. He felt at home in that moment of slow
change from darkness to unformed day, anywhere and
nowhere.

There was a splash as his line was taken. He gripped the reel
in his hand. Something big was pulling down. He hoped his line
wouldn't break. He let it run, then wound insistently. It turned,
this way and back, running to the bottom. Steadily he wound it
in until he saw it, barreling from side to side in flashes of silver, a
little Port Jackson shark, fighting hard as he hauled it over the
side. He held the shark flapping against the boards with his foot
as his knife went into its head and stilled it. Then quickly he slit
the belly open and let it bleed.

You couldn't buy or sell this fish, but you could eat it, being so
fresh. He cut the flesh away like a professional and packed it in

his bag. He hoped good luck had come to his boss at the Casino. They would eat fresh shark for breakfast to celebrate.

He cleaned his knife and put it away. Daozi. The Knife. As a kid he used to carve things from wood with a penknife. That's how he got the nickname. Then he graduated to carving stones. He was tough and agile as a youth and wanted to be a man of honour. His father got him a job with the Beijing police, but the force turned out to be more rotten than he expected and he quit. He and Ah Mo had grown up in the same block in Beijing, kindergarten kids together, starting each day with the same Red songs, waving little flags in the dusty exercise yard, marching up and down inside the green iron fence. But Ah Mo practised his violin when he went home and a teacher came, while Daozi, who was two years younger and left behind in the city when his parents were sent away to reform through labour, ran around the streets. The only structure Daozi knew came in letters from his father, telling him to obey those who were responsible for him. The son who had beaten and denounced him. That's why Ah Mo was the boss now and Daozi his loyal companion. That was the cord that bound him, a thick shadow that reached back deep inside him over many years.

As a policeman in Beijing Daozi had trained to a peak of fitness. He knew how to fight. But there was no order in the way the police ran things, only petty vindictiveness and small-time corruption. In those circumstances Daozi could no longer serve. He needed discipline and a sense of hierarchy. The only form of affection he knew was that attachment, expressed as obedience, and attachment was only possible to one master at a time. He left China in the panic that followed Tiananmen, when the whole country seemed to be descending into chaos. Ah Mo helped him come to Australia and got him a job in the cold room at the Sydney Fish Market. The guys he met there were fit too, from all over China. They were athletes – runners, boxers, swimmers. Maybe they made a wrong move in getting out at that time. China was a place for getting rich now. But they all had their reasons for coming here, Daozi and the rest of them, and it was too late to go back.

The shark's carcass plopped back into the water and a few gulls came screaming. Daozi watched it waltz from side to side as it sank. He walked back along the pier, yawning as the sun caught his face. The road went on round the harbour where the old train tracks ran and roses grew like weeds from the crumbling rock, Chinese roses filched from Europe-bound ships, run wild for many generations now, gold yellow and happy red. Daozi thought of the red flags he and Ah Mo used to wave as Young Pioneers, like thousands of other Chinese kids. He was a pioneer here too, in this other southern world, heading along with his catch of shark in the bag over his shoulder.

When he caught up with his boss, who was at home in his flat in Pyrmont with three thousand dollars of winnings after the night and hungry for breakfast, Ah Mo told him they needed to pay more attention to what that taxi-driver was about.

# Chapter XVIII

Zhou Huang's face stayed in Lewis's mind. Its silent message made a claim on him and in search of clues he found himself guided to the places where Zhou Huang had been. He took a fare to Campbelltown and with the tip the passenger added on he almost had the day's quota. He could justify making a detour back via the Pleasant Vale Recycling and Waste Depot. He had not been there since the morning he dropped Reg Spivak.

This time it seemed a more ordinary place, with people going about their business of dumping rubbish. The dump manager, however, was taken aback to see the taxi drive through the gates. Lewis had not called his friend to say that he was coming.

'What's up, mate?' asked Reg, scarcely pausing from his work. For him the taxi signalled bad news.

'Nothing,' said Lewis not very reassuringly. 'Can we talk when you have a moment?'

Reg was proud of the site. It was tidy and people obeyed his instructions as to where to deposit their unwanted stuff. The excavation, where the body had surfaced, was now filled and rolled smooth. Compactor trucks were dumping again today, from the ledge above a new pit. But because Lewis was there, Reg saw it as a re-run of that morning when Jimmy arrived with his gruesome load.

Lewis was taking photos.

'Did you ask permission?' called Reg angrily.

'Sorry sorry sorry.' Lewis put the camera away. 'It's nothing to worry about,' he told the old man. 'I just wanted to see the place again. It's different from what I remember.'

The ring of bush around the dump included some flowering gums that had burst into creamy masses. Cicadas were thrumming and kookaburras laughed. In that green glade under a brilliant blue sky, the intentness of people taking bags and cartons from their cars and dropping them in designated pits and cages took on the quality of a ritual dance.

'That was not a typical day,' said Reg. He frowned, looking righteously concerned. 'Did you see? There was another photo of the dead man in the paper, with a girlfriend.'

'I saw that,' said Lewis. 'What do you think about that woman?'

'Meant nothing to me. Never saw her before in my life.'

'That's not true,' said Lewis. 'She was in the black Beamer that day.'

'Bullshit,' said Reg. 'How do you know? You didn't see that. There wasn't time. You're making it up.'

'It's a guess,' said Lewis.

'The car was moving too fast.'

'I think maybe she was there,' repeated Lewis stubbornly.

'Anyway, the cops have been back,' Reg said. 'They're onto you. I said I couldn't remember the taxi company but they know you picked me up in Surry Hills. They reckon they'll find you with a thorough search. I look forward to seeing *your* picture in the paper next time!'

'You were already on television,' said Lewis. He understood that fear made Reg less willing to be friendly. The man was full of paranoid calculations. Lewis did not take it personally.

Reg scowled, walking away to the salvage shed. Books were lined up on a shelf. Ancient philosophy and myth. Russian novels. Speculative fiction. He said to Lewis that if he had the resources he could recycle ninety per cent of what came in. There was always a home for things no one wanted. There was always a use for waste.

'Can I take your photo in here?' Lewis asked, running along behind Reg, not letting him go. 'It's a great set-up. Like your own private museum.'

Reg softened a little at the idea. 'Maybe you should tell the police what you know. There's really nothing to hide.'

'I don't know the value of what I know,' said Lewis. 'I don't know what information is part of the picture and what is not.'

'You know,' said Reg sympathetically, 'ever since that day I keep finding things here at the dump and wondering if they are connected. Half the stuff on these shelves. I just don't know.'

There were vases and handbags and prints, lamps and artificial flowers and girlie calendars, radios and microwaves, plates and mugs, spoons and knives, fishing reels and big soft toys with popping eyes.

'Some of the stuff people left outside the gates after the story broke, while the tip was locked up. I don't know if they knew what had happened or not. A suitcase of men's clothes. Toiletries. A computer keyboard. A bag of golf clubs. Old pot plants and a bamboo stand. Even this – ' Reg pulled a Chinese-English Bible off the shelf. 'Nothing wrong with any of it. Like it was a kind of offering.'

The objects for sale stood in mute rows in the iron shed, clean but dull, as a dusty haze rose from the swept dirt floor. Reg posed in front of the neat display he had made, as if it all made sense to him, when in reality nothing much did. 'Tootle-loo,' he said with a grin for the camera. With his white beard and distinguished brow he looked like a trophy hunter, lord of his domain, standing amidst his conquests. But Reg was also something salvaged from the dump, a human being recycled one too many times.

Lewis knew he would be short of fares, but he had decided to take the rest of the day off. He figured Spiros, the owner of the taxi, still owed him for working two shifts in a row. He wanted to visit Kangaloon Native Garden which was not much further down the freeway from the turn-off to the dump.

The approach to the Garden was a winding route around the shoulder of a hill to stone portals at the top. Lewis drove in and parked the car. There was a map of the walking paths that he studied with no idea what he was looking for. He knew only that

Zhou Huang had worked there. On the map the asymmetry of the place looked appealing and Lewis was happy just to wander. But he did not grasp from the map the extent and contours of the terrain, nor the sudden gradations from one zone to another, from heath land to rainforest and scrub, all so flourishing and verdant. Lewis climbed to the highest point, then continued into a declivity where the path came to an end in a grove of flowering grevilleas. On the upper side, in an open space, an elderly gentleman was painting at an easel. He looked up at the intruder in an unperturbed way, then looked again, a little intrigued.

The man flicked his eyes in Lewis's direction as if giving him permission to approach. Then he returned to his painting until Lewis was close enough to see the easel over the man's shoulder.

'Sorry to interrupt you,' Lewis said. 'Can I look?'

The man went on painting. 'It's not at all finished,' he said gruffly as he moved to one side to allow his work to be admired.

Lewis stood with his head at an angle assessing the work in progress. Fire-coloured grevilleas whirled from the trunk in a feathery garland at the centre of which a face was depicted in repose against a white ground. Bigger than any of the surrounding bursts of flowers, the human features floated in a balloon, ringed by an aura of flickering, sticky fronds.

'What is it?' asked Lewis.

'Light, flowers and foliage,' said the artist.

'And the face?'

'It's a spirit of this place,' the man said, turning to Lewis with a questioning smile. 'What are you doing here?'

'Just visiting,' said Lewis. He recognised the face in the painting as Zhou Huang. 'Your painting is very good,' he said.

'That's kind of you,' the man replied. 'It's a nice day for the Garden, isn't it?'

'Yes,' said Lewis. 'It's a native garden. I never saw this one before.'

The man nodded, not entirely convinced.

'Do you sell your work?' asked Lewis.

'I do,' he said with some pride. 'There are people who collect my paintings. A couple from this series have gone to the Art Gallery.'

'The Art Gallery?' asked Lewis.

'The Art Gallery of New South Wales. They were accepted for a prize.'

Lewis had new respect for the man, a distinguished old-fashioned fellow who was accomplished at what he did. He seemed shy, formal, and at the same time inquisitive and almost overly friendly. 'You're a famous artist!' declared Lewis.

Jerome demurred with childish pleasure. 'Where are you from?' he asked.

'I'm Chinese,' said Lewis.

Jerome nodded with inward satisfaction.

'The man in your painting is Chinese, isn't he?' noted Lewis.

'You're right,' said Jerome. 'You don't know him, do you?'

Lewis laughed. 'No, no, no. You're a famous artist,' he went on. 'Can I ask your name?'

'I'm Jerome. Jerome Hampton.' He waited to see if the

name meant anything to the young man. Apparently not. 'And your name?'

'I'm Lewis.'

They stood for a moment in silence before Jerome picked up his brush and continued dabbing.

'There was a Chinese man who worked here,' said Lewis. The artist paused in mid-stroke. 'He was killed.'

'Truly?' said Jerome, turning to Lewis with a mask of sympathy. 'How awful! I don't know anything about that. Was *he* a friend of yours?'

'No,' said Lewis. 'I didn't know him. I just read it in the paper. Just another Chinese.'

'Oh dear,' said Jerome, shaking his head. 'That's terrible. Is that what brought you here?'

'In a way,' said Lewis. 'Anyhow, sorry to disturb you.'

'No, nice talking to you,' said Jerome, bringing the unsettling encounter to an end.

'Good luck with the prize,' said Lewis, cutting the air with his palm in a gesture of farewell.

From a vantage point at the top of the path Lewis was able to take a photograph of the old artist at his easel, dwarfed among the shrubbery. The lens zoomed in on the face in the painting, the likeness of Zhou Huang. Who else would the artist's model have been, here in Kangaloon Native Garden where the dead man worked? The trail's hot, thought Lewis, checking his watch. The Art Gallery in the city would close at five. That was his next stop.

An afternoon storm broke as Lewis reached the city centre. The harbour was pocked and grey, sucking in the light. He parked at Wolloomooloo and ran up the stone steps to the Art Gallery without an umbrella, drenched by the time he got there. He shook himself in the portico where people were cowering from the rain. He took off his bandana and used it to dry his hair, then he went inside and rode the escalator down through the levels of the building until he found the galleries where the entries for the prize were hanging: the Wynne Prize for a religious subject and the Archibald Prize for portraiture. To navigate those screaming walls was not easy. It was like a party at which everyone wanted to be noticed: politicians, entertainers, celebrities, and, in one self-portrait after another, the artists themselves, grinning and howling like Munch's *Scream*. The competitors painted large and bright in their clamour for the selectors' attention. There was little point in a Mona Lisa smile.

Around a corner in the second room Lewis discovered what he was looking for. The painting, labeled *Barely Buddha*, was larger than the canvas he had seen on the artist's easel at Kangaloon Native Garden. The subject was full length, nude, frontal, gold, with hands clasped in prayer as the figure walked through an explosion of scarlet and crimson grevilleas against a white light. It was radiant, reverential, full of longing for the naked male divinity.

Noticing Lewis's intense interest in the portrait, a pair of women moved in to have a look too. 'Jerome Hampton!' whispered one to the other, pointing at the label. 'I didn't know he painted.'

'He could *buy* the prize!' returned her friend. 'But it's not bad, is it? He can paint all right.'

Lewis waited for the women to move on before taking out his camera to record the picture, which he recognised as another portrait of Zhou Huang. He congratulated himself on his detective work. But a guard came waving his hand. Lewis bowed apologetically, saying 'Sorry sorry sorry' in his Chinese accent, and put the camera away.

The other work was a small, fully worked painting of Zhou Huang sitting cross-legged in a formal Buddhist posture, his hands formed in the *mudra* of blessing, one palm resting open on his knee, the other raised like a vertical knife to the front of his chest. Eyes downcast, ear lobes elongated, lips closed in a bud. His dark hair radiated in wavelets, and there was a gold cloth across his groin. The silver, green and scarlet of bush foliage pressed around him and behind was a dark recession of mountains topped by a shining night sky. In the foreground was a shoulder bag with an embroidered lotus on it and two Chinese characters, awkwardly copied but legible to Lewis as 'Zhou Huang'. There was the proof he needed.

The painting was labelled *Bong Bong Buddha*. It was intimate, tender, the composition leading the eye from gaudy outer circles to a point half-hidden in the shadowed gold pigment just below the belly where the life force had its centre. The skin was painted with erotic devotion. The modest scale made the picture into a private unfolding, a glowing still life that was also a rendering of living skin.

There was no one in this gallery, not even a guard. Lewis took the opportunity to photograph the picture, complete with label. He had no idea what Bong Bong meant. That would be his next search.

The rain was still splashing when the Art Gallery closed and people were herded outside. Lewis skipped down the stone steps to his taxi and sat there with the engine running and the wipers slapping back and forth across the glass as he gathered his thoughts. Zhou Huang was coming at him from all sides. Did he have a theory to fit the information he had garnered? He was suspicious of Jerome Hampton, this rich man with a strong artistic compulsion. Hampton must have met the dead man in the garden and painted him there. Yet he had not connected the subject of his painting with the Chinese worker who had disappeared and whose photographs had been published in the newspaper. Lewis wondered about the nature of the artist's relationship with his subject. He had transformed Zhou Huang from a gardener into an image of the Buddha. That was far from the 'pitiful rabbit' that Ah Mo had sneered at, far from the immigration informer. The man painted Zhou Huang as a lover. *Bong Bong Buddha*. Why was he killed in such a manner?

Rain dripped from Lewis's skin and hair on to the street directory that he opened on his lap. He turned to the maps of the outlying districts of south-west Sydney. Beyond Campbelltown and Macarthur Park and Pleasant Vale, beyond Kangaloon into the southern highlands where the escarpment fell away at the outer edge of the range. There it was. A place called Bong Bong.

'Nice work,' Lewis said to himself, putting the car into gear. You follow the trail and the clues are there. Sometimes. 'Ha!' he laughed out loud. He might be in the grip of delusion, or he might be heading right up shit creek as the Aussies liked to say.

# Chapter XIX

Without losing his rhythm Bernie could lift Jasmine into the air, hold her in his big arms and make her squeal. He made her breathe with him, mouth to mouth, and clench at the climax. He would be panting afterwards, his heart pounding fit to burst. Yet no matter how prolonged and athletic their sex, the white light did not return to rush up his spine and flood his brain. The kundalini would not come. Bernie lay there flexing his toes and listening to the night. Outside he could hear the cat on heat, its raw shrieks tearing the silence. Was it ecstasy or torture? That was the trouble with strays. If Jasmine was going to adopt that cat permanently, he would have to get it de-sexed. She lay peacefully against him, warm and heavy under the crumpled sheet. He turned away, unable to sleep, and she murmured a little. Her peace disturbed him. He got out of the bed and went downstairs. He put on some music, listening through headphones. Regurgitator. Radiohead at their most emotional, most metallic. He had been introduced to this music on the movie shoot, in

Arizona, out in the desert with that continuity girl who got him stoned. He thought about Jasmine's attachment to him. She was attentive, tender. He liked those things. She was different from the continuity girl, who was like a snake wrangler, never letting him get too close. But when Jasmine was asleep, he was unable even to stir her. What did she see in her dreams, her nightmares? She escaped into a different place altogether and became a stranger to him.

He turned off the music and sat in his robe watching videos until he could not stop yawning. The first batch of Oscar contenders had arrived. He had to send in his vote. He looked at the time. Three o'clock in the morning. Maybe he could sleep now. If he did not sleep, he would die. He went back upstairs and took a pill. Then he climbed clumsily back into bed, slipping in beside Jasmine's motionless warmth. He almost wanted her to wake, so envious was he of her healing slumber. She was breathing, but nothing else about her stirred.

Bernie was still asleep at eight-thirty in the morning when the phone rang. It was the police from a place called Pleasant Vale. A woman's voice, young and chirpy, was asking him if he was Bernard Mittel and if he lived at Centennial Park. Friendly but coercive, she introduced herself as Detective Constable Shelley Swert and asked him if he knew someone who went by the name of Jasmine.

'How did you get my number?' he replied groggily.

'We traced the calls to her answering service,' the policewoman said calmly. 'We found your account. It was a company account with an address in East Sydney and they put us through to someone in Los Angeles who said you wouldn't mind if we contacted you at home. Mr Josh Blane. Said he was your former employer.'

Bernie's stomach churned. 'I've been out of the country,' he said.

'Do you know Mr Blane?' The voice on the phone was switching from apology to interrogation.

'Josh Blane? Sure. A guy who wants to be a movie producer? Yeah, I know him. Did you say you're the police? What's your business with Josh Blane?'

'I'm calling from the Pleasant Vale police. Mr Blane gave us your number.' The woman's bright low voice was starting to sound amused. 'We'd like to ask you a few questions. If that's all right.'

'Now?' replied Bernie in his own joking tone.

'If you have time. Do you know this woman, Jasmine?'

'Yes, I do.'

'You've used her services?'

'Is she in trouble?'

'How many times?'

'Oh, I can't remember. Half a dozen times.'

'These are just routine inquiries, sir. We appreciate your co-operation. Did she come to your house?'

'Sometimes.'

'How did you find her?'

'How do you mean? What was she like?'

The policewoman gave a lewd chuckle. 'How did you come across her? Professionally speaking.'

'She was recommended by my osteopath. I have a bad neck.'

'Okay. Have you seen her recently? When was the last time you saw her?'

Bernie took a breath. It occurred to him that the conversation was being recorded. 'Just after I got back from LA. My neck was killing me. A pinched nerve. Maybe a week ago or more.'

'It would be great if you could give us an exact date, Mr Mittel.' Shelley Swert was at her most encouraging. 'Maybe you can work backwards.'

'Let's see. I left LAX on a Wednesday, skipped Thursday because of the dateline and got in on Friday night. Maybe I saw her on Saturday.'

'Thank you. Do you know where she is now?'

'I haven't been able to contact her,' Bernie said.

'You haven't seen her?'

'I don't know where she is.' He looked across the bed at Jasmine who turned and pushed her shoulders up against the pillows, pulling the sheet around her bare bony chest as she tuned in to the conversation. Her hair covered her face and her eyes were hostile and scared. 'Do you?'

'If you can help us with her whereabouts we would really appreciate it, sir.'

Jasmine brushed her hair out of the way nervously and stared at Bernie as he spoke. 'You'll be the first to hear,' he was saying. 'No worries. Happy to be of help.'

He hung up. Before he looked at Jasmine he let his head slump forward, the weight of his skull heavy in his hands. The nerve in his neck was biting again. There was too much going on that he did not understand. The cogs in his brain were grinding and crunching. Then he looked up at Jasmine with a wry arch of his eyebrows and said, 'Police.'

'Are they coming here?' she asked.

'Not yet.'

'I better go.'

'Is there anywhere you can go?' he asked. 'Safely?'

She shook her head. 'No,' she said, 'I don't think so. I have nowhere to go.'

'Then you have to stay here,' said Bernie, squeezing her hand. 'It's the only place, isn't it?' He lay his body on top of hers and whispered in her ear. 'Just stay here in bed. Just sleep some more.'

He pulled the clammy sheet over them as they lay there, as close as could be, joined by tension rather than desire. The shutters to the balcony were closed to mute the traffic noise and the room was stifling. Bernie rolled over. There was the squelch of skin unsticking. They could console themselves by making love but that would not dispel their apprehension of the situation enclosing them. 'We need air and light,' said Bernie, heaving himself up to open the shutters.

The morning was cloudless and hot. Jasmine preferred the darkness, although the heat oppressed her. She pulled the sheet over her head. While Bernie had slept, she had been kept awake by his snoring and by anxieties that wakefulness only intensified. She was worried. How long could she survive? In the pre-dawn light she had lain worrying, feigning sleep, and now again in the

hot morning she lay with her eyes closed, motionless, and still
could not sleep.

Then the doorbell rang, and rang again. There was the rapping
of the pineapple-shaped bronze knocker on the wood. Bernie
was the one to go. He padded down the stairs barefoot, calling
out 'Who is it?'. When he opened the door, he found the two
uniformed police officers. He was naked under his monogrammed towelling Four Seasons robe. They had caught him
completely unawares. 'I wasn't expecting you so soon.'

'Good morning,' said the woman, showing her identification.
'I'm Constable Swert, and this is Detective Sergeant Rogers,
Pleasant Vale police. Mr Mittel, I assume. I was talking to you a
little earlier.' The woman had more swing to her body than her
telephone voice suggested. She was a funky blonde in good
shape, set off by her sidekick, a blubbery oversize good guy with
a disappearing crown of carrotty hair.

'Didn't you guys believe me or something?' Bernie asked,
blocking the door.

'We were in the area for a meeting at Sydney Police Centre and
thought we'd take the opportunity to see if you were at home.
Since it's so close. And you are.' Shelley smiled sweetly. 'That's
where I was calling from.'

'Not that concrete bunker down the road?' Bernie said with
mock alarm. 'That's a scary looking place.' He was shifting his
weight from foot to foot, stalling.

'Can we come inside?' asked Shelley.

'Wow!' said Bernie. 'This is a first. Come right in. You'll have to excuse me.' He gestured at himself, conscious of his odour as he retied his robe more tightly and stood aside for the police visitors to enter the hallway. He pointed them to the front sitting room and opened the orange curtains for more light. 'Make yourselves comfortable. I'm still a bit jet-lagged, I'm afraid.' He hugged himself, wondering what happened next. 'Just give me a minute to put on some clothes.'

'You're fine,' said Shelley.

'Nice of you to say so, but I just need a minute, okay?'

He ran upstairs and found Jasmine curled up in a ball under the sheets. 'Police,' he said in a whisper. 'Go in the yoga room and shut the door. Keep quiet and keep out of sight.' Then he went into the bathroom and splashed his face, flushed the toilet, and reappeared downstairs a moment later in crumpled cargo pants and a half-buttoned shirt. 'Sorry about that. Now can I get you something to drink? Tea? Coffee? Something cold?'

They dutifully declined. No drink in it for the cops this time. 'It's a routine call,' Shelley said reassuringly. Her cropped hair had gelled spikes and the uniform of pale-blue shirt and tapered pants sat snugly on her frame. 'You're a star,' she said with a wrinkle of her nose, indicating his name on the framed movie posters hanging on the wall. 'Pretty impressive.' She was letting him know that they would not be aggro with a celebrity, not initially anyway. 'We're just following leads, like I said, systematically. Any information you can give might help us trace the missing woman's whereabouts.'

Bernie nodded like a panting dog in his eagerness to help. He ran through the story of his encounters with Jasmine, not varying from what he had revealed over the phone. Behind his eagerness, he was on guard. If the police made a move to look around the house, he would insist on ringing his lawyer immediately. The police needed a warrant to search a place and they had not produced one so far. And if they did produce a warrant, his lawyer must see it first. Behind his careful soft-spoken helpfulness, Bernie even grew slightly excited. It was like a film with a double frame. He was an outlaw to society in his own way, with Jasmine, his lover, hiding upstairs behind closed doors. He would protect her whatever it took.

Then he heard a sound behind him and he saw the eyes of the ginger-haired policeman dart from his notepad to the doorway. Bernie swivelled round a little too hastily and grinned with relief when he saw it was the cat. 'How did you get in?' he purred as the cat turned tail.

'Do you know anyone else who may have had contact with the woman?' the sergeant asked. 'Anyone else use her for massage?' His slack grin acknowledged that this was tricky business.

'No,' said Bernie. 'We never talked about that.'

'You said your osteopath recommended her?'

'That's right. Maybe you should talk to him.'

Bernie crossed his legs and tried to look relaxed about this interview that seemed to be going in all directions at once.

'What state was she in? When you saw her that Saturday?' Shelley frowned with concern. 'That was the last time you saw

195

her, wasn't it?' she continued. 'We're trying to get a handle on her role in all this.'

'All what?' asked Bernie dumbly. 'What's this all about, guys?'

'The photo we've released links her with a suspected homicide. A Chinese man found dead at the dump at Pleasant Vale. And now she's missing.'

After a solemn pause, Bernie said, 'Well, this is very serious.'

'From what you told me in the telephone interview you saw her *after* the discovery of the body at the dump. How was she?'

'She was just the same. I mean I was pretty wasted myself. Just off the flight. I wasn't looking for anything and I didn't notice anything to tell you the truth. But she fixed me up and I was grateful. She's safe, isn't she?'

'We don't know,' said Shelley.

Bernie blinked. 'What do you think happened to her?' he asked.

'No idea,' Shelley replied. 'We don't even know if she's in the country.' She paused, then rose to her feet. 'Well...thank you, Mr Mittel. You've been very helpful.'

'No problem,' said Bernie, trying not to hurry them out.

Shelley and Ginger lingered in the hallway, reluctant to leave with nothing more than they had brought.

'Nice house,' Ginger said inconclusively. 'Near the park and everything.'

'Will we be seeing you again?' Bernie asked, directing the question at Shelley as he reached across her to open the door. It was a foolish thing to say. 'I mean you know where I am if you need me.' He gave them a nod and they thanked him. But there was a degree of unease, a sense of unfinished business, as the two police officers said goodbye, putting on their hats and sunglasses and stepping out into the glare of the street.

From her dim silent box Jasmine could hear the muffled voices downstairs. She heard the cat miaow as if in sympathy. Looking down through the slit of light at the edge of the blind, she saw the cat jump from the wall to the courtyard and enter the house. She had forgotten to put out food. And Bernie had left the door open. She breathed deeply, rubbing her ankles together, trying to stay totally quiet. She wondered when her turn would come. Like anyone summoned to declare themselves, she feared the moment, while also longing for the resolution the moment would bring.

She had not called Ah Mo again, after keeping the lunch appointment in Chinatown. He made her promise to call every second day, but she had not done that. He wanted her to go to his apartment and drink tea with him and Daozi as a sign of her fealty. She knew he would not risk calling her. But he would be angry.

She was so careless, so naïve. So alone. She thought of Garlic Shoot. Huangzi. If she had married him and got her residency, there would be nothing to fear. She thought of Mengzi. He was too impatient, stirring her feelings in those late-night calls from China, speaking with such urgency, ordering her to help him. And his desperate desire to be reunited with her, his Lihua, far away across the south sea. How could she resist?

She was a good woman, she told herself, always ready to act with courage, but a stupid woman, believing her own dreams.

She looked up without expression when Bernie pushed open the door of the yoga room.

'They've gone,' he said, putting his arm around her. 'The coast is clear.'

'Do they know I'm here?' she asked, barely able to trust him.

'I covered for you perfectly,' said Bernie. 'It's risky. I guess they'll be back. It's like *Fifty-five Days at Peking*. Did you ever see that movie? Ava Gardner and Ropert Helpman? We're under siege, my empress. Look, I've been thinking, maybe you really should contact the police and just tell them what you can. They don't seem very frightening. They're not going to hurt you, Jasmine.'

'Then the Immigration Department will find me and send me back to China.'

'Oh yeah,' he said, looking devastated. 'I forgot about that.' That was one thing Bernie Mittel would never let happen. You never sent people back into the fire. 'There must be a way. You're not a criminal. Why don't I talk to my friend Andy about it? He's got a lawyer he uses for international cast and crew. Work permits. Visas. All that sort of thing. I bet he can fix it up. Whatever it takes.'

Jasmine held his hand, squeezing his skin so tightly it hurt.

'Owch!' he said. 'That's a Chinese burn.' He bit her neck playfully in retaliation, leaving teeth marks.

'No,' she moaned, 'no.' She slapped him. 'Stop it. That's enough now, Bernie. You help me, so I thank you for the rest of my life.'

# Chapter XX

Bong Bong was a puzzle of country lanes fortified by high hedges that hid the houses from view. Gravel drives, banked with agapanthus and periwinkle, led to dwelling places lost in scented foliage. Blue spruces and golden cedars dwarfed rustic cottages and mock-Tudor villas alike. Lewis found it creepy as he drove around looking for clues. There were pony grounds and parks, estates and retreats. Behind clipped hedges he caught darts of colour – a child running across the lawn, a woman in a hat bending to the soil, clothes flapping in the breeze – and the glint of vehicles streaming through leafy curtains.

The main street of the town was hung with baskets of miniature roses. Lewis parked the taxi and walked up and down. This time a fare had taken him as far as Liverpool, barely halfway, and he would be paying the day's contract money from his own pocket unless he was very lucky. He would not tell his family. It was money he could not afford. But he was on the case now, on a roll, like any gambler, and he felt compelled.

He found a vegetarian café and peered in the window. The woman working the espresso machine smiled at him. There were notices stuck on the glass inside, facing out. Among them he saw a flyer for the season's program at the Bong Bong Buddhist Centre. ALL WELCOME, it said. Lewis chuckled, pleased with his intuition, and went inside. A young waiter, who had a fork-tongued cobra tattoo down the length of his arm, pointed to a table and a chair strewn with cushions stitched with mirrors and beads. On the walls were little paintings of mermaids, butterflies and owls. Lewis ordered a latte and the woman at the espresso machine, a pierced, cropped madonna with rings under her eyes, set to work.

When the coffee came, he asked the waiter where the Bong Bong Buddhist Centre was.

'Do you know where the Buddhists might be, Pina?' the boy called back to the bar.

'They're at the top of Shepherd's Lane,' the woman said. 'Out on the road to the National Park. It's the old convent. Crystal House. The nuns have given them a space.'

'Is it open?' asked Lewis.

'Should be,' Pina beamed. 'It's a beautiful place.'

'What kind of Buddhists are they?' Lewis asked.

'There's an older woman and some blokes,' she said. 'They wear orange robes. A few of them are Asian. They come in here sometimes when they're on retreat.'

'They miss their lattes,' the waiter joked.

'We give them a discount,' Pina said. 'It's our donation.'

'They're addicted to coffee. You should refuse them,' said Lewis, 'if you want to earn karma.'

'Are you Buddhist?' she asked.

'Not officially,' said Lewis. 'I'm no religion officially.'

'Unofficially is better,' she concluded, taking his money. 'For all belief systems.'

Lewis drove out through the town of Bong Bong and turned off the main road into a single track that curved uphill. At the top were gateposts, a locked mailbox and a little sign that said *Crystal House*. He drove in through a canopy of pines and stopped when he reached a sign that said *Private Property*. The gravel was white, bordered by azaleas, their tiny leaves shining under the huge old trees. He got out of the car and walked up to the front porch where a modest wall plaque announced the Bong Bong Buddhist Centre. A stone crucifix was set above the main door. Beside the door hung an old brass bell. All was quiet.

The house was a sprawling villa with wings and attics, rendered, half-timbered, daubed in pale green. Lewis cast his eyes around the garden where magnificent conifers, blue, grey and gold, made islands of shade in the trimmed lawn. There were flowerbeds and pathways and, recessed among the foliage, statues and a shrine. He wondered whether to ring the bell.

While he waited he heard a rustle of footsteps. Then a woman appeared from the side of the house, frail, bright-eyed, venerable. She maintained her silence until she was close enough to bow to Lewis, hands clasped to her chest in prayer fashion by way of greeting.

'Welcome,' she said in a hushed tone. 'Did someone call a taxi?'

'No,' said Lewis, speaking at normal volume. 'I came to look.'

The wispy-haired woman put her fingers to her lips. 'We're silent here, except for what sometimes must be said. Are you wanting to join us?'

Lewis smiled. 'Your robe is beautiful,' he said.

The elderly woman dropped her head to one side like a coy schoolgirl. 'That's very kind of you,' she said in a stage whisper. 'I made it myself.'

The robe was a dusky apricot colour in a light, transparent fabric. It might have been a party dress, but in colour and transparency the material matched the crepe of her skin. The woman's hands fluttered and clenched into fussy little fists as she fondled the trimming braids. 'Welcome to the Bong Bong Buddhist Centre,' she said. 'I'm Nova Jewell. Our abbess. Now, how can I help you, dear friend? We are not open to visitors, I'm afraid.'

'I want to learn more,' said Lewis, seizing on the woman's good will. 'About Buddhism.'

'The best way to learn is to do,' said Nova. She was the queen bee of Crystal House.

'Do you have some information about your program?' Lewis asked respectfully.

'Come with me,' she said, opening the heavy front door and bundling him into the foyer where she produced a copy of the same flyer he had seen in the café. After a moment's hesitation, she also handed him a magazine.

'Thank you very much,' said Lewis. 'How many of you are there?'

'It varies. Some come for temporary retreats. Others come just for the day. Those in training stay here in residence.'

'What sort of people are they?'

'Oh, every sort of background!'

'Australians? Asians?' asked Lewis.

'We leave those labels behind,' explained the abbess. 'Those attributes of the self. We let them go in order to encounter the not-self.'

Lewis smiled, startled at her profound evasion of his question. 'Is it all right to look around?' he asked.

Nova Jewell stared at him, trying to read him. Was he a natural Buddhist, she wondered. For her, devotion was a labour. 'As I said, we're really not open to visitors. You may have a quick look on your way out,' she agreed, somewhat reluctantly. 'But please respect the silence. We try not to interrupt each other's meditations. We avoid eye contact.'

'Thank you,' he said. 'Thank you very much. See you again.'

The old woman bowed, cast her eyes down and held the door for him to go, closing it behind him.

Lewis stood on the porch and flicked through the magazine that the abbess had given him. In a black-and-white group shot taken on the front steps he recognised Nova Jewell in her swathe of gown, flanked by other figures in more orthodox Buddhist robes. He peered more closely. One of them looked like Zhou Huang. The photograph was captioned 'New trainees'.

The individuals were unnamed. Lewis checked the date of the magazine – last month.

Two men in orange robes and sandals came walking up from the garden. They were middle-aged men, their faces scored and blotchy, their heads shaven, their flesh sunken. They averted their gaze slowly as they passed, as if saying goodbye to the world of casual encounters was not yet easy for them. Lewis stepped out of their way and walked down one of the paths. In an open space of the lawn a large woman in a plain indigo dress stood in contemplation, her shoulders relaxed. She moved away as he approached. Gradually, as he made his way, the grounds became deserted. There were empty places where people had been moments before – the gazebo, the candle-shaped shade of a birch tree, the grotto where a statue of Jesus Christ bared hands and bleeding heart.

'So Zhou Huang was here too,' Lewis said to himself in defiance of the silence.

He grinned at the statue as he passed, its hands green with moss and holding water and bird shit. There was a wire gate that opened into the unkempt grass beyond the garden. He hoped only the statue noticed as he followed the path through the gate.

Immediately he was in bush that crackled and simmered in the late summer heat. The path led gently upward through an outcrop of rock. Lewis was drawn on. The undergrowth became thick heath, and boulders rose up higher than his head with ferns and gnarled banksias sprouting from their cracks. He was anxious about going any further when he reached the top of a ridge and a line of mauve hills became visible, dissolving into sky in the distance. Then closer at hand he saw something move. There was a figure ahead of him on the path, flitting between trees like a fleeing animal. The folds of an orange robe rippled against the blue. A shaven head turned away through green leaves. He hurried along the path, downward now, in chase. He had his camera out. On a lower shelf the path snaked round and he saw the shaven-headed figure again, moving between rocks and trees, orange against the blue.

'Hey!' called Lewis. 'Wait!'

But the figure did not turn.

Lewis reached the spot where the flicker of orange had passed. The split of rock was coated in bright orange lichen, the same vibrant colour as the robe. There were no footprints on the ground to disturb the earth and stone and tree roots and fallen leaves. He wondered if he was seeing things. A fleeting figure of slender build, a tonsured monk in Buddhist robes, a Chinese man? Why did he not answer? Was he Zhou Huang, the dead man? Had Lewis seen a ghost through the trees in this strange bush? Was Zhou Huang everywhere? There was a weird screeching and he looked up to see a pair of wheeling yellow-tailed black cockatoos. Was he hallucinating? The bush seemed to whirl about him. What he had seen was gone. There was no further trace, nothing for his camera to take, only the eerie flash of orange in his mind. Suddenly he felt quite alone, doubting his own senses – and doubting that doubt.

The taxi's tyres made a surfing sound on the gravel. Nova

Jewell watched in satisfaction from the window of her steeply gabled room in the upper storey of Crystal House as the taxi disappeared down the drive. The abbess was vigilant, suspicious, protective of what had been established at the Bong Bong Buddhist Centre with such difficulty. She hoped the young man was going away without taking anything that would disrupt the tranquillity of her world and the band of devotees in her charge. She did not know what he was after, or whether he was even really a taxi-driver, or who and what had directed his path to her. The thread of antecedents ran through her mind. She was sure it was not as met the eye.

When Zhou Huang sat for Jerome Hampton, he could pose motionless for half an hour at a time with no sign of any tension in his body. But Jerome could never capture him to his satisfaction. The more he admired that skin, the more he desired it, the more humiliated he was by his incapacity to come near. He had reached the limit of his artistry. He could not touch that pigment with his brush. It was a surprise, observed Nova Jewell, that such obsession should declare itself again in Jerome's old age, in an old man, in relation to the shy Chinese he wanted to paint. Zhou was polite with Jerome, but also cheeky and joking in his blunt half-learned English. Jerome appreciated that rough edge. He handled the boy's body freely, twisting it this way or that. Zhou never objected. While Jerome rubbed his charcoal into the paper, Zhou lay back against a pile of cushions, disguising any tension in a pose of compliance.

He liked to chat about the Buddhist sites of his native Hangzhou: *Lingyinsi*, the Temple of the Purification of the Soul, and all the stories associated with it over many centuries; *Hupaoquan*, the Leaping Tiger Spring; and the Yellow Mountain not far away, *Huangshan*, draped in a cloudy mantle of spirit and legend. Talking of Hangzhou, Zhou's pride would turn to wistfulness as his homesickness surfaced. He told Jerome about the little dragon dumplings that were sold on the street, and the green tea from the mountain slopes that cost dollars an ounce, and about his mother and father, plain honest people who had struggled all their lives. Tears filled his eyes and flowed down his cheeks as he spoke of how he missed them. He didn't move a hand to brush the tears away. He kept his pose.

When Jerome and his young Chinese friend visited the Bong Bong Buddhist Centre for the first time, one Saturday afternoon, Nova was cautiously encouraging. Her life's work was to bring the teachings of the Buddha and the benefits of meditation to her fellow Australians. She knew how hard the path was. She had been disappointed countless times. To be free of self was not simple, with maybe, at the longest possible odds, at the end of long dedication, a shattering moment of enlightenment. Awakening. It was the hardest thing in the world.

Nova Jewell had known Jerome Hampton a long time and she had seen his passions before. Her first job had been in the famous department store when his family still ran it. She had gone straight from the convent into Haberdashery at Hamptons'. That's where she made her name. At school she had been a questing and rebellious girl who often had the ruler on the back of her legs in punishment. Yet the nuns insisted that she had a vocation for a life of service. Her father, gassed in the Great War, had taken his own life with a shotgun. Her struggling, unbelieving mother told her that the family needed her daughter's wages from Hamptons' more than they needed the glory of a Bride of Christ. Nova's vocation, her mother said bluntly, was to pass ribbons and buttons through her pure fingers into the hands of paying customers.

Nova was senior staff in Haberdashery when young Jerome arrived on the shop floor to learn how the business worked. Jerome Hampton was a solemn, unconventional youth for Ladies' Accessories. Nova's grip was firm as she tugged him into the storeroom to share her insights. With the Hamptons' badge pinned to her crushed velvet jacket and her eyes glowing like rubies, she inducted him into the gossip about staff and customers alike. She was young Jerome's teacher, his soul mate and, on rare occasions, his escort outside the store to an exhibition or a concert.

Nova Jewell's art lay in the sidestep that a piece of braid, a silken tassel or a shining mother-of-pearl button could make from the straight path of existence. In the sixties, via a charming renegade Jesuit, she took her own sidestep into Zen. A door opened to the Buddha – her ocean, her harbour – and Nova went through. When Hamptons' was restructured and became a public company under new management, she resigned at last from Haberdashery and gave herself full-time to the spiritual life. Eventually she founded the Buddhist Centre.

She admitted that Jerome may have had a part in leading her to Bong Bong. His grand estate was nearby, a reference for her as she sought a home for her cause. At any rate, she and Jerome became neighbours. She valued his support and encouraged him to turn to her, changing his life from the barren ostentation of a rich man's high summer to a more profound, more inward autumn. Once again Jerome was her spiritual charge.

Jerome winked at Nova, scrunching his shoulders, as he introduced Zhou to the meditation group. The young Chinese man was a natural already as he went down into his third prostration, his face touching the floor, letting go of self in perfect obeisance. Zhou came regularly after that, always accompanied by Jerome but, Nova could see, with a commitment and an understanding of his own.

Nova was excited by the newcomer's potential. When he sat, untroubled, centred, the clouds scudding across the sky of his mind left no mark. She spoke of training him. On some days she could see that he was disturbed by tiredness and anxiety. She gave him Zen riddles to study and struck him lightly with her stick to awaken him. After a one-day meditation he did a two-day meditation in which he slept overnight and rose to sit again before dawn. But when it came to the three-day meditation, Zhou gave his apologies. That was more than Jerome could manage, Zhou explained. He would not attend without the older man.

Sometimes it was necessary to slay the Buddha in order to release the Buddha. As time went on Nova came to feel that her friend Jerome's attachment to Zhou was holding the young man back. There was resistance in the excuses Jerome found when he and Zhou did not to come to the session. They were sick with a cold...Zhou was needed for this or that...there was a picture to finish...Childish games! Nova saw the hang-dog look in Jerome's eyes. She knew he could be predatory.

Nova was determined to break the attachment, for everyone's good. So one day she took Zhou Huang aside and let him know that he could come to her, *by himself*, if ever he needed refuge.

# Chapter XXI

A car took the old couple to the station for the longest journey they had ever taken. The late winter smog hung low as they left Hangzhou. Another car was waiting to meet their train in Shanghai and an Australian consular official escorted them to the airport where their papers were stamped. They sat at one end of a row of plastic orange chairs and watched the planes on the damp tarmac. The things they needed for the journey were in a black vinyl bag with long handles. Fortunately they had brought along enough food. They shelled their hard-boiled eggs while they waited and ate sweet buns washed down with pungent green tea, catching the dark swollen leaves of Dragon Well in their teeth. Then they were ushered on board.

It was cold in the plane. They wore the grey wool-synthetic suits that their workplaces had provided, the man with a cream shirt and silk tie, the woman with a flower pattern crimson knit. They shrouded themselves under the blankets. Mrs Zhou had been in a daze ever since she got the letter informing her of her son's death. Her second son. Colleagues in the accounts office where she worked said she would get an overseas trip out of it, but she could not compute such a tragedy in terms of profit and loss. She had lost her two sons. There was no way to account for that, no way to balance the books. Mr Zhou received the news more combatively. They would seek compensation. They would demand justice. They would sue.

The death of their first son was traumatic – and never officially acknowledged. Their closed-off grief sat like a stone in their hearts. Mr Zhou's workplace had offered assistance to send their second son out of the country to avoid further trouble, on condition that the son sent money back. Mr and Mrs Zhou were simple folk who had seen too much change. They came from families that had moved off the land, joined the Revolution and marched into the cities to become factory workers for the New China. They moved into Hangzhou from their mountain village, scuffing the refinement of the historic city with their tough peasant ways. Loyal to the slogans of the day, they worked doggedly to improve their own lives within the grid that was laid down. The rest of the world was of no concern. Their sons were their heirs – an inspired zither player and an uninspired worker in a porcelain factory.

This journey to Australia was another Long March, Mr Zhou joked, as the attendant fastened his seatbelt. He fell into deep, open-mouthed sleep on the flight. Mrs Zhou was more unsettled. Now at last, after hours of shuddering darkness, the plane dipped down over reflecting sheets of blue and weird fingers of coastline. Chewing ginger candy to quell their motion sickness, they craned for a view of this place. They stared through dry sore eyes at the tilting suburbs. They were told that Australian officials would take any food or medicine from them on arrival at Sydney Airport, even their gifts of best quality tea. They made sure to finish the last of their buns, even as they sat waiting to disembark.

They were met by Detective Heidi Lee from the Asian Crime Squad and a Taiwanese interpreter called Pamela So. They were taken to a three-star hotel in the city and given glossy bright-coloured currency for meals and expenses. The interpreter gave them instructions for finding a noodle shop where they could eat and warned them to look carefully when crossing the road because cars drove on the wrong side here. They should obey the green and red walk signs at the traffic lights.

Mr and Mrs Zhou understood that next day they would be taken to see their son's remains. They were happy to make the hotel room their temporary home, closing the thick curtains to shut out the alien sky and sinking into an exhausted sleep in the soft bed that smelled of chemical cleaning.

Mrs Zhou dreamed of the time she gave birth to her first son in the local hospital. She was strong and thin in those days and had produced a fine fat child. Everyone laughed at the way the boy bashed sticks on tins as he grew up, revealing his musical ability. His mother sang to him and satisfied him, knowing in her pride that he would leave her. She heard those old children's songs again in her dream. Then another child was crying, an unasked joy, a second son, and she was the envy of all women.

This time the birth was not so easy. She was weak for months afterwards, but the baby was quiet and strong.

They named him Huang, after Huangshan, the Yellow Mountain they had climbed on an excursion during the pregnancy. He grew up a simple child who only reacted when things were disturbed around him. Her husband's old mother said he was like one of the village boys in the old days, a mountain kid, tongue-tied and sweet, with a spirit that came and went like the clouds.

Mrs Zhou lay in the strange bed keeping her son's face in her heart as the images of her life played. 'Time to get up,' she said at last, touching her husband with her foot, making him groan.

The old couple washed as best they could in the white bathroom and put on their grey suits, he in his shirt and tie, she in her embroidered jumper. They went down for breakfast and ate fried eggs and melon and orange juice and toasted bread, then they wandered up and down outside in the surprising warmth and humidity. The street was lined with parked cars and small feathery trees that flourished among the stained old buildings. Here and there was a tower of coloured glass that made them smile. They entered a shop and looked at the racks of magazines with big, blond naked people on the covers. The man at the till stood guard. In another shop with the smell of old onions and oranges they laughed at the trays of large bread loaves, each more than one person could eat. Mr Zhou took out the money they had been given and handed over a red note for a big blue packet of the local cigarettes: HOLIDAY. That was what the man next to him in the plane told him to try. Several times the price of Chinese cigarettes. Mrs Zhou scolded him. Why didn't he buy them duty-free?

Pamela, the interpreter, arrived on time and took them by taxi to Sydney Police Centre. She was a graduate of the National University in Taipei, she told them in her funny sibilant Mandarin. She had worked as a travel agent and married an Australian businessman. Now she had a job as an interpreter for the police and the law courts. She joked that she was Mr and Mrs Zhou's compatriot. The gulf between them could not have been greater. She wore a canary-coloured pants suit and high slingbacks and had a large diamond ring beside her wedding band. Pamela felt sorry for the old couple, who returned her sympathy with bemused contempt.

They expected they would reclaim their son's remains as ashes in a cardboard box. Instead they were brought before the police officer in charge of the investigation, Detective Superintendent Silverton, who gave them milky tea and questioned them about their son's reasons for coming to Australia. He found their answers startlingly vague. They had no idea what their son had been doing in the place other than struggle to survive. He was a good boy, they said. He had no enemies – although he might have had some friends who did not treat him well. They gave the detective copies of Huangzi's birth and residential papers, high-school graduation, medical and dental records, and the X-rays taken when he broke his arm falling off his bicycle as a teenager.

They were typical parents, Ronnie Silverton thought. They

knew nothing about their offspring. No wonder they had lost two sons.

After the superintendent was finished with them, the interpreter led the old couple down a corridor to Forensic. The director there bowed to greet them. He was small and chubby – like bread, thought Mrs Zhou, from eating too much of it – and spoke in a high whispering voice. Mr Zhou thought he might be a Japanese. But he was Indian.

The interpreter told Mr and Mrs Zhou to follow the director as he escorted them into the Forensic morgue. They passed through heavy doors that enclosed a cold, silvery, neon-lit chamber. The director gave an order to an attendant then paused for the obligatory warning to be translated. 'Not your dear one, merely his temporarily preserved remains...' It was a perfunctory act of counselling to ready them for what they might find.

In Zhou Huang's case the gruesome remains had been assembled and preserved in barely human form. In a bizarre striptease the attendant removed the opaque plastic sheets that covered each section of the body, starting with the blue, unblemished feet. The parts were laid out next to each other. Caked blood had been removed to reveal the contours of tissue. When the attendant reached the upper torso, the director asked to be reminded which of the arms had been broken, left or right, and where. Finally the covering of the head was removed. The hair on the skinned head had been grotesquely combed. Mrs Zhou started to howl. Mr Zhou joined in. They sagged, supporting each other. The interpreter stood back out of respect.

After a long minute the director signalled the attendant to cover the corpse again.

There was a waiting area outside the morgue with a soft-drink machine. Pamela punched out two cans of cola for them to drink. Mrs Zhou was shaking. The two old people were speaking to each other in Chinese with some urgency. The interpreter struggled to understand their Northern Jiangsu dialect.

'It's not him,' the woman was saying. 'It's not my son.'

'How can you be certain,' demanded the man. 'It doesn't look like any human being.'

'I am completely definite about it,' his wife said, mopping her eyes. 'He's my own son. I know his shape, his bones, his head. I remember his head from his birth that caused me such pain. That is not him.'

Mr Zhou looked round at the interpreter without meeting her eyes, noticing she was listening. All the money spent wrongly on bringing them there if the dead man was not their son? He told his wife to calm herself.

'What have they done with my son?' she wailed.

The Forensic director asked the interpreter what was up. Pamela said nothing. Then Mr Zhou gravely faced the interpreter and explained. 'My wife says those remains in there are not our son.'

When the interpreter passed this information on, the director rubbed his hands. 'Excellent,' he said in his high upward-inflected whisper. 'A false identification. That's where forensic science comes into its own. Identity or resemblance? Science or speculation? Nowadays we have DNA testing too. Perhaps that will be required. But even with that there is scope for human error.'

He had the X-rays and the other records they had brought in his hands. 'We'll hang on to these if we may,' he said, waving the wobbly envelope at the old couple. 'Thank you so much.'

The Forensic director asked the morgue attendant to double-check that there was no mix-up with the body for identification, then he hurried upstairs to compare the X-rays from China with the X-rays of the Pleasant Vale corpse. By early afternoon he could advise Superintendent Silverton that there was a mis-identification. The X-rays didn't match.

'We're back where we started,' said Ginger when the information reached the Pleasant Vale police. So much time had gone into this case already, and now even the basic facts were in doubt. He yawned, weary at the thought of all the hours ahead, and the receding prospect of solving it. That started him scratching his scalp.

'Not quite,' said Shelley, her interest revived by the new twist. 'And stop that neurotic scratching, Sarge! We know that Zhou Huang is missing, even if he's not the dead guy, and we're pretty sure he's mixed up in something. If it's really a wrong identification, maybe it's not an accident.'

'You move fast, Detective,' said Ginger, clasping his hands in his lap and chewing his cud as an alternative activity.

'It's only logical,' Shelley said.

Mr and Mrs Zhou sat in the noodle shop near their hotel. Their bodies were heavy, drained after the morning. As she slurped soup noodles into her mouth, bending low to the bowl, Mrs Zhou began to emerge from the state of paralysis that had seized her on viewing the body. Her shocked mind was starting to move. The revelation that the dead man was not her son had opened a way. There was uncertainty, and behind uncertainty lay mystery, and behind mystery lay fate, and behind fate lay possibility.

'He looked a bit like Mengzi,' she mumbled to her husband.

'Mengzi?' Mr Zhou spluttered. The woman was imagining things, hallucinating revenge on her son's enemy.

'A bit like Mengzi,' she repeated, 'wouldn't you say?'

Mr Zhou leaned forward to the woman who had been his sturdy, reliable companion for a lifetime. He did not want her mind to crack in this foreign place. 'Never say that to anyone again,' he ordered her.

'Guo Lihua would know what has happened to our son,' the old woman stated, seizing the kernel of things. That much was clear. 'Lihua knows.'

# Chapter XXII

Lewis adjusted the band on his ponytail, pulling it tight. As he sped back into the city from Bong Bong he had the airconditioning on full bore but it didn't make any difference. He was hot and uncomfortable and the hard afternoon light made the fanciful mood of the bush evaporate. Maybe it was some sort of Buddhist mind control by the old lady, he thought, that had caused him to see things. He accepted that he had not seen the face of the person who hurried ahead of him, only a flicker of orange.

When he got the car back to base, he complained to his boss that the airconditioning had still not been repaired. That was his excuse for not making his quota of fares. It did not explain the mileage.

Spiros raised his eyebrows. 'You got other things to worry about, mate,' said Spiros. 'Coppers have been here. They're onto you. They're waiting for you at home.'

'Which coppers?' Lewis asked calmly. 'I haven't done anything.'

Spiros handed Lewis a note. 'Your lucky day, mate. See what it says. Call Ginger Rogers. Her-her-her.'

Lewis looked at the message. 'Pleasant Vale police.'

'Hollywood calling,' laughed Spiros. 'Hop in. I told them you'd be back by six and they said they'd wait for you at home.'

'Are you handing me over?'

'You don't want to do a runner, mate. Not at this stage. Take it from me. You want to find out what they've got on you.'

Lewis wished he had gone to the police first. Although he was completely innocent, he did have something to say. He wondered how they had found him. It must have been what Jimmy said, the driver of the garbage truck that morning. It would not be Reg, he thought. Maybe Spiros had put him in.

'I need to keep the car to midnight. I've got half a day's fares to make up. Spiros, you owe me.'

'You been doing some stuff, man. Listen, I don't want my taxi involved in anything, okay?'

'Just driving a taxi.'

'Then I don't need to come with you,' said Spiros, relieved. 'You can take the cab and drive yourself. But don't keep those guys waiting.'

'Okay, I'm doing what you say.'

Spiros patted Lewis on the arm for luck. 'That's the way. Keep sweet with the coppers. Let me know how you get on. If they take you away, I'll need the car back tonight.'

'Thanks mate,' said Lewis sarcastically.

The police car was parked outside the house in the suburban street when Lewis drove up. Seeing it, Lewis realised that the tentacles of the situation reached to his family now, his brother, his sister-in-law, their two children, his old father. Mind your own business. He had not heeded his father's warning. Neighbours peered through their windows, their worst suspicions confirmed. The first thing he would tell the police was that it had nothing to do with the other people in the house, nothing to do with his family.

Ginger and Shelley were sunk deep in the moss-coloured sofa in the front room when Lewis appeared. They had tea and sweets in front of them and soft toys in their laps. Ming and Jack were climbing all over them. The kids liked the blue uniforms. Alan stood grinning in the centre of the room. Nancy was refilling their tea. The old man had moved from his usual place in front of the loud television and was enjoying the intrusion. Lewis was surprised by how cosy the two police officers looked: the big red-haired man and the taut blonde woman with a cool haircut.

'Lewis Lin?' inquired Ginger. He moved the big brown bear and little blue sheep to one side and shepherded the kids in Shelley's direction, glad of an excuse to get up from the sofa. On his third try he was on his feet, showing Lewis his ID. 'We'd like to ask you some questions.'

Lewis waited.

Shelley freed herself from the sofa too, telling the kids to shush. 'Is there somewhere a bit quieter we could talk?' she asked Nancy.

Immediately Nancy bundled the children and the old man into the kitchen, leaving Alan to turn off the television and shut the door. Lewis was alone with the police.

'What a warm welcome,' laughed Ginger. He liked the energy

and the guile of kids. 'We're sorry to find you at home like this, Mr Lin,' he went on. 'It shouldn't take long. Let's start with the Pleasant Vale Recycling and Waste Depot. Do you know the place?'

'The place where the dead Chinese was found,' Lewis answered, cutting to the chase. 'Yes, I've been there.'

'That's what we want to talk to you about,' said Ginger. 'Why did you go there?'

'I had a fare. I drove a passenger out there.'

'Can you remember when it was?'

'I think you must know that, if you know that I was there. Who told you?' Lewis asked.

'A few people saw you. If the taxi-drivers and the police don't work together, we'd all be in trouble.'

'So it was Spiros who told you?' said Lewis, feeling betrayed.

'An owner can't hide his records from us. We already had our own ideas. Now we're asking you. So can you tell us when it was?'

'The same day they found the body. Early in the morning.'

Shelley was listening and writing.

'Can you remember who the passenger was?'

'Sure. We were chatting. An old guy. Said he was going to work. Anything wrong with that?' Lewis did not want to dob in Reg if Reg had covered for him.

'You tell us, Mr Lin,' said Ginger with a relaxed smile. 'You mean the manager of the facility, don't you? Did you see anyone else there?'

'A garbage truck came in. I got my money and left.'

'So you didn't see the body?'

'I found out about it later on television.'

'Did you see anything else? Anything else that might be relevant?' Ginger was a patient, persistent interviewer.

'I thought about that after I saw the television news that night. I couldn't think of anything.'

'You didn't contact the police. There was a reward offered.'

'I didn't see anything. I had nothing to say,' Lewis explained.

'You didn't want to get involved?' Shelley offered.

'No,' said Lewis. 'Not I didn't want to get involved. I just didn't see anything. It was a strange place to me. Too far away. Taxi-drivers don't like those places where there's no one around. I just wanted to get back to the city. I felt sick for the guy – Zhou Huang – when I found out about it.'

Shelley sat forward. 'Did you know him?'

'He was a stranger to me. I read his name in the newspaper. You know it felt close to me because I was there. Just by chance. Do you have any idea who killed him?'

'We've made some progress,' Ginger said. 'Us and the Homicide Squad. They're handling it.'

'Have you interviewed a person called Jerome Hampton?' asked Lewis.

Shelley shot her eyes to Ginger. Lewis was pleased with their reaction. He had taken them by surprise. The tables were turned.

'Tell us about him,' said Shelley.

'Do you know the big painting prizes at the Art Gallery?' Lewis teased.

'Yeah yeah,' said Shelley.

'Well, there's a painting in the competition called *Bong Bong Buddha* by Jerome Hampton. It's a painting of Zhou Huang. I recognised him from the photo in the paper.'

Shelley was writing furiously. '*Bong Bong Buddha*, you said?'

'Any more?' asked Ginger.

'I guess he must have painted Zhou Huang at Kangaloon Native Garden where he worked. Maybe somewhere else too. Did you know that?'

'We've been in touch with Kangaloon Native Garden,' said Ginger, whose ears were burning with this new information.

'Jerome Hampton's a rich man,' Shelley said.

'Wait a minute,' protested Ginger. 'Why do you say he painted Zhou Huang somewhere else?'

'He's got no clothes on in the picture. You don't take your clothes off in a public garden.'

Shelley raised her eyebrows. Ginger folded and refolded his fingers, aware that Lewis was getting cocky. 'How come you've taken such an interest in this, Mr Lin? If you didn't even know the deceased.'

'Okay,' said Lewis, 'as a taxi-driver you see things. It looks like just another anonymous Chinese killing. The sort of thing that no one cares about. Wouldn't matter if it never got solved. But it could have been *me* who was killed. You could say I'm following the case out of self-interest.'

'How did you come up with the connection between Zhou Huang and Jerome Hampton?' Shelley inquired.

'I just found it by chance.'

'Is there anything else?' asked Ginger.

Lewis hesitated. He had given them enough to establish his good faith. 'What about the woman?' Lewis asked. 'The woman in the photograph with Zhou Huang?'

'What about her?' Ginger retorted. 'You tell us.' He was easing off in the hope of getting something more. 'You say we should talk to Jerome Hampton. Have *you* talked to him?'

'I saw him in the garden,' said Lewis.

'And what did he say?'

'He said nothing. But he was painting Zhou Huang's picture,' said Lewis.

'That's not a crime, Mr Lin. But thanks for the tip-off.' Ginger was keen to move on this new lead. 'We're sorry to disturb you and your family,' he said. 'That's it for now.'

'A Chinese homicide is no different from any other homicide,' Shelley said, shaking the taxi-driver's hand. 'Rest assured that we're doing everything we can to solve this. We'll be in touch again if we may. You're a good detective. Keep it up.'

The interview was over. Lewis grinned, flattered, still not quite ready to relax. For all his elaborate fears, the police seemed interested in him only for the information he could give. But he saw that things were closing in.

In the car Ginger felt his memories stir. It was nothing to do with the case. He told Shelley that Hamptons' was the grand old department store where he was taken as a kid to whisper his wishes in Father Christmas's ear.

'Did Father Christmas ever let you down?' Shelley asked.

'The important thing,' said Ginger, 'is to get to Jerome Hampton before Ronnie Silverton hears anything about this. He'll want that privilege for himself. Ronnie loves mixing it with the rich and famous.'

In their rapid departure the police failed to notice another car parked in the quiet street. In it, in a line of unoccupied cars against the grassed kerb some distance away, a man sat smoking a cigarette, smoothing his thin moustache from time to time. Daozi, in an old orange Toyota, was watching. He was doing his job, paying attention to the taxi-driver, as Ah Mo had instructed. No one took any notice of his inconspicuous vehicle, parked across the road a few houses along, not for the first time.

The police car told Daozi that something was up. He looked into the sky as the street darkened. A plane was coming in low overhead, its shadow bigger than a house. His car was in the flight path. The plane roared as it swooped in, low and on target like a shining bird that could brush a man aside in its wing-beat or devour him like an insect if he was its prey. Daozi remembered being inside such a plane and his own queasy, excited experience of dropping from the sky to this unknown land. He stared at the white undercarriage as if he might slit it open with his knife. Then the taxi-driver came out of the house. Daozi sank down low in the seat so as not to be seen.

# Chapter XXIII

The fronts of the high houses along the park were shadowy and mute under the streetlights. Trees rattled and the spikes of railings were tipped with a dim glow as cars thumped by closed gates and locked grills. In Bernie Mittel's house blinds were down and curtains closed over windows that faced out, downstairs a faint orange, upstairs yellow with a faint blue flicker. Other houses disclosed their interiors – packed, outlandish, intimate – with walls of books and paintings glimpsed through open shutters. Already passers-by were rare. The park opposite and the stream of cars made it an unwelcome street for walkers in the dark.

Jasmine and Bernie were stretched out on the couch upstairs watching the videos from the Academy. There was still a swag of films to get through. While he could admire other people's work professionally, Bernie considered that a lot of the movies were not worth watching. He had an open mind but he couldn't help knowing what he liked and disliked by his stage of life. Maturity was that tendency to make the judgement without even thinking about it. It quickly settled into prejudice. He liked picking where the DOP's tricks came from. He liked to identify the provenance of other people's work. It was like wine. He liked to know on which side of the hill the grapes were grown. He had a few bottles spread out on the table, young and old vintages, whites and reds, and a slew of glasses as he tasted, working the remote control and moving on to the next. Beside him Jasmine stuck to Diet Coke. She went red in the face if she drank too much wine.

The house was dark and secure with only a yellow light in the stairwell and the light from the screen reflecting back on their faces. The brightest light came from the high curved neck of the street lamp in the back lane. But Jasmine was alert. Above the soundtrack of the movie she could hear bougainvillea spines scraping the wall outside, a telephone ringing somewhere and fireworks booming in distant celebration. While Bernie was changing videos she went quietly downstairs to get herself another cold drink. On the landing she passed a narrow window, a black strip that looked out on the street. As she took the turn of the stairs, her legs, her tight shorts and top, her long black hair, the back of her head, and then her face were framed in the light. She went through to the kitchen and opened the fridge in a flood of illumination. The cat came rubbing against the glass, expecting food, mewing raucously. Jasmine hunched her shoulders. She would not unlock that door. Besides, she preferred the cat's wild nature. She didn't want it to become part of the household. She didn't trust its willingness to become domesticated anymore.

Then the doorbell rang. Jasmine ran upstairs and told Bernie not to answer. It rang again. But Bernie refused to be captive in his own home. He went down and checked through the peephole and when he saw Lewis Lin in his taxi-driver's uniform he opened the door.

Lewis had decided to take action. He wanted to cut through the web. After the visit by the police he realised that while things may be closing in they were also going nowhere fast. He needed to alert Bernie Mittel to the complications he was facing with the woman from Hangzhou, if, as Lewis suspected, the relationship consisted of more than therapeutic massage.

Bernie swayed and grinned, relieved to see a friend. After a few drinks he was ready to invite Lewis in for a glass of wine and some video-viewing too.

'I know you didn't order a taxi,' Lewis said, stepping into the hallway. He came straight to the point. 'I'm sorry to come to your house like this, but there's something I need to ask you.'

Bernie stiffened, struggling to bring his focus to the matter at hand.

'That woman I drove to Chinatown. You remember that?' asked Lewis. 'Do you know who she is or where she is?'

'Let me close the door first, will you?' Bernie retorted angrily. 'The whole street can see. Why do you want to know?'

'The police are looking for her,' said Lewis.

'What business is that of yours?'

'There's a reward for information. I saw her photo in the paper. I thought before I say anything to the police I should contact you. Is she your friend?'

Bernie looked Lewis in the eyes and asked, 'Is this blackmail?'

'Sorry sorry sorry,' said Lewis, appalled that he might have given the wrong impression. 'I want to help you. You are a famous DOP and you are a good man. I think you know where the woman is. She knows the dead Chinese man. His body was found at the dump. I think she has information about that. I think she knows.'

'Okay,' said Bernie. 'Can you leave me a phone number? I'll call you if I can help.'

The response was not enough for Lewis. He stood waiting in the hallway. The man was not cooperating. That meant the woman was near.

Bernie flushed slightly and touched Lewis on the arm. 'Look, I appreciate what you're doing. Don't go to the police until you hear from me. That's all I'll say, okay? It won't be long.'

All this Daozi saw, sitting on a park bench across the way, unnoticed in the darkness under the huge arching figs that smelled of fermenting fruit. He had followed the silver taxi that lay in the street outside the house and he watched through binoculars as the taxi-driver came and went in his blue uniform. He saw the middle-aged man with the beard open the door to let Lewis in and close the door to let him out. The taxi-driver was not there to pick up a passenger. Daozi smiled, drawing on the cigarette between his fingers and pulling on his baseball cap as he crossed the road to investigate.

Daozi climbed the fence from the back lane, jumped down into the courtyard and edged his way along the wall. He was careful not to upset the potted plants nor to entangle himself in the greenery. He looked up and in that moment the woman passed the narrow window on her way upstairs. At once he recognised her as Guo Lihua, turning in an oblong of yellow light, oblivious of being seen. Daozi pressed his back against the wall and watched. He was invisible in his dark jeans, dark T-shirt and dark trainers. The baseball cap hid his face. Then he heard a sound, close – a cat. The animal sprang across the courtyard with a hissing miaow.

Daozi was gone in a sideways lunge into the darkness. He hurdled a lattice fence that blocked the way to the front of the house. The gate clunked behind him as he ran down the steps into the street, unseen. He cursed the cat that cut short his visit, but he had found what he was looking for. His diligence had turned up results. Guo Lihua, thinking she was safe and sound, playing around upstairs with her new boyfriend, with no idea that they had traced her. Daozi had to admire his boss. By instructing him to follow the taxi-driver, Ah Mo had gone straight to target.

Daozi rubbed the line of his moustache, driving as fast as the orange Toyota would go to report his find. Ah Mo's apartment was across town in a slick development behind the Casino in Pyrmont, crammed in between old and made-over warehouses where the cutting dropped down to the fenced-off edge of disused docks. On his right was the city's skyline, like a gappy tiara at night. On the left was a view of the Glebe Island Bridge, towering against the dark in spears and blades of shining metal like a fortification.

He left the Toyota in the underground car park next to the Forester and went up to the apartment where he found his boss sitting by the open window with a full ashtray and his face the colour of plums. Ah Mo wore a white tracksuit and his violin was out of its case. He had energised himself by playing through the diabolic solo part of the Mendelssohn Violin Concerto, and now he was listening to a CD of traditional Chinese music. Played on zither and *erhu*, the old court songs of lament and betrayal spiralled out into the Sydney night.

Ah Mo greeted his loyal servant by telling him there was beer in the fridge. Daozi threw his cigarettes down and the two men sat side by side, smoking and sipping the frothy beer. Daozi told Ah Mo what he had seen. While he had been watching the house where the taxi-driver lived with his brother, he said, the police arrived, and then Lewis Lin himself. When the police had gone, Lewis drove the taxi to a house at Centennial Park where he spoke to a middle-aged Australian with a beard. After Lewis had gone, Daozi took a closer look at the house. Through a window in the night he saw Guo Lihua: Guo Lihua, who knew every-thing. What was the taxi-driver doing, going between the police and the house where she was hiding? Did the police know everything too?

Ah Mo's rage drove his brain into a frenzy of reasoning that quickly produced its conclusions. Ah Mo's lunch with Lewis was a set-up. The taxi-driver had an ulterior motive. He knew some-thing and was willing to betray his comrade, his compatriot, his friend, to the dogs of the foreign police. Was that it? So Lewis Lin dared to work against him. What Lewis knew could only be what Guo Lihua had told him. Lewis was expendable. He needed a warning to back off. Ah Mo pushed his nose forward at Daozi. The woman, if she was talking, was expendable too. Like Zhou Huang. She should have told everything to Ah Mo. There were ways of taking action, after all.

The plaintive *erhu* and fluid zither were like rock and water. Outside, where the city buildings met the harbour the rock was floodlit and the water was black, lapping, sluicing, always in motion. The air was warm, yet with the first bite of southern autumn.

Ah Mo reached for Daozi's arm and held it in a tight grip to instil strength. Ah Mo's skin was soft but each muscle and tendon in the violinist's hand was precise in its grip. He took strength in return from Daozi's arm that was like bone encased in bone.

# Chapter XXIV

'He'll probably tell you to marry the woman,' said Andy over the phone. 'That's usually what it takes to regularise things. Just don't get married without my permission.'

Bernie was calling to get the name of the lawyer Andy used to sort out visas for the imported talent on his television series. 'I promise I won't get married. I have no intention of getting married. Marriage is the furthest thing from my mind,' he told his friend. 'You know me. I don't believe in those external structures.'

'That's so seventies,' said Andy. 'Not how it is now.'

'Costs too much, anyway,' said Bernie.

'Marriage. Live-in. It's all the same these days.'

'I just want Jasmine in my life,' said Bernie. 'I trust her. Something's going on with her and I'm worried.'

'Don't trust her,' advised Andy.

'You're a cynical bastard. I want to trust her.'

'Then maybe you should marry her. Maybe it's time to try and do things differently.'

'And that's so now,' quipped Bernie. 'Okay, I get the message, mate.'

Bernie was at the cappuccino machine early next morning, washed and dressed in his stretchy grey Armani suit and black T-shirt, ready for the appointment with the lawyer. He told Jasmine to stay upstairs in the yoga room until he returned. He would be back by lunchtime. She must not show herself. The doors and windows were locked and the security alarm was on downstairs. The blind in the yoga room was down, leaving only a slit of light. No one must know she was there.

Bernie activated the roller door and eased the blue Volvo into the lane, full lock, careful not to scrape, and watched as the door rolled down again. He recalled Andy's words about trust as he turned into the road.

From the park opposite Daozi watched the man with the beard nudge his car into the thick morning traffic. There was no one with him. That was Daozi's signal. The day was already well advanced as far as Daozi was concerned. He had been at his work since before sunrise. This was the day he went into action. He knew everything now. He knew where the taxi-driver lived. He knew the taxi depot where the owner kept the car. And he knew that the police were circling. He crossed the road at the pedestrian crossing and ducked into the back lane where he could easily spring over the fence, making no sound as he landed. It was harder in daylight, but he was ready to take his time. Then the cat appeared, stepping along a window sill with a faint mew. The cat seemed to recognise him, jumping down and brushing against his leg, purring for food. He kicked the animal away, but it purred louder in protest, returning to rub his leg again. He kicked it once more. But it was hungry and this unwelcoming person might still feed her. With an arch and dip of the back the cat crossed the courtyard and continued to mew loudly outside the kitchen door for everyone to hear. Daozi pointed his knife at the animal to silence it. He could slit the cat's throat with one movement. But a shadow passed, a spray of the bougainvillea along the fence, scratchily casting its image in the heat, and that held him back.

Jasmine heard the cat. She knew someone was down there. She knelt on the floor and peered through the gap where the blind was not quite closed to the window sill. She recognised Daozi by the baseball cap he wore. She knew he had come for her. She saw his knife. She could not see anymore. She wanted to call Bernie but was scared that Daozi would hear her if she used the phone. Daozi would be prepared for the security alarm once he entered the house. But if she was already downstairs when the alarm was activated, she would have time while the siren sounded to open the front door and dash out into the street.

Daozi looked around and readied himself to enter the house. The cat rubbed past him, mewing again. He glanced at the upstairs window where someone could have been watching him. He looked down at the cat, amused by the solipsistic insistence of its hunger. Then he pulled at the door with all his force.

Making no sound Jasmine left the yoga room and crept downstairs. She was in the alarm zone. In a few moments it would go off. She proceeded down the hallway to the front door and unlocked the deadlock with her key, and then the security grill, and still the alarm did not sound. She heard the man break into the kitchen. She heard his steps on the tiled floor. He was coming into the hallway. They were face to face. For a moment they assessed each other. Daozi's moustache bristled, a sharp line, like a cut, across his square jaw. His eyes glinted incisively.

'Stop,' he said.

Her face, opposing him, was pale and alert with aggression. She was scared for her life. He brandished his knife, willing to administer justice in return for her betrayal of his master. Then the alarm burst into deafening sound, unsteadying Daozi for an instant, and Jasmine was able to open the door and tumble down the steps into the street.

Daozi sprang after her. She expected to find someone in the street, but no one was there. She ran along the road a little way and when the cars slowed she pushed out in front of them, bumping against them as they jolted to a halt to avoid knocking her down. Daozi followed. She wove through to the other side, arms out to ward off the cars. He was coming after her. Cars were honking, people putting their heads out, or winding up their windows in disdain.

'Help!' she cried. She ran along the path into the park. 'Help!' she cried, bumping into two men. 'He's got a knife.'

The two buff men in gym gear looked at her indifferently at first, not welcoming the intrusion. They were walking a tiny dog on a leash. Then the realisation of her predicament kicked in.

One man put a muscled arm around the woman to protect her and the other stepped forward, pumping himself up to block the assailant. Seeing this, Daozi gave a frustrated scowl, turned on the spot and ran off. This was not the situation he wanted. One of the men was chasing him, pushing with thick gym-fit legs. Soon he was closing in.

The traffic was streaming now that the lights had changed. Daozi slipped through without even seeing the moving cars and vanished round a corner to the lane where he had left his orange Toyota.

The man giving chase held back. He did not want to enter a lane alone with a man who had a knife.

'That's enough, Bruce,' called his friend from across the road. 'Let him go. That's enough.'

Jasmine was brushing her hair on each side of her face with both her hands, shaking compulsively. She was trying to compose herself as the man returned.

'He's gone, Barry,' said Bruce, hands on his hips, breathing deeply.

'What a thrill,' said his friend. 'I suppose we better report it to the police.'

'No, no,' said Jasmine. 'I don't want trouble.'

'Do it, darling,' Barry insisted, reining in the dog. 'For your own protection. Then it's on record. Next time there mightn't be any blokes like us around.'

'We're here if you need support,' offered Bruce.

'I've got to go home first,' said Jasmine. 'The house is wide open. I'll go to the police later.'

'We're your witnesses,' said Barry, picking up the dog, a miniature silky terrier, and cuddling it. 'Aren't we, girl?'

'Write down our names and numbers,' said Bruce, whose skin was flush with moisture from the exertion of running and the rush of adrenalin, 'then she can get in touch if she needs us. What's your name?' he asked her.

'Jasmine,' she smiled winningly.

The two walkers crossed at the traffic lights with their little dog and escorted Jasmine to the door of her house. The alarm was sounding but no one had taken any notice of it. She went inside and turned it off. She checked that there was no intruder in the house. She knew that Daozi would not be back yet. She reassured the men that she was all right.

'Great place,' said Barry.

'Thanks,' said Jasmine.

'You been here long?'

'It's my friend's house,' she said. 'Thank you. Thank you for your help.' She was shaking their hands eagerly. Big smooth moisturised hands. Pushing them out the door. Waving as she saw them on their way.

'Let's keep in touch,' they said. 'Bye-bye!'

Then she locked all the doors and called Bernie.

In twenty minutes he was by her side. She told him the story. The mewing cat. An intruder with a knife. Her two rescuers.

'It's getting way too close,' Bernie shouted. He was angry. 'We have to call the police and tell them everything. That's what the lawyer says. It will help you later on.'

The security company rang to report that the alarm had been set off.

'No need to send anyone,' Bernie snapped. 'We've already dealt with the problem ourselves. No thanks to you guys.' He wondered why they bothered. The voice on the other end said that ninety per cent of calls were false alarms. There was a service charge of $45.

Bernie and Jasmine sat at the kitchen table trying to work through the implications of calling the police. The lawyer had advised Bernie to do some checks before he decided on marrying Jasmine. Marriage would be the simplest way to get her permanent residency. As long as she didn't need a divorce first. If she was illegal she would have to go back to China anyway and reapply for migration as Bernie's fiancée...There was a process to go through.

'We had a really good meeting,' Bernie said. 'The lawyer's there whenever we need him. You're not married already, are you, babe?'

'No, I never married,' she said, giving him her sternest look. 'You know that, Bernie. That's my big mistake. I'm waiting for you.'

The doorbell rang and Bernie rolled his eyes. 'What now?' he exclaimed, sitting there incapacitated. It was turning into a farce, but he felt too heavy even to lift his own weight.

'Who is it?' Jasmine asked.

'How would I know? Another one of your mates? Or the cops? Shit!'

The bell rang again, then there was knocking. Bernie got wearily to his feet.

'Be careful,' said Jasmine.

Bernie grunted. Before he opened the door, he looked through the peephole as a precaution and there in the fishbowl was Lewis Lin again, peering back at him with a gimlet eye. Back already, sighed Bernie, recognising a further complication. Lewis was the one who had started all this, helping with the bags late at night. Never fall for kindness, thought Bernie, opening the door with a wide grin.

'Welcome, my friend. What are you doing back so soon? Bird of ill-omen!'

Lewis stood chided on the steps. 'Sorry sorry sorry,' he said with a worried look, as Bernie tugged him inside.

'I took the taxi back to my boss last night, after I left here,' Lewis explained. 'I picked it up this morning at six o'clock. Then I got a flat tyre. I changed it for the spare. Then I got another flat in another tyre. I took the two tyres to be fixed and the garage found nails through both of them. Two tyres. Two nails this long.'

He indicated the length of the nails with his finger and thumb and looked at Bernie in silence. His face was pale and drawn.

'No coincidence?' asked Bernie.

'I don't think so.'

Sunlight from outside came through the stained glass around the front door, falling in coloured shadow on the walls of the hallway, on their bodies as they looked at each other, with a pulsing sensation of menace.

'You're not safe here either, mate,' said Bernie. 'Someone just broke in here with a knife.'

'What happened?'

'A Chinese bloke in a baseball cap. He wasn't after me.'

'That's Ah Mo's driver. Looking for Jasmine.'

'A friend of yours, is he? Well, he found her.'

'Is she here?'

'Tell me what's going on,' begged Bernie. 'I can handle it.'

'Jasmine is the one to explain,' Lewis told him. 'Is she here? You've been hiding her long enough. She must tell you everything. How much closer do you want them to come? It's the body at the dump. Don't you get it? She knows what happened out there and she has to tell you. Or tell the police.'

Bernie called to Jasmine in the kitchen. 'Did you hear that? Can I bring him through? Are you ready?'

Bernie brought Lewis into the kitchen. Jasmine was at the sink. The kettle was gurgling and whistling. She unplugged it as she turned to face them. 'I'm making some tea,' she said, smiling in a struggle to maintain her composure. She was very agitated. 'Have some tea.'

Bernie pulled out a chair for Lewis. He stood with his shoulders drooped and his jaw jutting forward, watching as Jasmine filled the pot, set out the cups and poured the tea with delicacy. She was acting like the mistress of the house.

'You know Lewis,' Bernie said. 'The taxi-driver. He knows you.'

'Yes,' she said. 'Sit down, Bernie. Drink your tea.'

'Go ahead,' said Bernie, standing behind Lewis, 'if you want to ask any questions.' Jasmine's eyes flashed with annoyance. But Bernie was willing to trust Lewis because Lewis was Chinese like Jasmine and Jasmine was the one, when all the complications were done, who was going to put his totally messed-up life in order. If only they could sort things out. Besides, Lewis understood the superior contribution of the Director of Photography to the making of a great movie.

Lewis explained to Jasmine that he knew she was associated with Ah Mo. He knew Ah Mo's black BMW was near the Pleasant Vale Recycling and Waste Depot on the morning the body was found. So far he was one step ahead of the police, but the police were not far behind. And this morning there were nails through two of his tyres. That was a gift from Ah Mo who was not far away either.

'Ah Mo's *dangerous*,' said Lewis.

'I know that,' said Jasmine.

Bernie raised his eyebrows. 'So you know these guys? You know what he's talking about?'

'They nearly killed me this morning,' yelped Jasmine, her voice breaking with rawness.

'You better tell me, for Chrissake,' said Bernie, lunging to take her arm.

She evaded him, pacing the room, cupping her tea.

'Tell us what happened out there,' Lewis urged her.

'Go on, sweetie,' Bernie pleaded. 'You're among friends. Please, you have to tell us.'

'I tell you in Chinese,' she said, 'and he translate.' She flung her head disdainfully in Lewis's direction.

'Do you have a tape recorder?' asked Lewis. 'And some paper and a pen?'

'Good idea,' said Bernie.

'What you want that for?' Jasmine barked.

'Calm down,' said Bernie. 'It's just for us. So I can understand. I'm going to put you on video. The truth will set you free, honey. It will help us be together. Now sit down.'

Jasmine sat on a stool at the other end of the kitchen table while Bernie and Lewis set up their equipment, a mini-cassette recorder and a videocam. Jasmine looked distraught, hair covering her face, but she made no attempt to move away. Tears welled up in her eyes and she let them fall. She sat solidly but lightly, without artifice, brushing her hair aside as she began to speak in a quiet low voice.

Bernie sat down opposite her, slumped over the table. Lewis interpreted for him as Jasmine spoke. She avoided their gaze, speaking blankly as if to an interrogator. The equipment hummed. Now she had started she was not going to stop. Each strand in her account must be tied logically into place.

After a while Bernie reached for the teapot and replenished her cup. Jasmine took a sip and continued speaking. Words, like stones, tumbled out of her, one after another, syllable after syllable, in Mandarin softened by her Hangzhou accent, dropping from her mouth as she spoke herself blank and empty.

# Chapter XXV

Mengzi wanted to get rid of me. After all I did for him. Even after I cared for him. I lived with him in rooms that no one else would live in. The last one was under the freeway at Auburn. That place was a dump. When it rained the stormwater drain overflowed right up to the back door. It was like a sewer. There were snakes in the yard. The landlord never did any maintenance. The ceiling sagged like an old belly and we were worried it would fall in on us while we slept. Mengzi was like a caged animal. He said it was worse than his army days in camp on the Vietnam border. Our food was okay. I always cooked for him. But Mengzi got skinny and jaundiced from smoking too many cigarettes. Even his dragon tattoo started to shrink. His own energy ate away at him like acid. Sometimes he would hurt me deliberately. Bash me. Bruise me. But I never left him. I was that stupid.

Mengzi's old army gang in Hangzhou had connections with Ah Mo's network in Sydney. That's how Mengzi came to work for them. That much I know. It's a black little world. Mengzi would complain that Ah Mo didn't pay him enough for what he did and would ask me for money. Mengzi was gambling. He hated being poor in Australia. He said it wasn't fair, it was discrimination because he was Chinese. He bragged that he had been a soldier in the People's Liberation Army. Now he had jumped into business, he said, he would be a billionaire by the time he was forty. But it wasn't happening. That was part of his frustration. That's why he beat up on me.

Mengzi knew that Ah Mo was in contact with big money. He wanted a better cut. Mengzi was doing the risky work while Ah Mo was growing fat on banquets and never got his hands dirty. Mengzi would move the new arrivals into housing and find them jobs washing dishes to get them started. If they paid more, they could skip that stage and he would fix them up with a full hand of documents and a whole new life. People would put themselves in debt for a lifetime to pay for that opportunity.

Mengzi never thought of himself as free, even when he had food in his belly and money in his pocket and he was roaming all over the city making arrangements. He believed that Ah Mo was taking advantage of him. He did not want to be tied to Ah Mo or to me or to anyone. He never knew how much I gave of myself, over and over. I was just another thing that weighed on him. He thought by going alone he could show his true greatness. That was when he made contact with the Immigration Department.

They were using the Rockdale office to get new passports for the people who came in. It wasn't that difficult, but it wasn't straightforward either. I used to give free massage to some of the Immigration people. There was a big fat lady who liked me. Always wanted extra time. Mengzi used her to get to people higher up. He had a contact in Canberra called Dennis. In all those dealings Mengzi used Huangzi's name. He had come into the country on Huangzi's passport with the photo changed. I sent it to him. He used that passport for ID. On his driving licence he was Zhou Huang. He had Zhou Huang's Medicare card. He hated the name. He hated the idea that the real Zhou Huang was walking around somewhere. He always thought that Garlic Shoot was a pathetic little thing anyway.

He boasted that some of the Immigration Department people would let things slip by in exchange for money in a brown paper bag left in a toilet cubicle for them. That sort of thing. Finders keepers. Every now and then someone had to be caught to show they were doing their job. Not that they cared as long as they were being looked after. Mengzi played both sides. He didn't tell Ah Mo what he was doing and Ah Mo never asked as long as there was no trouble.

Then he told me he was giving up the place in Auburn. He told me to pack everything. He said he was taking me to live in a flat in the public housing complex at Pleasant Vale for a while. Maybe he had someone else. He always had others. He was only ever using me for his own selfish purposes. He promised that if I did what he said when it was over we would move to the Gold Coast and start new lives with new names and no one to bother us. I liked that idea. I should have asked some more questions.

He didn't tell me I'd be sharing the flat in Pleasant Vale with half a dozen fresh-off-the-boat Chinese pretending to be part of a family. It was ridiculous really. I shouldn't have been surprised when Compliance turned up there from the Immigration Department a few days later.

Of course I was an illegal. I had a temporary entry visa as Zhou Huang's fiancée but that had expired and I hadn't married him either. I was caught. They gave me seventy-two hours to leave the country.

When I contacted Mengzi he said it was much worse than I realised. Immigration had found out about all the other Chinese who were living in those flats on false identities. Ah Mo's whole operation was blown to pieces. They were moving people out before Compliance could catch them. He said that Garlic Shoot had dobbed us all in. Ah Mo's connections at Rockdale confirmed it. The dog was Huangzi.

I didn't know what to believe. Why would Huangzi want me sent back to China? Mengzi said it was jealousy. But I said nothing. Ah Mo was angry, said Mengzi coldly. Ah Mo accused Huangzi of betraying his Chinese brothers for some small favours from those Australian officials. He shamed the heroic memory of his elder brother's sacrifice at Tiananmen. There was no behaviour more despicable.

Mengzi laughed like a devil. When I saw how the situation played to his advantage in so many ways I knew that he was the one who had gone to the Immigration Department. He had betrayed Ah Mo and sold me. Using the name of Zhou Huang.

He didn't care. He never cared. That hurt me most. In that moment all my love for him turned to hate. But I kept my mouth shut.

I went to see Ah Mo in his apartment in Pyrmont. I didn't tell him my suspicions of Mengzi. I complained to him that the Immigration Department had caught me and I had to go back to China straightaway. Ah Mo was still fuming. He said that Zhou Huang was the informer. He asked if I knew how to contact the little worm. I replied that I was prepared to help him teach Zhou Huang a lesson. He smiled at that. He told me to bring Zhou Huang to a meeting with him. Daozi was there too. I remember the way his eyes met Ah Mo's. We agreed on a time and place. Ah Mo told me that Zhou Huang must not suspect anything. I knew they were planning to make him confess and then to kill him.

I asked if Mengzi could come along too. Otherwise he would be suspicious of what I was doing. Ah Mo didn't really like that idea. But he accepted it.

I met Garlic Shoot next afternoon at the Macarthur Park Shopping Mall. He said it was better for me to go back to China, within seventy-two hours, like they said, or else I would be arrested. He gave me the money for the plane ticket. He said he could come back to China and find me. He was a simple soul but he kept promises that were only words to other people. He would never let go his dream.

I told him that Ah Mo wanted to kill him. Because of what Mengzi had done. I told him to hide. I didn't know what to suggest. I said he should get help from his rich Australian friend, the artist who lent him the money for my ticket. I told him to find somewhere safe.

Garlic Shoot was deeply moved by my concern for him when I was in so much trouble myself. I urged him to disappear. He smiled strangely. He told me to go, go quickly, and to tell his parents he was fine. That's how we parted.

# Chapter XXVI

That same night Mengzi and I caught the last train from Auburn to Pleasant Vale. Mengzi was edgy and excited. I could sense his complete contempt for me, as if I didn't exist anymore. Ah Mo and Daozi were waiting for us in the black BMW, parked outside the Chinese restaurant there, the Green Dragon. It was late and the restaurant stayed open specially for us. Ah Mo ordered expensive dishes. We picked at our food. At one point when Mengzi left the table Ah Mo asked me what had happened to Zhou Huang. I said that Zhou Huang was already there with us. Ah Mo wrinkled his brow at me. I said that Mengzi was that man. Mengzi was really the informer. 'Check his ID,' I said.

Ah Mo's face cleared as if in a moment of sudden enlightenment. He knew Mengzi's nature. In a flash he saw it all.

Daozi made a phone call and by the time we left the restaurant there were two other Beijing brothers waiting for us outside the restaurant. Mengzi and I went with Ah Mo and Daozi in the Beamer. The other guys followed. Daozi drove to a park somewhere. It was a dark and empty place. Only perverts would be around at that time of night and they would avoid us, a gang of agitated Chinese. We walked in among some thick trees, then Ah Mo asked me again where Zhou Huang was. I pointed at Mengzi. 'That's Zhou Huang,' I said.

Mengzi looked really confused. He laughed for Ah Mo's benefit. He couldn't believe what I'd done. 'Don't joke about it,' he said.

Ah Mo nodded to Daozi who grabbed Mengzi. Mengzi tried to shake him off and the other two men stepped forward. They held Mengzi while Daozi slipped his hands into Mengzi's pockets and searched him for ID. He pulled out the passport. I knew it would be there. He gave the passport to Ah Mo who opened it and looked through it carefully. It was Zhou Huang's passport with Mengzi's photo. That was proof.

Then Daozi found the driving licence in the name of Zhou Huang, again with Mengzi's photo. Mengzi said he could explain everything, and Ah Mo said that was good, he wanted to know everything, and he proposed that we all go somewhere we wouldn't be disturbed to hear the whole story.

Daozi had a knife in Mengzi's back as the men dragged him back to the car. I couldn't meet Mengzi's eye. I hated him, but he looked so pitiful, that big-talking man, just a human being. Ah Mo sat in the back seat with Mengzi. He had a gun. I sat in the front next to Daozi as he drove. The other car followed. I don't know where we went. We drove for nearly an hour. We went to the freeway and I thought Mengzi would try to signal for help from other cars. But no one paid us any attention. Daozi drove fast. Then he came off the freeway and drove into a forest. It was some very remote place where no one would ever come. A place with no name where there was a public toilet and a concrete table and a neon light on a pole. Some sort of picnic spot surrounded by trees. 'Not bad,' said Ah Mo, commending Daozi's choice as Mengzi was manhandled out of the car. 'You're at our mercy,' Ah Mo told Mengzi. 'If you don't cooperate, we'll just leave you here.' Daozi was flicking at Mengzi with his knife. Ah Mo laughed out loud and offered Mengzi a bottle of cola.

Mengzi said he needed a piss. Maybe he thought he could run away. Daozi gestured at the toilet block with his knife. Then he said that Mengzi could piss where he liked. Mengzi looked like if he unzipped himself to piss Daozi might cut his dick off.

Then Ah Mo told him he should be comfortable. It was going to be a long night. 'We want you washed clean,' he said. 'You're going to tell us everything until there's no more lies left.'

'I'm not Zhou Huang,' Mengzi shouted in panic.

Daozi jabbed at Mengzi's clothes with the knife, not caring if it cut. 'Who did *they* think you were?' asked Ah Mo.

Mengzi tried to fend Daozi off with his bare hands. 'It wasn't me. It was Zhou Huang,' he shouted. There was a slice of blood across his palm from Daozi's knife. I put my hand over my mouth, frightened I would scream.

'Did you think you could take over from me?' Ah Mo asked. 'You couldn't even hold on to the money I gave you. You're a flea. You used information I trusted you with and now you have caused all this trouble. We want you to tell us what you did. Everything.'

Daozi's knife nicked Mengzi's face. 'Ask *her*,' he yelped, pointing at me. I turned away.

They put a gag on Mengzi and forced him to his knees. He was squirming and groaning now as Daozi cut at him until his clothes were ragged and falling off his body, exposing bare, bleeding skin.

Then Ah Mo told me to get in the car. I had seen enough. I was afraid that I would be next. There is a limit to what I can take responsibility for. How could I know that what I did would lead to something so pitiless and terrible?

I waited by the car, listening, watching them by the picnic table in the circle of light. While the other men pinioned Mengzi, Daozi removed the gag and Ah Mo began his questioning. It was precise and calm and Mengzi did everything he could to cover himself. He invented. He lied. His answers were inconsistent and Ah Mo got angry. He wanted a full confession. That was essential in front of the others. It was a disciplined and controlled ritual, but Mengzi became more and more desperate.

They dragged Mengzi into the toilet block. They had a rope. There was more shouting, then the noises changed. Moans not words. I heard Mengzi begging. I heard him call my name. Then there was a thumping sound. Kicking. It went on for a long time. Then there was silence. There was never any gunshot. They must have used the knife.

Ah Mo came out first. He had washed himself in there. He was drying his hands and face on a white handkerchief. He looked composed in the neon light. I heard the cry of a strange bird, an owl maybe, a low repeated cry. I was sitting in the car by then, low in the seat with my head down, hiding my eyes behind my hair. I heard the crackle of leaves underfoot as Ah Mo approached the car. I was terrified, assuming it was my turn. He opened the door and spoke to me. 'We cut his face off,' Ah Mo said. 'It's a warning to you this time. You didn't see anything. You are with us and you will never go against us.'

I nodded. I thought I was going to be sick. I got out of the car and walked a few paces and threw up on the grass.

Daozi came out of the toilet. His face was set, with no expression. I couldn't guess what his intention was. He held up something. I couldn't believe it was a piece of skin. It had the shape of a vest and the dragon on Mengzi's back was visible, the tattoo done when he was stationed on the Vietnam border, in a town full of soldiers where you could get anything you wanted. Ah Mo gave a satisfied grin. That was the most horrible thing of all.

The two other men carried a black garbage bag across to the car. They opened the boot and put it in. Then Ah Mo told them to go. Daozi got a can of fuel and burned his blood-soaked clothing in the bin. I saw him change into his clean clothes. He was strutting about restlessly. Ah Mo pulled out his cigarettes. There was time to enjoy a smoke. Ah Mo was relaxed, loose, supremely confident. He was not worried by anything. I got back in the car. My mouth was dry. I felt myself retching but there was nothing more to come up but the taste of bile. I watched Daozi prowling in a kind of torment. He saw me. I'll never forget his look. He thought I was laughing. By the time we left that place, the sky was already pale and light was returning. But the smell in the car was horrible. I felt like I was sweating evil through my skin.

Dawn brought houses into sight. The sun bounced off iron rooftops through the trees. We were on a winding sealed road that looked almost suburban. I wondered how we were going to get rid of our load. It was more and more of a risk as we headed closer to the city. We passed one of those big garbage trucks on that country road. It was stopping at wheelie bins along the roadside and emptying them into its crusher. Daozi drove to the end of the road to a rubbish dump. The gates were locked. He swore. The dump should have been open. He looped the car round and drove back fast along the road. There was a spot where a bin stood by itself with an old sofa dumped beside it. The house was out of sight at the end of a drive.

Daozi stopped the car and hopped out. He heaved the bag from the back of the car and rested it on to the sofa. He checked that there was room in the bin and lifted the bag in. He had not noticed that the sofa was covered in thorny canes that caught on the bag and tore the plastic. Blood was dripping out. As he stuffed the bag into the bin he got his hands smeared.

'He's dumpling stuffing. He's shit. He's compost.' Those were Ah Mo's words. 'There's nothing left in the world of that person without a name who made the mistake of calling himself Zhou Huang,' he said.

Daozi put his foot to the floor. As we sped towards the city we were nearly wiped out by a head-on collision with a taxi coming in the opposite direction. Daozi cursed the stupid Aussie driver. That was Lewis.

They dropped me on a street corner in Chinatown. Ah Mo said he appreciated my cooperation. I took that as a threat. He said he looked forward to inviting me to eat lobster with him. He expected we would work together more closely now that obstacles were out of the way. It was good to overcome difficulties, he said. He told me to be at the restaurant at twelve the day after next.

I bought some new clothes in Market City and checked myself into a cheap hotel. I hadn't slept for twenty-four hours. I hadn't been sleeping well before that either. I called Huangzi's number, the real Huangzi, and the man who answered, Fu, said he had gone out the previous evening and had not returned. I called you, Bernie, and left a message. Thank God you were there when I called again. I was pinning my hopes on you.

So Jasmine continued, hollowing herself out in her confession. Lewis translated the stream of Mandarin. As she went further into her story, Jasmine rose to the occasion, lifting her head, tilting her face, bending her mouth, marking the rise and fall of her intonation with the sinuous lines of a stage recitation. Bernie sat in a dazed, disturbed silence as he absorbed what she set before them, the monstrous and unshapely missing pieces of a narrative that spread dark defacement into the time and space they had shared.

'I'm not guilty,' said Jasmine. 'I wanted to pay Mengzi back.

But not like that. It was out of my control. If I tried to stop them they would have killed me too. Or left me out there in the wild.'

Bernie looked at her, wondering where the truth lay, the final judgement of her behaviour. He looked at Lewis for a response, an interpolation, for something more than the hesitant translation of fluid words. He looked at the tape as it spun in revolutions too fast to see. He felt the warmth, the occasional click of the video-cam for reassurance. Was the answer in there, in language that he could replay and perhaps one day come to understand?

'I saved Zhou Huang,' Jasmine said.

'Then where is he,' asked Bernie, 'if he's not the body on the dump?'

'I don't know,' said Jasmine, shaking her head sorrowfully. 'I haven't seen him again.'

'I think I know,' said Lewis.

And Bernie, who could not help his love for Jasmine, let his mouth fall open in a dumb grin. If he could believe her, then perhaps he could trust her, now that he knew the worst. 'Truly?' he asked, clutching at this hope. 'If you can find him, Lewis, it proves her story. Take us to him if you can.'

# Chapter XXVII

Silently at sunset they came, removing shoes and socks as they entered the incense-filled darkness and found a space on the floor to sit. Not many. Only a fraction of the fifty or so that made up the sangha of the Bong Bong Buddhist Centre. Nova Jewell had found over the years that most people only dipped in and out. Sitting was hard. Phases of painful cross-legged meditation broken by creaking steps around the room. Submission to routine made it easier. Still, a few came, wandering in from the garden or from their rooms or up the gravel drive from outside. Time was suspended in meditation and not otherwise marked at Crystal House. Yet the hours were observed as if a continual unconscious counting of the breath measured the infinite flow of moments. They assembled punctually, welcoming the practice.

After a few days the newcomer had found his rhythm too. He came in, bowed to the Buddha and Nova Jewell, and, placing his cushion, sank to the wooden boards, face to the wall, hands settled in his lap, head inclined, eyes half closed, and began to steady his breathing. That was the way to empty his mind, to be rid of attachments, to let his old self go. His thoughts scudded across the sky of his mind like clouds, his desires, his anxieties, gone, until his identity was nothing more than an illusory form against a void.

Then, when Nova clapped her sticks, he rose, stretching awkwardly, adjusting the orange robe, and paced the room with springy steps. He had found his place. The abbess could not help a smile of satisfaction.

Approaching her seventy-fifth year, she was scarcely more than skin and bone. It was not only her diet of grains and vegetables and sometimes wine with sweet biscuits, but also that her wiry body was readying for its end, though she felt no illness. She was proud of her life's work, but she had failed hitherto in one thing. She had not found a successor. Her friend Jerome Hampton had promised her that he would ensure the financial survival of the Centre, but he was not the spiritual leader it needed. Jerome was unreliable. He used his spiritual practice opportunistically. But Nova was a believer in the hidden order of things. She understood that Jerome was also being used opportunistically for the completion of a larger pattern.

And so Zhou appeared that night, asking if he could stay. He came with no belongings and begged that his presence be kept secret. Jerome was not involved in the decision. The young man said he wanted to become a monk. When she explained what was involved, he replied that no amount of rigour would deter him. He was ready to abandon a world he hardly knew. He was leaving his life behind.

Nova recognised in Zhou the essence of the transmission from East to West and back again that gave her life its meaning. It was a matter of some urgency to her. She was growing old and there was no other master to call on. She would devise a teaching of her own, no matter how unorthodox. In an ultimate Zen act she would create a new lineage from her to him, tacitly acknowledging Jerome as the unwitting vehicle. There was a braid of connection that wound all the way back to Haberdashery at Hamptons', across decades, precisely for this purpose: a breakthrough to the true path.

On the first morning she asked Zhou if he was sincere. Then she began his training. He put on the orange robe and the sandals and shaved his head. She saw that he was gifted. Surprising, and yet no surprise. He would prove to be a true fire among the inconstant souls on her list. He would bloom like a lotus from the mud of the blind, shallow, too easily distracted society in which they found themselves. A fine successor.

The afternoon sessions were reserved for their dialogue. Nova Jewell drilled the novice with the profoundest questions. There were puzzles and riddles that could crack the self open like a walnut, as she had been broken open by the revelation of her destiny long ago, a young woman selling buttons and bows to seekers of just the right finishing touch in the great city department store.

After the evening session they would eat together at the polished table in the dim dining room that had an image of the bleeding heart of Jesus hanging on the wall from the era when Crystal House was a convent. The other devotees in residence sat with them, including two remaining nuns, a mother-and-daughter-like duo who had never been separated from each other. Both silver-haired now, virgins conceivably, they did the cooking. Brown rice and cheese. Apple crumble. Minestrone. After a few such dinners Zhou began to help with the food, using more salt and flavour than they were accustomed too, chilli and soy and stir-fry. In a short time a changed routine was established. Nova ate the new dishes with relish.

During the day the young man worked in the garden. He more than earned his keep. He knew something about native plants and liked to wander in the bush behind the house, observing trees and shrubs. It was his walking meditation, he earnestly explained to Nova. She noticed that his ear lobes were lengthening, like the Buddha's.

Outside did not impinge. The one thing she had to guard against was letting strangers see the novice and upset him with their questions. And Jerome, of course. She had to keep the boy hidden from Jerome, his original patron. Jerome normally came on Saturday. That day, and whenever other people came, Zhou slipped out the back in his orange robe and sandals to follow the winding rocky path that climbed into the scrub, moving as fleetly through the trees and ferns as any bush creature.

He knew when to come back.

Now the evening session was reaching its conclusion. Those sitting formed a facing circle and recited the Four Great Vows together. Then they prostrated themselves three times, taking refuge in the Buddha, the Dharma and the Sangha. After the third prostration Nova Jewell's gaze flashed like a darting bird to the young man. She had allowed him a week to meditate on the most powerful, most ancient Zen *koan*. *Before your father and mother were born, what was your original face?*

That afternoon he had given her his answer.

He understood that, once free of the ignorance and craving that gave birth to him, his original face was enlightened nature itself: the Buddha nature shared with all sentient beings. He was no longer holding on to the woman, Guo Lihua. He had let go his jealousy of Mengzi. He was released from the heavy awe of his dead zither-playing elder brother. Free of obligation to his old parents. Released of responsibility to build the family's fortunes in this foreign land. Unburdened even of distant China. Loosed from his losses. From simpleton he was reaching a state where he was purely simple and free. One day, near or far, he would achieve enlightenment.

He was the one. Nova Jewell was grateful beyond her dreams. Accordingly, as master to student in a ceremony between themselves that afternoon, she conferred on him his monk's appellation. It reflected the aspect of the Buddha that his particular being manifested. He would answer to nothing else. As he rose now from the third prostration she spoke his new name to the Centre for the first time. She named him Original Face.

# Chapter XXVIII

Ginger was at home asleep when the call came, with Toni beside him, both of them dead to the world. Shelley was preparing for bed with her late night tae kwon do routine. It was rare for them to be called like this when they were off duty so they took the summons seriously and headed in to the Pleasant Vale police station at once. They found Lewis Lin waiting for them with Bernie – and Jasmine. It was a multiple surprise to find that the taxi-driver and the DOP were connected and to have the woman they also knew as Guo Lihua delivered into their hands. A major break-through in the case had come to them on a plate. After a cup of instant coffee, they were wide awake. Pleasant Vale was gloomy at night, but the light in the station was painfully bright as they took down statements from each of the three parties. Jasmine's was the longest. Lewis said if they missed anything he had it all on tape. The woman was more elegant than they expected, more sophisticated, ready to laugh at herself. But as it got late her eyes began to droop. She was running on empty, Shelley said.

Lewis had left his taxi in the street outside Bernie's house in Centennial Park as a decoy. Late at night, he had left the house with Bernie and Jasmine in Bernie's blue Volvo via the roller door to the back lane. He had directed Bernie at the wheel through a maze of inner-city streets until he was sure they were not being followed. Then they headed for the freeway.

Lewis had a plan to lift the darkness away from themselves. It depended on bringing the police in. Lewis figured that the amiable coppers from Pleasant Vale would be grateful for any lead and would be ready to defend them if there was any trouble.

Ginger couldn't wait for morning when he would call Superintendent Silverton to let him know of the latest developments. Next morning at nine, when the detectives at Sydney Police Centre were sloping into work. Nice one for Pleasant Vale. But for now it was a matter of agreeing to go along with the plucky Chinese taxi-driver's plan. That was the deal. If it didn't work out, they would bring the woman in for further questioning next day.

Lewis left the police to make their arrangements while he went with Bernie and Jasmine to the Bong Bong Country Motel. It was the only place that had a vacancy over the phone. They took two rooms and rang for pizzas. The pizzeria was the only place open at that hour. Bernie had brought a bottle of red wine from his stock at home. It would all be over soon, Lewis thought. The motel bed smelled of smoke, chemicals and floral perfume. He fell asleep watching late-night television, impatient for the morning. At 5 a.m. his alarm clock beep-beep-beeped. He rose, washed his face and put on his black jeans and a black T-shirt to match.

Gear for Zen. The pre-dawn was cool as he knocked softly on Bernie and Jasmine's door to let them know it was time.

The blanket of the sky was lifting over the massy conifers as Bernie turned into the driveway to the Bong Bong Buddhist Centre. The old house was another dark mass in the pungent air. Lewis gave a thumbs up for luck to Bernie and Jasmine as he crept in through the open front door. He removed his shoes and socks and padded silently over the floorboards to the Meditation Hall. A single candle was burning in the darkness on an altar table beside a spray of flowers and an image of the Buddha. Nova Jewell sat cross-legged at the head of the room, distinguishable by the crook of her neck and her drooping shoulders. She recognised the visitor – the taxi-driver – and nodded to him ever so slightly. Lewis gave a little bow of the head in return and, as his eyes adjusted, he found a space for himself between the dark figures sitting cross-legged on cushions around the perimeter of the room. He settled into a meditation posture and tried to stay calm as the light came up slowly through the curtained windows. The birds in the trees outside were carolling joyously, magpies ascending and swooping in chimes of song.

After ten minutes a clapper sounded and the devotees rose from their mats with a grating of stiff joints and stood facing the wall with their hands clasped in front of them. At another clap of the wooden sticks they turned to the right and began a slow walk, one behind another, around the room. Their feet brushed the floorboards. Passing the table where the candle darted they could smell the flowers and the incense that wafted from a trio of sticks in a holder. The presence of the visitor provoked a ripple of curiosity that was palpable even as they walked with their gazes unfocused and their minds void. The walk gave Lewis his first chance, from the corners of his eyes, to glimpse who was there.

They resumed their seats for another ten minutes' sitting, then there was a second walk. Lewis hoped that the timing of the practice would work with the timings he had set up outside. The final ten minutes of sitting commenced, with bodies heated from the concentration of internal energy, stiffness transcended, and the abstraction of the atmosphere at its most intense. By the time they finished it was light.

Another sounding of the clapper from the abbess was a sign for everyone to stand and face inwards to each other for the recitation of the Four Great Vows. Lewis looked softly across at the Chinese man who was standing opposite him with downcast gaze. He was the man presumed dead – warm, alive and breathing deeply. Lewis could not help an ironic smile as he looked at the serenity of the man's expressionless face and the smoothness of his skin in the muted golden light. He wondered if the man knew how many people were in pursuit of him.

But Nova had noticed the attention the visitor was paying to Original Face. Her intuition was right. She had suspected the taxi-driver's motives from the outset. After the prostrations were complete, Nova struck the gong to bring the session to an end. People started shaking themselves loose. They picked up their cushions and mats and put on their shoes and went out into the light. The day was theirs. But Nova hooked a finger to beckon

Original Face. He went to her and she whispered in his ear. The room had only one door. He passed through it, head bowed, hands clasped against his orange robe, avoiding the gaze of the people in the hall.

'Zhou Huang!' called Lewis. His voice broke the prescribed silence like a hammer striking a nail.

But the monk did not respond.

Lewis stepped after him, catching hold of his robe as he went to slip through the front door into the garden. 'Are you Zhou Huang?' he asked.

'No,' he said, shaking his head. 'No!'

'Then who are you? Who are you?' repeated Lewis in Chinese. 'What is your name?' The monk stared with a faint detached smile, seemingly untroubled by the way Lewis had fixed on him. 'If you are not Zhou Huang, *who are you?*'

'Who is it that hears?' the monk replied. 'Before my father and mother were born, who was I? What was my Original Face? That is my name.' Then he placed his two hands together over his chest and shook them in thanks before quickly turning away through the front door of the house.

Outside in the shining sunlight Jasmine was waiting to greet him. 'Zhou Huang!' she said, coming forward. 'Garlic Shoot!'

Then he could no longer keep from responding. He burst into a grin of recognition when he saw her, there in front of him, not spirited away to China. But he was a monk now, apart from such things, so he just stood and kept grinning, letting the changes that had happened to him sink in for her.

'How are you?' she asked. 'You're safe?'

'I was meant to be dead,' he replied. He had seen his own photo in the newspaper, named as the deceased.

Ginger and Shelley were watching from the police car that was parked under the trees in the driveway of Crystal House. They had reluctantly agreed with Lewis to stay in the car until they were needed. When the figure in orange emerged they took it as their signal to come forward. They marched up the gravel to introduce themselves.

'Your father and mother will be very pleased to see you,' said Ginger as an opener. He could not wait to tell Silverton that he and Shelley had found the dead man alive.

Sitting on a bench under the hundred-year-old Himalayan cedar, its leaves a pyramid of silver-blue in the centre of the garden, was Jerome Hampton. He had arrived there with the police who had called in the small hours of the morning to ask him a few questions. He gave a wave, taking pleasure in the sight of this young Buddha, looking near anonymous in the guise of a monk. But he kept his distance. He told the police he did not want his name or his picture in the paper. Those long ear lobes, he noted, observing Zhou. Nova Jewell had taken the boy – that was clear. But equally the young man had accepted her haven of his own volition. He had gone through the gate, discarding the likeness that inspired Jerome's paintings as a snake might shed a skin when changing from winter to summer. Jerome accepted that. He saluted the police for finding his missing friend. Any misunderstanding had been cleared up. He had killed his attachment to Zhou and was free to go, yet he lingered under the trees, waiting for a word with his dear friend Nova.

Original Face felt the warmth of the sun on his skin. He was heated from within too, and burning a little from the attention. The abbess stood beside him protectively. The police were making arrangements to 'borrow' her monk for a while. She had no choice but to comply, although she was put out by their invasion. Then she looked at her protégé as he prepared to go, feeling the tug of her own attachment to him, and understood that this was the moment when he was being announced to the world.

Original Face parted from Nova Jewell with a solemn bow and was escorted to the police car. The lines of blue and white agapanthus along the drive nodded as he passed. The reviving scent of pine flushed the air in the grounds of Crystal House. Nova stood at the top of the stone steps. She had a wry smile for her old friend as he crossed the grass to her.

'I compliment you on your powers,' Jerome said. 'You have the gift of recognising potential.'

Nova laughed with much larger force than she usually allowed herself. 'Thank you, dear boy,' she replied. 'We're all potential. I saw that in *you* all those years ago.'

'You saw it in yourself,' he said, 'which is far more important.'

She opened the palm of her right hand, followed by the palm of her left. The skin, jaundiced and creased, seemed to be laced with golden threads in the morning sunlight. She shrugged, turning to go inside on the expectation that Jerome would follow.

# Chapter XXIX

Fancy lighting made the dated purple and greens and metallic greys of the carpets and upholstery and sleek chrome furniture of the conference room at Sydney Police Centre look sumptuous and bright. The concrete bunker was closed to the outside world, yet the potted plants were glossy on a diet of air and water. Usually the daytime shift grumbled into work, scrutinising the nasty surprises of the night. The appearance of a monk in an orange robe seated at the head of a long table made a happy exception. Detective Superintendent Silverton was claiming the success as his own. He had his junior staff on hand to fetch donuts and croissants and tea or coffee for the visitors. Ginger and Shelley sat back with smug pleasure and allowed themselves to be waited on.

The police photographer paced up and down in the doorway, testing his equipment. Lewis was there too, by special permission, following Ginger's intercession. They were all waiting. At last a call came to say that Mr and Mrs Zhou were on their way.

'Thanks, Heidi,' said Silverton, relieved.

The young monk sipped the milky tea and let the sweet donut soften in his mouth. Then Heidi Lee put her head around the door to check she had the right room and ushered in the old couple.

The people around the table rose to their feet in witness of an occasion that had a simple human gravity beyond its professional significance for them. The photographer moved in, and Lewis with his camera. Pamela, the interpreter who had accompanied the old couple since their arrival from China, stood to one side with a wide grin, squeezing her hands in front of her as Mr and Mrs Zhou came to their son in an ecstasy of recognition.

'Ma! Pa!' said the young man in orange, stretching out his arms to them.

'Son,' they said, clasping him. 'Son!'

Mrs Zhou cried as she held him. She had never believed he was dead. She knew that the body lying in the frozen basement of the building was not him. Now in the continuation of her dream she was able to affirm that he was living and returned to her. Lewis brought the focus of his lens in close on the joyous certainty on the mother's face.

The father smiled at his son and nodded doubtfully, as if it might all be some trick. He had been taught to regard reincarnation with suspicion. That's what this might be. He could never have conceived it as literally as this transformation of his disappointing younger son into the radiant presence at the centre of the room. The old man's face wrinkled at the bitter puzzle of it all, a first-born son's brutally unexplained demise

273

and a second son's reappearance in the flesh and bone that he was holding in his hands.

It was indubitably Zhou Huang, who looked a little removed from the intensity of the moment, his eyes closed in contentment.

Those involved with the case felt their own umbilical connections stir – Ginger and Shelley, Heidi and Pamela, even Ronnie Silverton whose old mum was about to celebrate her eightieth birthday in a retirement village on the Central Coast. Lewis wondered to himself how people were supposed to deal with the separation of parents and children that life impelled with its constant pulling away from the starting point. He thought of his old father, sitting all day in front of the television in a suburban Australian living room, and his dear mother, dead of cancer not a year before. But then, he thought, life had a dimension of its own, as broad and impersonal as the sky, where people were free of all connections and attachments.

Mr and Mrs Zhou sat at the table beside their son and an eager question-and-answer followed in their Hangzhou dialect. The interpreter shrugged her shoulders. The exchange was untranslatable. The onlookers turned away. It was a moment to joke amongst themselves before the routine work of the investigation resumed.

Then the superintendent let Lewis know that the time had come for him to leave the room. Lewis had the photo he wanted. Behind him he heard a police voice begin. 'Please state your name, address and date of birth.' Then Pamela's sharp rendering of the question in Mandarin and the low murmur of a reply as a junior officer escorted Lewis out of the secure area and down the corridor.

Original Face told the story of Zhou Huang in a detached sequence of simple sentences, how he came to Australia, how he had an understanding with Guo Lihua, how he met Ah Mo in the Chinese Democracy League who helped him apply for refugee status when his visa expired. Refugee status was easy for the brother of a Tiananmen martyr, and once he had permanent residency he brought Lihua to join him. She planned to open her own clinic. But the sweetness he hoped from the relationship was not there. Mengzi still controlled her, and as soon as she could she went out on her own to earn her own money. She took with her his new Australian passport. He couldn't refuse her anything. She said it was for safekeeping. He didn't need it the way he lived, sharing a house with other Chinese students, labouring at Kangaloon Native Garden. No one questioned his identity. In the larger community he didn't exist except as a faceless occupier of space.

Then she stopped returning his calls. He guessed she had used his passport for Mengzi to come and join her. He wondered if Ah Mo had helped with that too. When Ah Mo tried to enlist him to his cause, for the sake of his brother's memory, he replied that he could be of no use. He was a gardener.

He struggled to learn English. Confined to his own space, he had walls around him. He drifted into himself, or his not-self. Quietly awakening within him was an interest in the teachings of Buddhism.

When she needed money Lihua would come looking for him. She called him quite unexpectedly one night. It was an emergency, she said, appealing to him as a true friend.

He met her the next afternoon at the Macarthur Park Shopping Mall. She told him that the Immigration Department had given her seventy-two hours to leave the country. Mengzi had given her away, using Zhou Huang's name. She smiled uncertainly at him. He had brought the money she needed, borrowed from his friend. He told her it was better to go voluntarily than be deported. That way he could follow her to China and marry her, then bring her back to Australia as his wife, to start a new life. No, she said, not now. There was something else, something dangerous. Ah Mo was displeased with Zhou Huang. His ventures were in trouble because Zhou Huang had betrayed him. So Ah Mo believed. The one who caused him to lose face was really Mengzi, hiding behind Zhou Huang's name. But Ah Mo didn't know that.

What she said scarcely made sense, but Zhou Huang accepted her story because it showed how she cared for him. She warned him to go into hiding immediately, to tell no one where he had gone. She would let his parents in China know he was safe. She was so afraid that Ah Mo would kill him. She held him by the hand and their faces were close. Her eyes shone as she called him Garlic Shoot. Then she was gone.

He went to the Buddhist Centre at Bong Bong that same evening and spoke to Nova Jewell. He said he wanted to take refuge. He asked her to keep his presence there a secret, and not even to tell Jeremy where he was. He was following Lihua's instructions completely. Nova felt a glow of self-satisfaction. Regarding the young man's spiritual development, she considered that she had a higher claim than Jerome. She agreed to his request unconditionally. Not hers to question the tortuous paths to enlightenment. The surprise visitor could stay there and commence his training, if he was genuine. He nodded his head and she let him in.

'*Benlai mianmu ruhe?*' The young man repeated the ancient Zen riddle for those gathered in the conference room.

His parents smiled. The interpreter translated the words. 'What is your original face?'

'So Zhou Huang took refuge in the Buddha,' Original Face concluded, 'and today you know.'

'Thank you,' said Silverton, giving the signal for the tape recorder to be switched off.

'It's the other side of the picture,' commented Ginger. 'When you put it together with Jasmine's statement.'

'Do you want the girl to come in?' asked Shelley.' She's outside.'

'She's given us everything she's got,' said Ginger. 'It's all in the transcript. Ah Mo's our man.'

'That's right,' said Silverton smugly. 'The squad's onto him. I'm expecting him to be apprehended any minute. I'm just waiting for the call.'

'You mean while we've been hot-airing here there's an operation in progress?' Ginger blurted, incredulous that information was still being withheld from the very officers who had delivered Homicide the case.

'Nice work, Superintendent...' said Shelley.

Ginger glowered at her as if she were betraying their team of two. Was she sucking up, hoping for a promotion out of Pleasant Vale?

'Or another stuff-up,' she added flatly.

# Chapter XXX

Ah Mo was always the one with the greatest belief in himself. He had the greatest belief in what he could achieve, and what his buddies and classmates and colleagues and compatriots could achieve, what the Chinese people could achieve when their energies were harnessed and their aspirations forged and tempered. Even when his plans changed, even when they failed, he was still able to see himself as a great figure. His loyal henchman supported him in that, his lieutenant, Daozi, the Knife. When the situation went against them, it was merely the test of the superior man. So now as Ah Mo and Daozi emerged from a long downhill night at the Casino, stripped of the wad of cash they went in with. The money had grown to quite a pile at one point, and Daozi had tried to drag his boss away, in vain. The superior man risked everything, redoubling the odds. They were down to the last packet of cigarettes as they walked back empty-handed to the Pyrmont apartment against the drift of morning workers.

'We'll go to Fatso's for breakfast,' said Ah Mo. 'He owes me one.'

Daozi ambled alongside his master, the gambler's companion who rejoiced or commiserated according to circumstances. He liked to watch money come and go, sticking sometimes like glue, other times running away like water. Information was the same, he thought, staying tight for a while then leaking.

The trouble with Immigration had changed their business. Old arrangements ended, new ventures were not yet ripe. Ah Mo had been the boss of the Sydney operation, working through the travel agency in the same Chinatown building as the video hire, where the Chinese Democracy League used to be. Ah Mo never knew the identity of the philanthropic landlord. He was not given any more information than was strictly needed. He was never sure who his friends were and who his enemies, accepting that they were shifting quantities anyway. But links back to Beijing were acknowledged, even to the School of Music where his genius had first emerged. His friends knew about his patriotic, well-placed parents. And about his family ties to Taiwan. Money came from there too, in the form of sponsorship for the fund-raising concerts in which Ah Mo had played when he first came to Sydney, and other connections in the chain of documents and tickets and boats and planes and transfers that enabled people from Hong Kong or Vietnam or wherever to have a new life in a new country under a new name. There was one famous occasion when a boat from Fujian sailed right into Botany Bay in the middle of the night and landed its cargo of people on the beach, quite undetected, before it sailed away again. Ah Mo's network provided a complete backdoor migration service that was still cheaper than the half-million dollars required up front by the Australian government for business migrants. And those who made it never forgot their gratitude. That was part of Ah Mo's method too. They were bound for life in the age-old way.

Luckily by the time Immigration was in a position to act on its information, everyone in the public housing at Pleasant Vale had been safely moved elsewhere. Even the latest arrivals, who were living apprehensively with scarcely a word of English, had been deftly moved on and were now secure. Ah Mo's side of the bargain had been honoured, even with a traitor in their midst. An inferior man who brought shame on all his brothers, the once trusted one, the informer who went outside the circle. He had been punished, defaced, destroyed in his turn. Ah Mo would not even think his name.

But he did think of the other Zhou Huang, the man whose name had been borrowed, the dumb kid from the factory in Hangzhou with none of his brother's talent. Ah Mo's efforts to find him had failed. He had disappeared. Lihua said she didn't know where he was. He was probably alive somewhere, not dead, whatever people thought. But Zhou Huang didn't count. He knew nothing. He was a void, not an enemy. He was merely lost out there in the suburbs of this endless land. And that gave Ah Mo a strange kind of comfort.

Walking through this warm, empty, hungry morning with Daozi beside him, up the hill from the old waterfront warehouses through a cutting of sheer rock, with gulls wheeling and shrieking over his head, Ah Mo felt he was the hero of a lonelier, longer revolution than Tiananmen. He had been a rallying point for countless Chinese students when they first came to Australia, adrift from the motherland, lost in confused dreams. Now he was part of the larger struggle of the masses to improve their lot. He must turn his own fortune around, spin the wheel and be ready for the next opening chord. Ah Mo flicked his cigarette butt into the gutter and began to whistle. Beethoven. The Eroica. Last movement.

The whistling gave him away.

After he left Sydney Police Centre, Lewis joined Bernie and Jasmine who were waiting outside in the blue Volvo. He still wanted to beat the police at their own game. He wanted to get to Ah Mo first, and Jasmine knew where Ah Mo lived.

Lewis did not know what he would say to his Beijing compatriot. He felt a residual obligation to warn him. Maybe Lewis owed him a chance to escape the justice that was coming to him, foreign justice. But it was also a matter of letting Ah Mo talk, letting him explain, hearing out his own high-minded justification of all he had done. That might serve as a confession, Lewis insisted to Jasmine, who was keen to cooperate in bringing Ah Mo to court. They did not know that Silverton's squad was already on its way.

Bernie saw that, in legal terms, Jasmine needed to establish her own innocence. He needed to satisfy himself of that too. He was still digesting her revelations, coming to terms with her past, or was it her present? The person she proved to be, having been forced into a desperate corner. Bernie had to renegotiate her in his own mind, and his emotional commitment as well. He figured he was committed. She was just too good. He wanted her to show the world her virtue and courage. That meant helping to bring in Ah Mo.

They drove to the flat in Pyrmont and buzzed the intercom. When there was no answer they checked the underground car park. The green Forester was there. Lewis recognised it from his lunch with Ah Mo. The orange Toyota was also there, Daozi's car. They crossed the street and found a coffee shop on street level with a view of the harbour from where they could watch the entrance to the building and see the balcony of Ah Mo's apartment. They would know if Ah Mo returned. Lewis figured it would not be long before the police were there too. Then they heard Ah Mo whistling Beethoven with correct tempo and trilling gusto. They watched from the coffee shop as the two men crossed the road, nonchalantly dodging the cars.

'It's them,' whispered Jasmine. Ah Mo. Daozi.

'What are we going to do?' asked Bernie. 'Are we going to confront them?'

'I don't want them to see me,' said Jasmine.

'You and I can go,' Lewis suggested to Bernie.

Bernie flinched. 'The two of us against the two of them. Isn't that a bit dangerous?'

'I want to see their faces,' Lewis said, 'when they open the door and there we are.'

Ah Mo and Daozi went into the building and a couple of minutes later Daozi appeared on the balcony opening a packet of cigarettes. Lewis stood outside the coffee shop and zoomed in on the first draw of the cigarette with his camera. Daozi's eyes, half-closing with weary relief, surveyed the sparkling blue water of the morning harbour and the hazy shores beyond. Ah Mo joined Daozi, leaning against the rail as he took a cigarette. Lewis captured both their faces on film, up close, before Ah Mo glanced down and looked straight at him. What a great shot. Then Ah Mo pointed, speaking out the side of his mouth, and Daozi shouted and lunged back inside, out of sight, pulling Ah Mo after him. As he did so, a police car came to a halt at the entrance of the building and four uniformed officers jumped out.

Ah Mo stepped out on to the balcony again, ready for the spectacle of Daozi dashing across the street below to grab the camera that Lewis had pointed at him. Instead he saw the police. There was a buzz from the intercom. He ran into the stairwell, just in time to warn Daozi.

'Let's get out of here,' said Ah Mo, pushing Daozi down the stairs.

They got to the basement and ran through the car park to the Forester. With Daozi at the wheel they were out of the building before the police had found a way in. The security bar lifted and the green AWD sped up the ramp to the sunlit street, almost skittling the police woman who was stationed at the entrance. She caught a glimpse of the Chinese faces through the tinted glass and yelled to her colleagues.

'Hey! That's them!'

Bernie turned the nose of the Volvo out of the lane, poised to follow as the Forester swung left and the police vehicle slid into motion behind it. The woman on the street transmitted back to base. Bernie honked his way across the oncoming traffic as, up ahead, the Forester shot the red light and headed west in the direction of the fish market. There were any number of escape routes. Roads flew under and over, some ramping into dead ends, blocked by water, concrete or NO EXIT signs, others looping back. In this corner of the city transport and commerce crisscrossed like a dish of eels.

Daozi took the way that would get them the greatest distance in the shortest time, out to the Glebe Island Bridge. He was speeding up the arc of the bridge too fast to see the traffic up ahead stalled in a tight jam and a truck slewed across all three lanes. He slammed on the brakes not quite in time to avoid crunching into the car in front, causing a chain collision down the line. When he tried to back up he was rammed from behind.

He could hear the police siren. The police car chasing him had switched over to the lanes of oncoming traffic and blazed a way over the bridge until it was level with them.

Ah Mo cursed. He made his decision, giving Daozi a parting clasp of the shoulder, opened the door and jumped out. Weaving through cars, he reached the fenced walkway along the edge of the bridge, high over the water, and ran, glancing behind to see if anyone was after him.

The police saw Ah Mo running. A young constable gave chase, calling to the man to stop. Ah Mo kept running, weaving and darting, his shirt tails flapping, like a black and white bird on the wing. The police officer stopped and pulled out his gun. He aimed shakily at Ah Mo. He was out of breath and puffing. He shouted again for the man to stop.

Daozi was torn between staying with the car and running too. He heard more sirens as reinforcements approached the bridge from both sides.

Bernie's car was further back, engulfed in the traffic snarl that extended from one side of the bridge to the other.

'I can't see anything from here,' Lewis said. 'Wait for me.' He got out and wove his way on foot ahead through the stationary traffic. He crossed to the walkway where he had a view to the other side. He heard the first gunshot. He clambered on to the security fence with the lens to his eye as he leaned forward.

There was a second shot and a third. Ah Mo had climbed up on top of the fence that was meant to stop people jumping from the bridge. He stood swaying on the ledge above the water. He would not be caught. There was blood on his shirt. Then he hurled himself forward, as if his fate might turn again at this very last moment, as he plunged into the emptiness below. From the windows of dozens of stalled cars, people peered, leaning out, lifting their sunglasses in the strong morning light for a better view. Car radios blared, oblivious of what was happening. Some saw the man go, others watched as he descended, turning slowly, as if performing for them, a single dark figure falling from blue to blue. In the last instant, as if in a final cadenza, Ah Mo's limbs splayed, his body resisting its ultimate end. Then he was gone. There was a collective sigh, a shielding of eyes. The man was way out in the middle. He could not swim. The gunshots, aimed above his head, may have missed, but the drop from the main span of the bridge was too far for the man to have survived unharmed. Anyone who swam out from the side to rescue him would not have got there in time. His arms flailed in the air as he drowned in the murky brown water.

Ah Mo had chosen his own death, joining the other victims of struggle who had loosed the tie of life in this smiling harbour. That included numbers of his own countrymen who had walked this fine new bridge in the pitiless hours of the morning when their luck at the Casino failed them one last time. It included people from many other places stranded on this foreign shore, as uncaring as it was benign.

The young constable who had fired the shots looked down. This result was unexpected. His police colleagues hurried over and clapped him on the back, stood with him, not too close. It was not meant to happen this way. They were supposed to bring the man in. They had blown it.

Daozi hit his head in helpless despair against the fence from which Ah Mo had fallen. Then just as quickly in one low whirling movement he backed away, seeking in retreat to counter the wave of people craning forward to see the body of the drowned man bob to the surface darkly, as if it might have been a shark.

Forget about the boss and the Forester. Forget about everything. Just escape, he told himself. But it was too late. The police were there, behind, in front. They had him in their net.

'My God!' said Lewis when he got back to Bernie and Jasmine. He was eager to see what he had in his camera. That last photograph was a bonus, but he asked Bernie to take him back to Centennial Park where the taxi had been parked all night. Spiros had been making furious calls to Lewis's brother in his effort to locate it. Lewis needed time to placate people, but first he wanted to get to his darkroom.

When he was done, Lewis let Bernie know he had a spectacular photo. He would be unlucky if anyone else on the bridge had caught the moment better. Bernie got straight onto his mates in the media. It happened in time for the television news that night, with Lewis's image superimposed on helicopter footage of the chaotic aftermath on the bridge. It appeared in the early editions of the papers. The police were happy to announce that they had a man in custody. 'Tiananmen Dump Slayer Death Plunge' read the morning tabloid headline. Underneath, filling up most of the page, was Lewis's photo of the fall, inset with an aerial shot of the bridge, its span and webbed stays at an angle to the ribbing current that pressed out from the harbour to the sea. Divers had so far failed to retrieve the body.

# Chapter XXXI

Ginger and Shelley were seconded from Pleasant Vale to Sydney Police Centre to prepare the case for the coronial inquest into the murder. They managed it in such a way that Jasmine was declared a friendly witness and no charges were laid against her. She had been getting even with a bad boyfriend. Shelley would not condemn her for that and Ginger considered that she had gone only so far in the wrong direction but no further. The coroner's report commended her integrity and valour.

Later, when the case against Daozi as an accessory to the murder came to court, the presiding judge praised Jasmine's commitment to the values of life in a democratic society.

*It was out of my control*, she repeated in the witness stand. *If I tried to stop them they would have killed me too. Or left me out there in the wild. At what point does responsibility begin? At what point does it end? At what point does responsibility, or lack of responsibility, become guilt? At what point does my action or lack of action count? When does it make a difference whether I am there or not there? I am innocent.*

The judge had paused over these remarks. He frowned, wanting to make sure he understood what she was saying. Certainly, as the legal aid lawyer for the defence insisted, there were gaps in the investigation. There were questions of timing, of cause and effect. There were other ways of looking at the Chinese woman's involvement. If she had not been there, would a man have been killed so cruelly? Did her presence add to or subtract from the vendetta? But Jasmine was not on trial, and both the man who ordered the crime and his victim were dead, as the judge reminded the jury, wondering what message they would take away for their own life management. Deception and self-deception, good luck or bad luck, blinded judgement and clear-eyed survival instincts: a jury might see the hapless woman differently from the judge. But the judge could not entirely discount her character references nor the general testimony to her gifts of caring and healing. If there was ambiguity in her position, it had been highlighted neither in the prosecution's case against the man who wielded the knife nor in the defence's legal argument. They should therefore not be reflected in the judge's summing up. So the sentimental judge came down on the positive side of the ledger, smiling at the beautiful Chinese bride-to-be as she stepped gracefully from the witness box to rejoin the man who had allied himself with her.

Bernie put out his hand to pull Jasmine back by his side. He was beaming too. Having made the decision to support her, he was unerring in his public display. Yet the unspoken uncertainties of the court left exposed the doubts that the Oscar-winning cinematographer must face in relation to the woman he was taking as his partner. That was what journalists with a taste of blood in their mouths wanted to ask outside the court.

Jasmine hugged Bernie tightly as a clam as the reporters pressed close. Bernie scratched his beard a little. To this point his unwavering support had been a matter of public presentation. Now he had to ask himself what judgement he made, what it meant to love someone, or trust someone, equivocally, and how this equivocal judgement might make the woman feel in response. He considered what he would have to live with, about her, about himself, about the secret sources of their own well-being. And all of this he summed up by saying, 'We're very happy. Thank you!'

They scuttled to the car park and drove home. But before they went inside, Bernie asked Jasmine to take a walk with him in the park. She had got off scot-free. But before they crossed the threshold of his house to the next stage of their life together, he wanted to talk to her. He led her across the road and down the avenue of figtrees that smelled of fermenting fruit.

'Can I ask you a question?' he began. 'Do you feel regret for what has happened? Do you feel any remorse?'

Jasmine gave a clear, clipped answer. 'It is behind me,' she said. 'It is the past.'

'I need to know whether you are still that person?'

'I am this person,' she said. 'Am I the person you want? It doesn't matter who I was before, or who you were before, or where we have been. What matters is who we are now, together.'

They were heading for the Federation Pavilion. Bernie separated from Jasmine and trod the grass to the domed edifice, part neoclassical monument, part spaceship. He strode in and out of its smooth sandstone columns, his face slashed by sharp shadows. He saw that there was no way his doubts would ever be answered. If he needed her, he had simply to accept her or not. Only it wasn't simple.

'Someone has pissed in here,' she said, turning up her nose as she entered the rotund structure, following him around its curve.

'It was built to celebrate two hundred years of this country.'

'Two hundred years. So short,' she said flippantly.

'So *long*,' Bernie groaned.

'What does the writing mean?' she asked, pointing to the letters incised in stone above.

'*Mammon or millennial Eden.* It means we could be tied up in the same old nets of greed here and let the past trap us or we could make a new and better start. It's *your* message.'

Jasmine laughed. 'That sounds great.' She went to Bernie, put her arms around him and laid her head on his chest. 'I will make you happy, Bernie. You know that, don't you? I promise you.'

That was when he saw that his aversion to getting married had to turn through one hundred and eighty degrees. If they married each other, they would know where they stood. The new contract would make the past little more than an old movie that had died on its first release, he figured, a land of previous incarnations, like China. The bond between them would remix the light and dark of their souls.

'Phew, you're right,' he said. 'It stinks in here. Let's go.'

They turned their backs on the commemorative folly and, as they headed back across the park for home, he put his arm round her. He took refuge in her, as she took refuge in him, with a love that would be as unquestioned as it was unquestioning from now on.

Bernie shaved off his beard for the wedding day and put on the shiny new suit he and Jasmine had bought together in Oxford Street. He was filled with well-being. No matter what may have happened in his career, his life was rejuvenated, which was far more important. He felt confident with Jasmine that he had another fifty good years.

She had given him some green oil to use in the tub, a herbal potion from her home town that oozed its fragrance at every pore, making him healthy and potent. With every breath the scent reminded him of his new life. It may have been slightly too sweet, but it was always with him. For Bernie the green oil was like air freshener, overwhelming any lingering doubts.

Jasmine said that in Chinese culture the greatest thing that could happen to a man was to father a child at the age of eighty. With nearly forty years to practise, he joked that he might just notch up that good fortune. He had only to close his eyes and inhale and he could feel the energy rising up his spine, strong despite the sleek weight of belly he carried – the mark of prosperity, Jasmine assured him. That energy was her gift. He had only to feel the heat of her body against his skin and the colours of the world heightened, the hooded serpent starting to stir. He knew that the *kundalini* would return *one* day.

Bernie and Jasmine were married on a Thursday morning at the Registry of Births, Deaths and Marriages in the city. The lawyer had been right. Marriage solved all the problems. In time Jasmine would be a citizen with her own Australian passport. She was immediately entitled to enrol in a recognised diploma of Traditional Chinese Medicine that would allow her to practise in an authorised clinic. Bernie had arranged all that and had paid the registration fees in advance.

The wedding party filled the basement function room for the no-frills ceremony. The walls were painted with blue sky and some fluffy white clouds, and a bunch of scarlet gladioli erupted from a fluted white plinth. Into the airconditioned chamber oozed a bridal waltz as the celebrant appeared from behind the plush red curtain. She was a diminutive official of Philippine background with a brisk manner. The bride and groom stepped forward with Lewis Lin and Bernie's friend Andy, the television producer, as witnesses on either side. The guests moved close – Lewis's family, Ginger Rogers and Shelley Swert, and Cloud, Bernie's daughter, who had flown over from Adelaide. And Original Face. As arranged, after she had said her part, the celebrant invited the Buddhist monk to step forward and bless them.

Original Face stood before the couple in his orange and scarlet robes. A string of wooden beads dangled from his arm. He steadied himself, silently acknowledging the bride and groom.

Solemnly, with closed eyes, he began to recite the Four Great Vows until his low chant filled the basement room. Then Original Face snapped his eyes open and, looking at the man and woman with refreshed vision, gave them the *mudra* of blessing. He bowed to them with half a smile on his lips and resumed his place. The celebrant took charge for the concluding exchange of declarations. Being a professional romantic, she announced in triumph, 'Bernard, you may now kiss the bride.'

Bernie's tongue went straight down Jasmine's throat. Andy popped the cork on a bottle of French champagne and Lewis flashed his camera as they walked out into the daylight.

A car was waiting there, not for the bridal party who would walk the short block to the Chinese restaurant, toasting themselves in tall flutes of bubbly all the way, but to take Original Face back to Bong Bong. Original Face seldom left the Buddhist Centre since assuming the higher role that Nova Jewell had ordained for him. Still in mourning for her passing, still learning, he concentrated all his efforts on the burdensome task of becoming, one day, an abbot in her footsteps. Jerome Hampton helped in practical ways, such as providing his car on this special occasion to enable Original Face to visit the external world and release Lihua to her new attachment. The driver sat patiently in the No Standing zone. Jerome was unseen in the back, happy to have the monk's company for the ride. Now, wrapped in orange, the young man joined his benefactor in the back seat. He turned his breath inward, stilling the pain in his heart as the car slid away.

Jasmine looked more elegant than ever in a tight cheongsam with the skirt slit to the thigh. It was auspicious red satin picked out with white sprays of blossom. Her hair was twisted up in a loose chignon and her face was painted and powdered in a combination of delicacy and invincible strength. Bernie wanted to mess up her mask and eat her. She bent into him as she wobbled unsteadily on her high heels, taller than her new husband. A little of the champagne dribbled from her mouth down her neck and soaked into the line of her bodice. The day was a landmark in her life and she was happy, exultantly happy. She had telephoned her parents back in China the evening before. Her family rejoiced with her. Deservedly, after everything, she had made it.

The Golden Harbour restaurant in the middle of the day was a noisy, crowded sea of eating, drinking humanity. Large groups surged by, children borne aloft, families, tourists, business parties, sweeping in, drifting out. Tables never stopped moving, stripped, covered and reconfigured. The waiters in black and white dealt out crockery, set down wet hot teapots, delivered trays of frosted drinks. The women in pink uniforms pushing their trolleys and opened steamer baskets for examination, smiling only when someone said yes to a dish and they could punch the order with a stamp. While people all around were finishing late breakfast or starting on business lunch, Bernie and Jasmine embarked on their wedding banquet.

Their table was like an island in the heaving ocean of the restaurant, or a boat on which the wedding party floated, squeezed together, with the bride and groom as the centre of attention. Cloud sat on her father's right, and Lewis's old father sat on Jasmine's left, then Alan and Nancy and the two kids, and a place for Lewis who was on his feet taking photographs. Andy sat next to Cloud, with his wife Margo beside him. Cloud, a stylish waif with wispy blonde hair, a strong jaw and nervous confidence – was no longer the child they had known. She called her father's marriage 'an interesting thing'. She was curious about Jasmine, who said Cloud would be her little sister.

Ginger and Shelley sat opposite the bridal pair, like an old couple, enjoying an event that also counted as a day's work for them. And on Lewis's insistence Reg Spivak was there too, the manager of the Pleasant Vale Recycling and Waste Depot looking spruce in a crimson blazer and the bright Mickey Mouse tie he had saved from becoming landfill.

'You started it all,' said Lewis for all to hear, pointing his camera at Reg. Reg waved him away.

The dishes came thick and fast: snow-pea sprout dumplings and pork-stuffed taro balls, ginger-steamed scallops and braised pigeon, noodles and a huge red-glazed snapper, plate balanced on plate on the overflowing table.

Showing Bernie how, Jasmine took a chicken's foot with her chopsticks, dipped it in the sauce and chewed the pale stretchy flesh until there was nothing but tiny bones. Bernie picked up one and dropped it, tried again and nibbled vigorously before letting the thing slip half-finished into his bowl.

'Good,' she asked, dabbing her lips with a cloth.

'Not worth the trouble,' he said.

'The trouble is what makes it taste good,' she laughed.

'Sounds like police work to me,' quipped Ginger across the table. 'The trouble is what makes it fun.'

'I'll drink to that,' laughed Bernie, clinking his glass with each guest in turn. It was why he was there, why they were all there. 'To trouble,' he smirked, giving his new bride a wink before he sculled the champagne.

'Count Ginger out when it comes to the chicken feet,' added Shelley. 'He's strictly a vegetarian.'

'Oh is there enough for you to eat?' asked Jasmine.

'Sure,' said Ginger. 'Rice – and mango pudding. That's all I need.'

At the end of the banquet a wedding cake with a burning sparkler was presented to the bride and groom. Eyes turned to their table as the knife came. Bernie felt better than ever as he passed his arm through Jasmine's and they cut the cake together. Then, as the pieces of cake were passed around, he wanted to propose an extra toast of his own.

'To Lewis,' he said, raising his glass, 'and your photography.' Bernie had lined up a photographic agency for Lewis and was trying to convince him to take his photography more seriously. If one photograph could make the front page of the daily paper and earn good money, why not more? 'One day soon you will take those photos out of the darkroom and make them walk and talk. You'll be shooting movies yet, Lewis, and I'm here to help you. Cheers!'

Lewis blushed. Bernie had stumbled into his most private dream. 'No-no-no,' Lewis stammered shyly.

But Bernie would not let it go. 'Hey, Andy, say you agree.'
Bernie saw himself as the mentor of a new cross-cultural generation, the legendary guru Bernie Mittel – it was one way to
salvage his sagging reputation – and once he was seen at a few
fashionable events entwined by a gorgeous Chinese woman half
his age with a sharp smile and the wit to match, film-world
wannabes would start detouring through tables in restaurants
just to be in his sight lines.

'He's the same old Bernie,' Andy laughed affectionately. 'Sure
Lewis, if Bernie says so you have no choice except to become a
DOP and win an Oscar.' That was a future they were all prepared
to believe in around the table. On dreams come true, at an
occasion such as this, was their faith in the world founded.
Accordingly they raised their glasses, all except Lewis, who
refused. 'Sorry sorry sorry!' he said.

'Cheers, Lewis!' toasted Cloud enthusiastically. She liked this
Chinese photographer who had taken more photos of her than
of anyone else at the table.

The detective sergeant stood up, patting his belly after his
second mango pudding, and proposed his own toast of thanks
to Lewis on behalf of the Pleasant Vale police. 'If you don't
make it to Hollywood, mate,' said Ginger, 'there's always police
work. You'd be good detective material. I'd write the reference
myself. And now, I'm sorry to say, Shelley and me have to get
back to work.'

Reg made a move then too. 'Time for me to go, folks.' He
thanked the bridal couple for inviting him. 'It's his fault,' he

gestured to Lewis. 'This happy ending. It's the last time I get in his taxi.'

'I'm quitting,' said Lewis. 'I'm not driving that taxi again.'

Reg tapped Lewis lightly on the chest. 'Just don't forget us, mate. It's a crazy world. You never know when you may need the taxi. Anyway, you know where I am. Down at the dump. See you all there.' With that Reg swung his backpack over his shoulder and went to catch his train.

Alan and Nancy took Ming and Jack and the old man home, thanking Bernie for his hospitality. 'You're Lewis's family, so you're our family too,' said Bernie. He was drunk, exaggerating the ties between people. 'Like Andy here is a brother to me.'

But Andy's wife Margo had detoured to another table in the restaurant where she spotted the head of the top-rating radio network lunching with a government minister. No doubt they hoped to be incognito in the Chinatown throng. The pickings were too good for Margo to miss. She worked as a fundraiser for the children's hospital and was always on the lookout for an opportunity to extort a donation. She gave a wave to the curator of Asian art from the Powerhouse Museum who was lunching at the next table with her husband, an ex-diplomat turned China consultant. Margo knew everyone in Sydney. That left Andy stranded as he aimed for the exit.

'I'm sorry your mother and father are not here,' Bernie said to Jasmine. 'At least I've got my daughter to give me away.' He smirked at Cloud who had moved away from the table and was standing with Lewis.

'We can have another wedding with them in China,' Jasmine laughed. Her hair was coming adrift. She was having a good time.

Bernie picked up his glass. 'Absent friends,' he said for whoever was listening.

'Absent friends?' asked Jasmine. 'Who are the absent friends? What does that mean?'

'It's just a phrase,' explained Bernie. 'A tradition.' No one was left to reply to the toast, as the customary phrase cast a momentary shadow over the table, filling the space with those who were absent, friends or otherwise. Family members, associates. The women in his life – Noni, Wanda – were not there. And Zhou Huang – the missing man was someone else now. Bernie stood there with his raised glass. Then he drank, awkwardly, put the glass down and let his head slide on to Jasmine's shoulder. She wriggled free of Bernie's weight. It was time to pay the bill and leave.

The waiters came and removed everything but the tablecloth and returned with a platter of sliced orange and watermelon. Bernie and Jasmine sat on one side of the table and Lewis and Cloud on the other. A sense of those whose places were now empty made the story that Jasmine had told in Bernie's house replay in Lewis's mind. The newlyweds were snuggled up to each other in double happiness. Lewis admired the skill with which Jasmine had told her story. The admiration made his skin tingle with discomfort as he looked at her, her face draped by her lustrous black hair as she kissed the man's neck. The past was gone. The knowledge of how they had reached this moment would be their bond and power for life. Lewis turned to Cloud beside him. They seemed to hit it off. Cloud was sucking on the fresh, crisp red watermelon. Lewis picked up a piece and followed suit.

# Chapter XXXII

Mind empty. Energy harnessed inward. Daily life flowing easily. No excess of strength. Food, shelter and clothing provided. No need of protection, now that he had established himself. Companionship – in games of table tennis and chess. Observant in body, clean in spirit. Heart open.

In the mornings he mowed the prison grass. That gave him enough money for cigarettes. In the afternoon he read and wrote. The years turned in the old circle. The bristle on his upper lip grew tougher. In winter the ground was sometimes white. The cold chafed his skin and made his cheeks like apples, just as in childhood days in the faraway north. In summer he could not sleep for the heat. The bush surrounding the prison made the air fragrant. He could smell the smoke when the bush burned. There were mosquitoes here, but he had no wish to escape, even when summer rains swelled the river and flooded the valley and the prisoners were moved to higher ground. That was the ideal opportunity to seek release from

the boredom and occasional brutality of the place. The greater
test was to stay.

He could not avoid doing his time. It was karma, he said, the
return of things. Even here in this exile, so far from his birthplace, he was close to his real home, close to the beginning of
himself. In his green prison uniform he blended in, free of the
desire to roam.

Daozi had no knife in prison. Therefore he should have had
no name. But he kept the name he brought with him, which
became Dazza to the guards and the other inmates. The Knife
was now something he carried in his mind. It was the sharpest
edge in existence. In one move it could cut his ties to the world.
Peel him loose and leave the world to be. Blades of grass, rising
and lying down as the mower passed.

Where he was was what he had been waiting for. He was
neither angry nor bored. He could excite himself with
contemplation. He did not even have a sense of waiting. At
times, even here, in the full transparency of what he had
done, he was able to know the joy not of himself but of all that
was not him.

Daozi smiled with ironic understanding, sitting on the bed in
his solitary room. The sky passed beyond the barred window. He
rubbed his lip, roughly shaven where the moustache had been,
out of habit, as a reminder. Of them all, he was the one to bear
the burden of punishment. He preferred that condition to the
woman's. Guo Lihua. He had heard her speak in court. She was
an actress. She was working off what she owed in another way, in

this life and subsequent lives. She still had release to earn from her own distorted yearnings.

In the end he would have no debts. He would be bound by nothing. He would lift from the earth and fly like the blue heron he imagined crossing the sky, making his visits without knowing why or where.

He thought of Ah Mo, his soul condemned to further cycles of suffering. A homeless spirit, washing endlessly from shore to shore. He thought of Mengzi with biting remorse, his dying a torture arising from previous cycles of unknown craving, unknown greed. He thought of all the other creatures who had experienced violence at his hands. That had been his dark delusion, a condition he was unable to reverse. He had been the vehicle of cruelty, as now he was the vehicle of atonement. Ultimately he would be set free from what he had done.

Alone, without identity, in the green outfit of an Australian prison, he atoned for suffering. That was the inside of his outside experience. That was the reality of doing his time.

There was only one way to skin a cat, he acknowledged, though people always wanted to believe otherwise. There was only one way to be human. Once the human form was lost, it was hard to find it again. Here in prison, he was looking. Reading and writing, he was making himself a new skin of thought. He wrote to the Buddhist Association, asking for books and materials. They passed his letter on to a monk who wrote back in Chinese. From there a regular correspondence developed. Daozi was an apt student with time to write. The monk responded with diligence and compassion and a sense of humour. The prison where Daozi sat in his cell was not far, as the crow flies, from the Bong Bong Buddhist Centre. It transpired from their letters that they experienced the same weather patterns. The prison regulations would have allowed a visit, but neither ever suggested that they should meet face to face. The monk was too busy, he said. The founder of the Centre had died, a venerable Australian woman, and the monk had taken over as her successor. For the time being he would neither make nor receive visits. It was enough that they should share their fundamental nature in gifts of books and pages of script conveyed between them by postal workers. Their minds were bouncing off the same satellite. It was even closer as the blue heron flew, the monk said.

Daozi depended on advice. He would ask for the monk's help:

*Even someone who has committed the worst crimes is a buddha if he transforms and becomes enlightened*, wrote the monk.

That presented Daozi with his greatest challenge yet. Could he make that instant hurry? It was not even something he could earn by waiting with the utmost patience.

Then the monk wrote: *When you delude yourself and degenerate into evil ways, even the buddhas and patriarchs can't help you.*

That was to remind the imprisoned man.

In the next letter the monk wrote: *One moment seeing your own mind…leads eventually to enlightenment.*

That was to encourage him.

Daozi wrote back thanking his correspondent. He was ready to accept guidance, if the monk would be his new master. He asked the master his name.

The reply came: *Your own mind is the fundamental nature of all sentient beings. It has never changed since before your parents were born, before your own body existed. It is called Original Face.*

So that was the master's name. Daozi looked out the window at the sky. He seemed to hear a beat of wings. The great blue fish-catching heron was lifting off. Closing his eyes, he saw the bird fly into the distance, shrinking to nothing. He rubbed his face and his eyelids with his fingertips and opened his eyes again. The bird was still there, in the afterimage of a blue heron where the bird had been.

# Acknowledgements

*The author is grateful to the editors of* Antipodes, refo *and* dimsum *where sections of the novel appeared in an earlier form, and to Ah Xian, Rick Farquharson, David Ingram, Rosemary Creswell, Lesley McFadzean, Claire Roberts and Bob Wyatt, and especially Ivor Indyk for help and encouragement. Italicised sentences on pp.306–7 are adapted from* The Original Face: An Anthology of Rinzai Zen, *translated and edited by Thomas Cleary (Grove Press, New York 1978).*

*This project has been assisted by the Commonwealth Government through the Australia Council, its arts funding and advisory body.*